COLOR OF LIES

GENERATIONS OF SECRETS, BOOK 2

Abbe Rolnick

Color of Lies
Generations of Secrets, Book Two

Copyright © 2013 by Abbe Rolnick. Second Edition, 2018

All rights are reserved. No part of this book may be reproduced in any form; by any electronic or mechanical means, including photocopying or information storage and retrieval systems, without permission in writing from the publisher, except by a reviewer who may quote brief passages in a review.

For permission to reproduce selections from this book or to order copies, write to Sedro Publishing, 21993 Grip Road, Sedro-Woolley, WA 98284. http://www.sedropublishing.com or http://www.abberolnick.com.

Cover Photos taken by Jim Wiggins
Design & Prepress by Sally Dunn Design & Photography
(www.sallysuedunn.com).

Editor: Sara Stamey (www.sarastamey.com).
Copy Editor: Ariel Anderson (www.arieledits.com).

The characters and events in this book are fictitious. Any similarity to real persons, living or dead is coincidental and not intended by the author.

Library of Congress Control Number: 2012904793
Rolnick, Abbe
Color of Lies/Abbe Rolnick—1st edition
ISBN: 978-0-9845119-14

Other Books by Abbe Rolnick:
River of Angels, 2nd edition (2018), Book One in Generations of Secrets
Cocoon of Cancer: An Invitation to Love Deeply (2016)
Tattle Tales: Essays and Stories Along the Way (2016)

Forthcoming;
Founding Stones, Book Three in Generations of Secrets

A Novel of Cultural and Environmental Conflict

COLOR OF LIES

GENERATIONS OF SECRETS, BOOK 2

Abbe Rolnick

*"Open your heart, soften your eyes,
Between your truths, a story unfolds."*

—*AR*

Dedication

*To my family and those who
have become my family.*

Acknowledgements

Color of Lies would not have existed but for the glimpse of a woman dressed in white, seated in a wheelchair, rolling herself along the tarmac at the Concrete Fly-In. Thanks go to the hardworking volunteers at the Concrete Fly-In, the Civil Air Patrol, and all the pilots. Special thanks to Carl Lindberg for his great explanations of the CAP procedures, as well as to Ralph Black, and those at the Heritage Flight Museum in Bellingham, WA.

Jim, your sense of adventure and openness to learning aided my thirst for knowledge. Without your encouragement and thoughtful readings of the manuscript, the book would still be an idea.

As always, to those in my writing group—Barbara Defreytas, Iris Jones, Mary Stone, Terry Parakh, and JoAnne Chavre— your careful listening kept the voices honest.

A very special thank you to Sara Stamey, my editor and friend, who understood the ideas behind the words.

Contents

Prologue

Chapter 1: **Dinner Plate** 13
Chapter 2: **Mountain and Molehills** 19
Chapter 3: **White Lies** 23
Chapter 4: **Arms of Steel** 27
Chapter 5: **Gone Fishing** 31
Chapter 6: **Moonshine** 39
Chapter 7: **Cast in Stone?** 47
Chapter 8: **Waste Not, Want Not.** 53
Chapter 9: **Missing Pieces** 63
Chapter 10: **The Flight of the Hummingbird** 69
Chapter 11: **Scree.** 75
Chapter 12: **Skid Road** 83
Chapter 13: **Two-Way Communication** 91
Chapter 14: **Baa, Baa, Black Sheep, Have You Any Wool?** 99
Chapter 15: **The Moon Is Made of Green Cheese** 103
Chapter 16: **Mourning Dove** 111
Chapter 17: **Flying Without a Compass.** 119
Chapter 18: **Walking on Eggshells** 125
Chapter 19: **Citizens of a Community** 133
Chapter 20: **Diablo: The Devil Made Me Do It** 143
Chapter 21: **Squaring a Circle** 153
Chapter 22: **Hinges and Handles.** 163
Chapter 23: **Nerve to Feel.** 171
Chapter 24: **Neighbors** 181
Chapter 25: **Trust and the Future** 191
Chapter 26: **Find the Loophole** 199
Chapter 27: **Attitude: Stable Position.** 209
Chapter 28: **Concrete Command Center** 219
Chapter 29: **Bird's Eye Perspective** 229
Chapter 30: **SAR-X: Search and Rescue Exercise** 243
Chapter 31: **Connections Concomitants** 253
Chapter 32: **Beginnings Never End** 265

Reading Club Questions
Preview of Founding Stones, *Generation of Secrets, Book Three*
About the Author

Prologue
Truths Swept Under the Sand

Off the coast of Puerto Rico, two months and six days before the city of Hiroshima rose in a cloud of nuclear haze, a practice bombing mission went terribly wrong. A young man in a rowboat witnessed the sky explode and waves plow into the wings and tail of a metal bird.

As a local fisherman, he knew to hurry with patience. Waiting for the waters to settle, for the wind to carry the flames away, he studied the pilot struggling to inflate a raft. He paddled toward the crash site, a mile out along the point of the Borinquen coast. The engines in the B-29 Bomber must have failed, and the pilot missed the approach to the longest runway in the Caribbean, Ramey Air Force Base.

In the midst of chaos and black smoke, screams rose from three of the thirteen crew members as they sank below the surface, caught in the plane's fuselage. Of the ten remaining crew, five men scrambled into the plane's raft, leaving five stranded. Sirens sounded from the air base. The young fisherman focused on one man who dove below the surface, frantic. He popped up and then dove again. Obscured by the veil of smoldering oil, the fisherman hid from view. The rescuers from Ramey Air Force Base scooped up four of the remaining survivors. As the air base's crash boat and plane's raft made their way to shore, the fifth survivor surfaced.

The fisherman rowed to his side. He reached down, grabbed the frantic diver's forearm, and hauled him aboard. Not a man of many words, the fisherman said in his best English, "What are you looking for?"

Out of breath and in despair, the survivor coughed and sputtered, "Cracks. This plane carries a nuclear bomb."

A sheen of oil covered the spot where the plane sank. Both men stared as the waves engulfed the black hole of danger.

The fisherman passed him a bottle of rum. "My name is Tuto. And yours?"

"Spencer T. I'm the engineer, the person responsible for the crash."

Tuto picked up his oars and rowed along the coast to shore. The wind caught the boat as they headed inward to a small cove. He watched the man called Spencer T brush a tear from his eyes.

"By now, your plane has sunk 120 feet below the surface."

Spencer T held his head in his hands. "What have I allowed to happen? I am such a fool. There is no going back now, too much secrecy, too much destruction. I . . ."

Tuto strained to hear the engineer's lament, but the wind carried off his words.

12

Chapter 1:
Dinner Plate

Maria studied her aunt JoAnne, who had taken the leader's seat at the head of the table. She chose a chair at the opposite end with three settings between them. The two faced one another, giving Maria a clear view of her aunt's plate and her aunt a direct sight line into Maria's face and plate. Maria chose her spot so she could spy. Not with malice—no one deliberately hid anything in this household—but to uncover truths among the peas, potatoes, chicken, and rolls.

Maria had arrived late last night from back East. Anything past the Cascade Mountains was East in her mind. She could see the signs of the Pacific Northwest in the table setting: lacking a tablecloth, a forest green placemat framed each setting. Rosy red tulips with yellow centers, mixed with pale white daffodils, graced the middle of the mahogany dining table. Fern sprigs circled the beeswax candles.

Maria felt pleased to be back home in Concrete, Washington, where she could depend on the subtle complexities of their simple life. As Maria took her place, she noted her aunt's nod, an indication of approval as well as a gesture to be alert. JoAnne wore the white linen dress, a sign that Maria was still in her favor, and she had pulled her hair back in a low bun with a black velvet ribbon encircling stray hairs. Around her neck, a scarf of red tulips hid the necklace of hearts, a necklace rarely worn and even now obscured. Her wheelchair, concealed by the adaptation of padded armrests with a cloth that matched the sofa and armchairs, fit snugly under the dining table.

Maria had been gone for over a year, and this dinner was a valiant attempt at appearing normal.

"Pass me the chicken, will you, Maria de la Via?"

Maria de la Via was a nickname that JoAnne used when she needed Maria to be on her best behavior. Ever since Maria was little, they would pretend that she came from an aristocratic family from the Deep South. In order for Maria to learn her manners, JoAnne would continue the ruse when they dined with influential families from town. Now at twenty-six, Maria found this game annoying. She had come home because of a frantic phone call: JoAnne needed to fly to the Caribbean on a "mission."

As Maria passed the roasted chicken, she watched for signs of why her aunt had invited this group of people to their home. She knew that the chicken on the platter was from their own yard, since JoAnne held a strict food philosophy. Never eating meat or poultry outside of their home, she had a mantra: "If you can't grow it and kill it, you shouldn't eat it." For that reason alone, the town thought JoAnne was a finicky eater, or worse yet, a vegetarian. Roasted chicken was reserved for family and friends who appreciated the hard work of raising, slaughtering, and cooking.

"Good to have you back home, young woman." It was their old neighbor, Russell. At eighty-eight, he looked kinder and sweeter than ever and had clearly dressed up to be here. His white hair no longer covered his head; the few strands left stood up to salute the sky and competed with his beard, which refused the edge of a razor. He wore an old blue shirt that showed the wear of buttonholes frayed from washing. The shirt complemented his blue eyes that could still penetrate a stranger's soul. Today, they peered out from behind the bouquet of flowers he had strategically placed at his setting. Even though JoAnne had made peace with his gossiping ways, he still shied from her sharp eyes. He must have brought the flowers as an offering, since tulips and daffodils were his specialty.

As Maria passed the chicken, she winked at Russell. His thin lips curled upward until JoAnne looked at him. Maria felt an undercurrent of disapproval. Something was going on.

"Please, help yourselves," JoAnne directed. "Spencer must have been delayed."

Each of the guests took a helping of chicken. Of the five settings, one seat to her aunt's left remained empty. JoAnne was a stickler for timing, and Maria wondered who was this Spencer who would receive her aunt's wrath?

Molly McCain sat opposite Russell with her head down as if praying. She was almost the same age as Russell, but meaner and uglier. Maria could almost hear the hushed whisper of warning from JoAnne: "Unkind thoughts beget unkind actions." Molly and her aunt had been feuding over property rights since Maria was four. Why, after so many years, was Molly here eating with them?

Molly took the chicken and the potatoes, peas, and applesauce, piling the food in the center of her plate. She heaped the food so high that her chin touched the edge and stuck there, defying anyone to mention the obvious. Nothing had changed in her world of greedy entitlement.

After the mysterious phone call of a week ago had brought Maria home, she had expected a heart-to-heart conversation alone with JoAnne, not this odd dinner party. Intrigued, she studied her aunt's plate for clues.

JoAnne's peas were scattered around the edges of the potatoes, a clear sign of nerves. She usually made pictures or circles before devouring them one by one. Today, they were strewn with no pattern, cast off. Clearly without appetite, JoAnne cut each piece of her chicken until her plate was filled with bite-sized chunks.

After the silence of mouths chewing, the swallowing and sipping of wine, Maria finally caught her aunt's eye. The green flecks that peppered JoAnne's hazel eyes flashed a warning. Not sure if it was anger, fear, or excitement, Maria kept her head bent. Although she was starved, she couldn't eat. A missing guest, no toast or words of thanks for the meal? Despite her good intentions of keeping quiet, words spilled from her lips, "Let's all make a toast to—"

Before Maria could finish, JoAnne clicked her wine glass with her fork, "A toast to seeing old friends."

Maria almost spilled her wine. Russell was their benevolent knight not ever quite dressed in shining armor. He was nosy and a nuisance and always trying to propose to JoAnne, and when that didn't work, he'd go on a drinking binge. He lifted his glass of red wine and winked at Maria.

Molly peered up from her plate. Instead of lifting her wine glass, she grabbed at her glass of water and raised the goblet in the air. "I guess we are old, aren't we?"

After all these years Molly could still twist words to suit her.

Maria sipped her wine slowly, letting the rich earthy flavor warm her throat as the wine made its way down. She took another taste, nodded at JoAnne, and said, "I like your choice tonight. Is this from the winery downriver?"

"Yes, it's the first bottling since the new owner took over the old Tar Heel bootleg operation."

At this, Molly's glass slipped. Ripples of water flowed toward Maria's plate, which acted as a dam, diverting the water away from her lap but toward JoAnne. Maria sopped up the table with her napkin and righted the glass. Russell winked at Maria again. JoAnne wheeled her chair slightly away from the table. Coconspirators, they were up to something.

As if on cue, the front door opened, and in walked the mystery guest. JoAnne swirled her wheelchair toward the door, and Maria admired her aunt's enduring elegance and strength as she whisked herself around. More than forty years without the use of legs, and she made Maria feel clumsy.

"Speaking of the devil, here is the new vintner. We didn't wait for you, Spencer, but we haven't even finished our first course. We were just sampling the wine from your grapes. Let me introduce you. Everyone, this is Spencer. Spencer, this is Russell, the gentleman who follows me around like a puppy, my neighbor Molly, whose property butts up against the river, and my beloved grandniece, Maria de la Via."

Everyone nodded from their seats. Maria, hearing her aunt's warning code, stood up with wet napkin in hand and walked over to the front door. But the man—probably in his thirties—had already bent down to kiss JoAnne on the cheek and was wheeling her back to the head of the table as Maria approached. She stared at the closeness between her aunt and Spencer, wondering why she hadn't heard of him before. A twinge of jealousy hit as her aunt blushed at his attention.

Maria thought if she were to use a color for what she was feeling, she would not pick green or red, but more of an orange infused with the white light of dawn. This Spencer, a tall tanned figure looking the part of an outdoorsman, walked with the grace of knowing one's self. His smile took her by surprise. Maria was used to looking for smiles through the lips or the eyes. When she played poker with the other pilots, she could judge when they felt the luck of the cards, when they felt happiness. Spencer's smile came from his hands, his gait, the way he held his shoulders.

Maria impulsively held out her wet hand to shake. Spencer nodded a hello and seemed to ignore Maria's hand as he returned JoAnne to the head seat at the dining table. Maria pulled her hand back and crossed her arms. She felt irrelevant, as if this person had slipped into her home and family and taken her spot.

Holding back her irritation, she modulated her voice to a low pitch, one of JoAnne's tricks to soften words. "Obviously you know my aunt, but I am sorry to say I have no idea who you are. I am at a disadvantage."

"I think your aunt planned this dinner so I could meet all of you."

Before Maria could respond, Molly chimed in, "And why would she do that? I have no interest in meeting a young hooligan who grows grapes, steals water, and takes over property that he has no rights to."

Spencer took his time to respond. After filling his plate with chicken and salad, he took a bite of each, then a sip of wine, before saying, "You do jump to conclusions. Should we break down each of your declarations one by one, challenge each other, and stomp off, or just enjoy a good meal?"

At this, Maria couldn't help but smile at her aunt. No one had ever put Molly in her place so quickly.

Chapter 2:
Mountains and Molehills

The sweat dribbled down her neck and onto her chest, and Molly's face burned as she made her way to her car. JoAnne never could accommodate her guests. Making her walk down the driveway was just downright inconsiderate; someone ought to have fetched her car. Who did she think she was?

Already she was out of breath. With all the extra weight she had gained over the years, her walk was more of a waddle. As she passed the row of bordering shrubs, Molly plucked the blossoms off all the bushes, an unconscious act, something she had been doing since her teens. The bright crimson petals of the rhododendrons fell to the ground. *Red, red, red; my mother is dead.* A horrible thought, but it only made Molly smile. Now she needn't worry about visiting or covering her tracks. Besides, as the only daughter, she was entitled to the money. Her brother was too stupid to deal with anything. Her mother's death couldn't have happened at a better time. Now she'd have enough money to see a specialist for her lungs and thyroid and live in the style she deserved.

This dinner party had been a farce, and Molly sensed that JoAnne was trying to get back at her. Indignant, she opened the door to her silver Eldorado, and eased herself between the seat and steering wheel. Even with the seat pulled back to the furthest notch, her belly felt confined. For years, Molly had watched JoAnne thrive after her fall down the scree off of Baker Lake hillside. JoAnne couldn't possibly know the truth about that night. Molly had kept quiet and would continue to do so, no matter what. Besides, JoAnne was just fine, better than she was herself.

Driving east on Highway 20, Molly made a mental count of all the businesses she had worked at: the gravel pit, the cement factory, Seattle City Light, Northern State Hospital. There were too many, and she hated them all. Most of those jobs only lasted a few years, not like her favorite job with the Skagit River Telephone Company. The Quackenbush sisters were busy owners with multiple businesses. When they became ill and could no longer attend to the switchboard, Molly had relished stepping in, with full control of the switchboard and the accounts.

Her right eye began twitching. Her heart raced. She took a few deep breaths as the new doctor told her to do, but her blood pressure still rose as she drove through the gate to her now-defunct sheep farm. The sign overhead had been carved close to forty years ago from logs she acquired from the Tar Heels in exchange for keeping quiet about their bootleg operations. Now faded with years of sun, the bold letters spelling McCain Sheep Ranch threatened Molly. She couldn't put into words the threat, but since Spencer had moved in down the way, she felt spied upon.

She preferred having the bootleggers as neighbors. They were drunk, ignorant, and could be easily persuaded by her demands. Being on the wrong side of the law made them malleable. How dare Spencer challenge her in front of everyone at JoAnne's dinner party. He may have inherited that property from his uncle, but his property rights were her concern. Spencer was too smart for his britches. His snooping had to be stopped. He was worse than his uncle and not as good looking.

Another flash of heat passed over her body. A nagging pull caused her heart to skip a beat. The doctors said this sensation was an irregular heartbeat, but Molly knew better. Problems, complications, meddling, this was nothing but a nuisance. If everyone would just mind their own business. This was all JoAnne's fault. And bringing Spencer to dinner, as if JoAnne didn't think Molly would remember his uncle, that stupid man who had finally given up on JoAnne—she was a fool.

Just before Molly pulled into her garage, she paused to look over the valley to the Skagit River below. The mountains loomed in the background, her own hill setting her above the floodplain. The fading light cast shadows that seemed to move with the wind and clouds along the valley floor. Without her binoculars, Molly couldn't quite feel at peace. Living alone had its advantage, but lately she felt a sense of ill ease, as if she was missing something, or just that something was missing.

Her garage opened into her main foyer. Before she entered, she checked the string set at mid-ankle. No disturbance; no one had ventured in. Satisfied, she blobbed her purse onto the kitchen counter.

She was out of breath and hungry. Dinner had not satisfied her appetite. She took a chocolate-covered caramel candy from the dish on the counter, unwrapped the cellophane, and curled the wrapper under her sleeve. The chocolate had half melted with the summer heat, leaving the caramel chewy and sweet. Without thinking, she devoured half the bowl. Smudges of chocolate lined her lips, and wrappers fell from her sleeve as she made her way to the sink.

The phone rang, startling her from her sugar reverie. "Oh, shush your noise. Whoever is calling can damn well wait."

Ignoring the phone, Molly refilled the candy bowl and stared out the kitchen window. Absent from her view were telephone lines. Years ago, all the lines had been buried along her driveway. The poles and skirts of wire were just nostalgic memories now, but back when telephone service first came to the valley, the tall spars of trees and crisscrossing of wire meant you were well off.

She remembered the first time the sisters who owned Skagit River Telephone Company were called out to fix the telephone lines. Nell did all the heavy work, and Glover usually stayed behind. This time, Glover was in the hospital, and the whole switchboard fell to Molly. Oh, what sense of control she felt, answering the rings, connecting two callers. At first, she dropped a few calls by accident. Later she would drop them on purpose.

Finally, the ringing ceased and Molly's recorded voice rasped, "This is Molly McCain. I don't want to answer the phone. If you feel the need to communicate with me, send me a letter. But if you must, leave me a message."

"Hello, Molly, I know you are there. We have to talk. The bank wants to foreclose on the ranch, and they are questioning me about other holdings. I'm worried about the gravel pit. Molly, answer your damn phone."

She was almost tempted to pick up the receiver. Instead, she took out three muffins from the refrigerator and smashed them with her fists. Her brother was incompetent, always making mountains out of molehills. She tossed the muffins in the garbage can, just like she used to do when they were kids.

Chapter 3:
White Lies

Russell didn't have far to go after dinner. Years ago, he'd have walked through the field and crossed over the creek, but now he had given in slightly to his age and drove his trusty green truck down the gravel road two miles past the creek and into his driveway. Tree frogs chirped in the wetlands, and wind blew up the river from the Salish Sea. He always left the light on in the kitchen to welcome him back home. Although he'd lived alone for more than thirty-five years after his only sweetheart, Emma, had died, he still missed her warm greeting.

Within seconds of slamming the truck door, he heard the yapping, singsong bark of Maya, his aging mutt lab. She stood at attention, eyes on him, tail swishing, as he opened the kitchen door.

"Quit your barking, you ungrateful dog. I brought you some leftovers. I could barely eat watching that old witch Molly gobble her food down."

Maya obeyed, sitting on her back legs, tail wagging and eyes alert. Russell emptied the leftover chicken and potatoes into her bowl. Waiting until Russell gave her the signal and patted her head, Maya limped over to her dish, sniffed, and ate.

"Good girl, you might as well eat it all. That JoAnne is a great cook, and she'll be off soon enough on a big adventure to Puerto Rico. You'll miss her as much as I will."

Russell didn't believe in locking his doors and usually left all the outside doors open in case a neighbor was in need, or now more likely if he was in need. The door to the basement was another story. This he kept locked up. From behind a wood panel next to the fuse box in the foyer, he unhooked a long antique key to his shop. During the war, he had reasons to lock the door, but now it was more to hold on to his memories, or not to reveal them. He'd collected many as a salesman traveling up and down the Skagit River, laughing at all the stories and the gossipy news his customers insisted on telling him in the guise of facts, informing him of half-truths. Some facts he now wished he could forget.

"Damn it." He had to jiggle the key just right for it to work—it had to be close to sixty years old. "Maya, aging is the shits. Creaky and leaky—that is all we are. Come on, let's go downstairs and work."

Work was a wide concept for Russell, encompassing everything from gardening, birding, and fixing motors, to building radio-controlled airplanes and listening to his ham radio. Working for Skagit Equipment had paid off, as he not only sold the various tools but was responsible for knowing how to work and fix them as well. His basement was organized by projects. All his gardening tools filled one wall. The rakes, shovels, hoes, and his favorite dandelion puller were all outlined in green paint so that he knew where to put them and whether or not they were loaned out. Bins of potatoes, carrots, and bulbs were stacked one atop another. The lawn mower and wheelbarrow were out in the garden shed, but he kept his essential tools away from the riffraff.

He was a stubborn man and still remembered when the house was robbed, just garden tools and some wire and stuff. "Maya, stop your growling. All that happened before your time."

Russell growled irritably to himself. He flicked on the light at the head of the stairwell and took twenty tentative steps down as he hung onto the handrail. He noted that the handrail was as shaky as he was, had been since last month, but he had more important matters to deal with. When things calmed down with JoAnne, he could tend to repairs.

Ignoring the garden section, he walked on till he came to another small door. This door was almost invisible, with his wrenches, hand-saws, and hammers outlined and covering the magnetic pressure point that released the latch.

Maya sat patiently until Russell reached behind the wrench and the door swung open. A crackling noise came from the center of the room. Even before he switched on the light, Russell headed for the table. The crackling meant someone was broadcasting. With a pull on the over-head chain, a small bulb gave off a faint light. He checked his watch. Either they were early tonight, or someone else was broadcasting on his wavelength.

Taking the receiver in his hand, he pressed the talk switch. "Copy over, this is Hummingbird. Do you read me?"

Chapter 4:
Arms of Steel

A hush had fallen over the house after the guests said their goodbyes, and JoAnne let the tiredness settle in. Maybe the dinner had been a bad idea. Maria was still in the kitchen rattling the dinner pots, clearly upset and confused. JoAnne decided to let her rattle the dishes some more before she ventured out to talk with her.

Guiding her hands along the worn wheels of her chair, JoAnne headed outside to her vegetable and flower garden to admire the sky. The air was warm with summer, dusk just settling in. How she loved the summer when days stretched and nights shrank. Nine o'clock, and the sun still hovered above. All the garden paths accommodated her wheelchair, flattened river rocks leveled with concrete to create the feel of a paved walkway. Russell had helped her with the bird feeders, and even at this hour the stellar jays swooped in while the rufous hummingbird drank sweet nectar from the feeders. Thank goodness for Russell, always there for her. His motto was, "Look your problems straight on. Everything can be fixed, as long as you are prepared."

If only that were true. JoAnne stared up at the sky, the promise of stars. Her butt ached from sitting so long, and her mind felt the same ache of time, the strain of words and deeds not understood. She hated admitting her age—not that she cared about looks, but by admitting she was closer to eighty than seventy, she had to accept that time might just stop her from finding truth. No, she wouldn't allow that. Age was relative. Her mind was still sharp, and her physical strength was beyond most women her age. All she had to do was keep learning, keep active.

"Aunt Jo, where are you? I've finished the dishes."

"Maria, come out to the garden. I'm watching the rising of the stars."

JoAnne waited until the lights of the kitchen flicked off and she heard the swish of the swinging back door before she wheeled herself around to face Maria.

"Come here, my sweetness. I didn't mean to disturb you this evening with a crowd of people for dinner. I know that took you by surprise, but I need you to see clearly what's at stake. Sometimes explanations fall short of the truth."

Maria looked at her aunt and sighed. "Aunt Jo, I owe you my life. If you hadn't rescued me, I'd be a delinquent or worse. But you do get me mixed up sometimes. Which truth are we talking about? Is it white, or blue, or red, or black?"

JoAnne cringed. "Do you remember the last time you sat on my lap and asked me to tell you a story?"

Maria finally cracked a smile. "I know exactly the last time I crawled up your wheelchair and plopped down on your lap." Every year when Maria had come home from boarding school, even when she was too small to reach JoAnne's arms for a hug, she'd scramble up the wheels and give her kisses. She'd earned her other nickname, Monkey.

Maria bent over and kissed her aunt on the cheek. "I'm too big to sit on your lap now, but I get the sense that you might just want to sit on mine. What's going on?"

"The last time you climbed up was when you were fourteen. It was a happy and sad day for me. You still gave me kisses, but I knew that I was no longer the center of your world. You had your own mission in life." JoAnne had waited for her on the tarmac, dressed in what Maria called her welcoming outfit, a white linen dress and white hat. She sat for hours waiting for the plane, and it finally arrived late after a lightning storm. She was worried, but no, Maria sauntered out with a big grin, bubbling over with how the sky lit up and the pilot skirted the rods of the gods. "Tell me, do you still see the adventure in flying?"

"Yes. But you are doing what you always do when you aren't ready to answer me. When do we leave for the island, and why?"

"I will keep my promise to you, the promise of yet another story." Maria had asked her for this each time she'd returned home. "I'll tell you how I fell."

"Each year you tell me the story, and each year it changes."

"Yes. There are many versions of truth and many versions of lies."

JoAnne turned her chair around and pushed herself away from Maria and over to the swimming pool. The sun still cast a warm glow over the patio, the last rays before it set. Without a word, JoAnne maneuvered her chair over to a concrete ramp covered with a rubber mat. Locking her wheelchair in place, she hoisted herself up by her arms and gently let her bottom down on the rubber. Throwing off her dress, she pressed a button along the ramp. Warm water trickled down the center of the mat so she could slide into the pool. Just as her legs touched bottom, JoAnne folded her torso so her center of gravity changed and her arms extended. Synchronizing each breath with a pull and a glide, she propelled forward. Her legs lifted upward, skimming the water's surface. With grace and power, her arms of steel released her from her imprisoned legs, and she flew as if she had her wings again.

After a couple of laps, JoAnne came up for a breath and called out to Maria, "Go visit Spencer. He'd like the company."

Maria gave her a half salute as she returned to the house, and JoAnne was left to her own thoughts.

Each lap took thirty seconds. JoAnne could hold her breath for two laps, a far cry from her younger days when she competed on the swim team. But then she had her legs, and the laps swallowed one another. JoAnne hardly ever thought of herself in terms of her legs. Her fall from the mountainside was an unfortunate accident, and regret, blame, self-pity took up too much energy to pursue. Then a letter delivered only a month ago from across the ocean had changed her thinking. That, plus a frank talk with Russell and the discovery of a latent illness in her town, made her realize that what followed her injury had been a sequence of manipulations that no one wanted to review. Least of all herself.

JoAnne deepened her pulls, cupping her hands, stretching her arms as if she could stretch the truth. Anger, for the first time in more than thirty years, overwhelmed her. Bringing her arms together, she dipped below the water's surface, undulating with her body like the waves of an ocean. She could almost feel the pull of past currents, the salty kisses of another time, but there was no sense in letting what was gone dictate her mood. With only a few weeks before the annual Concrete Fly-In, she had lots to do.

Ending her swim with her signature handstand, JoAnne dove five feet down to the bottom of the pool and pushed up with her hands. Her legs, buoyant and light, lifted in the air. An observer would see only her toes, not JoAnne's triumphant smile.

Chapter 5:
Gone Fishing

Maria stumbled out of bed, her eyelashes glued together with what JoAnne called fairy dust. She had slept fitfully with images of running, dark corners, the old feeling of heat burning her feet, and the world slipping as if she were falling off a cliff. Quickly, Maria ran the hot water, placed the washcloth under the faucet, and applied the warmth to her eyes. Old nightmares popped into her head, but the heat melted the crystals of fairy dust from her eyelids and with it, the past fears.

Instead of reassuring her last night, JoAnne had churned up new fears of abandonment, erasing Maria's hope of a simple life at home. But she knew better than to push—answers always came slowly with JoAnne. The first question unanswered was this character, Spencer. Taken aback by JoAnne's boldness in bringing him into their home, without her even knowing of his existence, and then to tell her to go pay him a visit, Maria tensed in outrage.

Pulling on a t-shirt and running shorts, she stretched her body with lunges, push-ups, and the balance pose of the tree. Standing on one foot with arms stretched to the sky, Maria counted to fifty. When she fell over as she reached twenty-five, she started the pose again. After three attempts, she gave up.

Balance eluding her, she figured a good run along the river would clear her mind.

The only noise in the house was the ticktock of the tall mahogany grandfather clock in the dining room. Long ago, it had lost its hourly and half-hour dong, but the ticktock of each minute still echoed off the walls. Maria pulled a notepad from the kitchen junk drawer and wrote:

Aunt Jo,

Hope you slept well after your swim. Gone for a run by the river. Fishing for answers, call me if you need anything, I've got my cell.

Maria de la Via (I'll behave myself).

The sun skimmed over the horizon, rising ever so slowly as if stretching to wake up. Maria noted her good position on the road and smiled at finding no one in front of or behind her as she drove along Highway 20, an event rarely achieved once the weather turned nice. Soon the hikers and tourists of the season would crowd the road, but for now Highway 20 belonged to her. She hoped that her favorite river run would also be empty. Just by mile marker 100, the road veered slightly and a small white building, tucked behind a weeping willow tree, greeted her. Once an old railroad ticket stop, St. Francis Church now offered wayward travelers a place to be close to God and a connection to all creatures. Maria never went inside, where rows of pews faced a bare altar and, through the window, Sauk Mountain. Her church was outside. All she needed was to see the views of Sauk Mountain, green fields with cows, and across the way, her river. This to Maria was heaven. She parked her car and made ready for her run.

In her one-year absence, the running path along the river had remained free of brush. Whenever she returned home for a visit, she kept the path weeded, using an antique machete to whack the weeds back. With no money in the county's coffers for maintenance, Maria volunteered her labor. Now seeing it in such good condition triggered a sense of loss as well as relief. She wondered who had taken on the project while she was gone.

Sweat dripped along her short bangs onto her neck and trickled down the sides of her shirt. The faster she ran, the stronger she felt. Maria thought of JoAnne, bound in her wheelchair since before she could remember. Swimming to her aunt was just as powerful as running. Maria ran harder, mimicking the strong arm strokes of her aunt's crawl with that of her own pumping legs. They both worked their bodies for mental clarity, and Maria had started running because her aunt swam.

When she had first moved to her aunt's home, Maria was angry and confused. All she had was her aunt's address, a name she had found in her mother's old purse. She was a runaway, an adolescent, too young to know better, and her hitchhiking experience had gone wrong. Maria could still feel the rush of adrenaline when the police had found her intoxicated. Just thinking back to those years caused her pain, a deep side ache. She ran faster, forgetting to look at the river, forgetting to look at all. Her right foot came down on a root, and she found herself facedown on the path. As she brushed herself off, she heard a voice she recognized.

"Didn't your aunt ever teach you to look where you were going?"

Spencer stood on the riverbank with a fishing rod in his hand. Maria spat out mud and glared. How stupid of her not to remember that his vineyard was just minutes from here, across the highway and up the hill. If she thought JoAnne had blushed under his care last night, her face by comparison must have resembled a freshly cooked beet.

Trying to regain her footing, she said the first thing that came to her. "You must be the one keeping the brush off the path."

"All but the root you tripped over. I do apologize."

"I didn't mean to sound ungrateful. I have been clearing the debris for years, and I appreciate all your work. I wasn't paying attention to where I was going."

Spencer remained in fishing stance, pole held loosely in his right hand. "Never take a step before you know where the next foot will land."

Maria burst out laughing. She had heard that saying so many times when she was growing up that she had been thinking the same thought. Being prepared was an ingrained trait from her aunt and from her training as a pilot. She had even won awards as a model pilot—able to take care of all contingencies—and earned honors at the academy.

"Did I say something funny?" He wasn't smiling.

"No, I was laughing at myself. Do you mind if I sit for a minute to recover from my encounter with the earth coming up and grabbing me? That is, if you don't mind company while you're fishing."

"First tell me why you were laughing, and then I'll let you sit on top of my ice chest."

"Aunt Jo always said that to me. Not always in the same words, but when I was a kid going to pick berries, she'd ask me where the bowl was to hold the strawberries. Or if I was going for a walk, she'd ask me what I'd do if it rained. I had to know how to change the oil in the car, change a tire, and even know the weather plans for a week so that I'd be prepared if the wind shifted."

As tension visibly eased in Spencer's shoulders, a smile crept along his lips. Last night, he had acted more freely with her aunt. Maria preferred that confidence and intimacy to this more formal side.

"I got the saying from my great-uncle, for whom I'm named. I owe my good fortune to him."

"I guess we have that in common. My aunt is my good fortune." Maria gazed out at the river. Ice fields from Glacier Peak were melting, muddying the water. The Sauk River, laden with glacial melt, joined the Skagit River not far up from here. She wondered if Spencer was a good fisherman, good enough to see the fish in murky water. "Did your uncle teach you how to fish?"

"Are you asking me if I'm a good fisherman?"

Spencer's eyes were lit up now with amusement. Maria didn't know how JoAnne had met him, but she could see why they got along. He had that rascally, devilish air. Not quite a smart aleck, but maybe one who pushed himself and knew his limits.

"My uncle taught me to fish rivers," he added. "Not these rivers, but the rivers of the tropics. He taught me how to be patient, to see riffles and pools beyond rocks and know depth. He taught me to smell the wind and the rain. He taught me to know more than less about anything I attempted. So, Maria, the fact that the river is cloudy this morning doesn't mean that the fish aren't there. They're hungry just like you and I are hungry. The small fish, the insects, they all move even with the silty water. I know where they are even if I can't see them."

It was Maria's turn to grin. She had baited him and then reeled him in. Spencer knew it, too. Maria thought they may have been flirting, but she was out of practice and couldn't be sure. She had caught him bragging, and that clearly wasn't his style. Now he blushed. The red mixed with his tan, and his dark hair shone. He lowered his gaze.

She crossed her legs on the ice chest and stared out at the water. She let the river flow through her, ignoring the urge to talk or bombard Spencer with questions. The silence felt like a blanket. Maria always slept with a blanket, not for warmth but for the weight. She needed something to hold her in place, to keep her safe, to make sure that she remained tethered to the world.

Spencer finally cleared his throat. "Time to move on. Birds are in the bushes, and it's my sign to go back to work."

Maria jumped up from the ice chest, startled at his voice, startled that she had let her guard down. "I don't usually zone out like that."

35

No smile answered her, only a look to keep quiet. Motioning toward the bushes, he pointed. All Maria heard was a "witchity, witchity" song, and then two common yellowthroats flew out.

"These warblers act like my alarm clock. Since I took over the vineyard, I fish each morning before my chores. Their calls let me know when it's time to leave. Last week, I found two of the birds dead. The week before that, I found three others."

Maria turned her back to the river and faced Spencer. His jaw tightened. His eyes held her gaze, transmitting a message of anger and alarm.

"Is that why you came over last night for dinner?" she asked.

"Yes and no."

"Tell me about the 'yes' part, and I'll ask you about the 'no' part later."

"When I first came back to take over the farm," Spencer said, "I noticed some oddities in the soil, though nothing alarming by itself. The phosphates were up, the potassium lower than normal. There was a chalky residue. I tested and retested the minerals, trying to create the right balance for the topsoil."

Spencer paused as if putting together a puzzle. He looked at the river and the trees, a breeze running through the leaves. A bald eagle flew above, taking advantage of the gentle breeze from the west, gliding before it swooped down to fish. Maria knew the feeling of gliding, the balance of air over the wings moving so fast that the plane lifts past gravity's pull. She'd find the place where the wind cradles the plane, stabilizing almost without her guidance. But as a pilot, she felt like an impostor—the eagle's flight represented nature's perfection.

It was her turn to clear her throat. "Doesn't every vintner have to work the soil to create the perfect balance for the grapes to thrive?"

Spencer sighed. "I only have my suspicions. My tests on the soil now seem safe, but I found traces of elements surrounding my property that are toxic—toxic enough to make small birds sick and die."

"Who would contaminate the soil?"

Spencer's face hardened. His fishing demeanor gone, his body tensed as anger surfaced. "I'm more concerned with how it got contaminated. Knowing the 'how' would lead us to the person responsible. Then we can determine if the 'why' was intentional."

Maria's stomach turned at the sternness in his voice that almost felt like a reprimand. His words held a remembered tone of abuse, not toward her but toward her mother. Maria had run from her home thirteen years ago to escape that meanness. Her mother had a habit of bringing home men with opinions, with sternness that morphed into verbal and physical beatings. Unconsciously, she put her hands to her ears.

"Maria, did I offend you?"

Her heart thumped—an adrenaline rush, fight or flight. Spencer moved closer, and she readied herself for verbal blows. None came. Soft sky-blue eyes, weather lines, and the steadiness of a kind heart met her eyes. Again Maria had misjudged.

She took a breath. "You seemed aggressive, and I felt it was directed at me."

"Your Aunt Jo mentioned that you sometimes get skittish. I am angry, but not at you."

"What else did Aunt Jo tell you about me?"

At this, Spencer stepped back, started packing up his fishing gear, and shot Maria a look. "I think that comes under the category of your 'no.' You asked me why I was at dinner last night. Russell, JoAnne, and even the old sourpuss Molly have noticed birds dying on or near their properties. The dinner was meant to open up a dialogue concerning the cause. That didn't happen."

Spencer busied himself loading up his truck—buying time, or

dismissing her? Only minutes before, she had felt the urge to flee. She ran in place, stomping the ground, then planted herself firmly in Spencer's vision.

"Then the other reason you were there involved me?"

"I'm not so sure I want to tell you. Now you look like you'll hit me."

Maria sighed, a balloon slowly releasing air. Deflated, she smiled.

"JoAnne also said you were *learning* to be patient. The other reason I was there last night was to meet you. Apparently, your aunt needs us to get a plane ready for you to fly back to Puerto Rico after the Concrete Fly-In."

"That's why I rushed home. What I need to know is why I'm flying to Puerto Rico and why you are involved."

Maria couldn't figure out what bothered her more: not knowing why she was going to Puerto Rico, or why JoAnne had confided in this man who seemed to know all about her while she didn't have a clue who he was. More importantly, Spencer appeared in control. Without thinking, she grabbed Spencer's arm. "If you want me to trust you, you have to tell me the truth."

He placed his hand over hers and stared into her eyes. Again, her shell of protection slid off. She saw why her aunt trusted him.

"I only know parts of the truth. Your aunt knew my uncle when they were younger. He still lives in Puerto Rico. We, your aunt and I, met by chance last year when I moved back to open the vineyard. When she saw me, she thought I was my uncle, and she nearly fainted."

"Okay, so you look like your uncle. Why is that so unusual?"

"Would it strike you as unusual, if someone thought you looked like a woman named Monica?"

Maria's jaw dropped, and tears filled her eyes. This time she ran, not from fright but from shock.

Chapter 6:
Moonshine

Russell massaged his lower back as he got up from kneeling in the garden. He'd lost most of his garlic to some blight. The leaves were yellowing, and black spots stained what should have been healthy green stalks. Next year, he'd dig up the whole bed and bring in fresh soil and manure. Garlic failing to produce, two years in a row, he couldn't accept. Just like he couldn't accept the age spots on his exposed arms or the gnarling knuckles that kept his hands perpetually knotted in a fist. The doctors had already tried reworking his veins to help his heart pump better, but refurbishing his body didn't work like the garden.

He held his hand up to his brow and stared toward the sun. Already it was past the north corner of his property. His stomach growled, letting him know that lunch was long past due. He looked down at Maya sleeping in the shade of the apple tree.

"Guess we best head back to the house. A man's got to eat sometime. Come on, girl."

His house sat on a small knoll where he could look out at the valley and the river. Walking up from the garden, Russell took his time, holding on to a long iron rail that followed the wood rounds he used as stepping-stones. His breath wheezed in and out, echoing a hollow repeat. Maya waited after each step, making sure he was okay.

A blue truck was parked parallel to his own. Russell smiled, knowing whom he'd find inside.

"It's about time you came in for something to eat. I decided to make us some grilled cheese sandwiches, baked beans, and dogs. No offense, Maya."

Spencer patted Maya's head, and she nuzzled in to his side. Russell sat down at the dining table without saying anything. Although he was physically moving slowly, Russell's mind flitted back and forth.

"By your silence, I'd think you didn't want visitors," Spencer said.

Russell held up his hand, motioning for Spencer to slow down. "Can't a man just catch his breath? Besides, I'm thinking."

"I can tell. Your eyes are flickering back and forth like a hummingbird."

At that, Russell cracked up. "That's funny, I use Hummingbird as my call name because Emma used to say that if I was wound up, and thinking, a hummingbird couldn't compete with my mental energy. The first time she said it was when I came home perplexed about one of my accounts upriver. At that time, the only quick way across the river was to take a small ferry. Logging meant logs were everywhere. I was selling the Talkie-Tooter to one of the bigger companies. This was an electrically actuated steam whistle for the donkey to let the tower know when to pull the logs up. I came home pacing and couldn't keep still. Someone had stolen it the night before. I couldn't figure out how or who did it."

"Did you ever figure it out?"

"Yep, it was one of your distant cousins, Ronald. He is long gone now, passed away. The Tar Heels had a bad reputation back then, some deserved, some not. Your cousin came to me the next day with some fresh moonshine, as a way of apologizing. Seems that they wanted to use the Tooter to signal if the sheriff was coming, give everyone a heads up."

"Did it work?"

Russell got up slowly and went to the cupboard. From the top shelf, he pulled down a ceramic jug and two shot glasses.

"Try some."

Spencer poured two shots and swallowed his in one gulp. He let his tongue linger over his lips. "Sweet, strong, best 'apple pie' I have ever tasted."

"Yep, Old Crow can't beat this stuff. Ralph felt bad that he had caused me trouble. He might have sold his moonshine illegally, but only because he hated the 'Revenooers.' Prohibition was over, but it didn't matter. All Ralph wanted to do was log, but when he lost his job, he went back to what he knew. The local whiskey makers back then didn't have a good recipe, but Ralph's recipe came with him from North Carolina. It was all in the corn. He might have skirted the law, but he meant no harm to me."

Spencer held the jug in his hand, rolled it around and looked inside. "You mean to tell me this 'apple pie' is over sixty years old?"

At this Russell bent his head down, trying to keep from laughing. "Every year since then, I've gotten a jug on Christmas, even after Ralph died. One of his relatives leaves the moonshine on my porch. Ralph was an honorable man. I kept quiet about lots of things he did. As long as he hurt no one, I trusted him. His intentions were pure—not like Miss Molly. Everything she does is meant to harm."

"Speaking of harm, I found five dead warblers this week."

"Did you take them to get analyzed? Nothing will happen until we can show there is a toxin. I thought we might have interested Molly in the issue, as she has lost most of her sheep. But she showed no interest in the subject at JoAnne's house last night. She'd rather have a riggin-fit over your vineyard. For some reason, she feels she has the rights to your land. I don't trust her. She is like a bull choker reaching out to destroy anyone in her path."

"My uncle warned me that she was a pest."

"Your uncle didn't know what JoAnne and I found out since his departure after World War II. Molly McCain has been up to no good for years. That is part of the reason JoAnne and your uncle lost touch. I heard things years ago and paid no mind to the gossip. At my age, you hate to think of evil. I am not a cynic, but my newest revelation is that lies are an incurable addiction. Molly can't see beyond her greed."

Spencer set the food on the table. He drew two glasses of water and pulled up his chair next to Russell.

"I didn't come here to talk about Molly. I'm worried that I upset JoAnne's grandniece. Maria was jogging this morning and ran past my fishing spot."

Russell waited for more, but Spencer kept eating his sandwich, as if his statement was enough to give Russell a clue.

"Spit it out, Spencer. I am a dying man. Either eat or talk."

"Maria didn't think it was odd that I looked like my uncle or that she looked like her aunt. I told her she looked like Monica, and she ran like a hunted deer."

Russell shook his head, pushed his beans into a pile on his plate, and stuck the hot dog in the middle.

"For a smart man, you sure know how to put your foot in your mouth. Didn't JoAnne warn you that Maria was skittish about her past? She hasn't seen her sister, Monica, for over fifteen years, not since Monica left Maria with her drunken mother. Maria knows nothing about her sister, nothing about the years of prostitution in Puerto Rico or that she is even alive."

At this Spencer dropped his fork. "Oh, dammit, no wonder she ran. I had no idea about any of that. Monica owns a restaurant near where my uncle lives. If she was a prostitute, she isn't one now. When JoAnne told me Maria was skittish about her past, I thought it was because Maria was a runaway. I take people as they are, not how they were. Damn, not only is my foot in my mouth, it feels like I tracked dog shit inside my house. How do I recover from that?"

Russell sat back on his chair, tilting it slightly onto the back two legs. After taking another swig of moonshine, he cleared his throat. "Looks like you and this chair have something in common. You both are missing some limbs, some truth and understanding. The flight Maria and JoAnne will be taking from the Concrete Fly-In to your esteemed island isn't a vacation. It is what you call a healing trip."

"I guess I just picked at the wound."

The kitchen chair crashed backward onto the floor. Russell stared up from the floor with a startled grin as wide as the rows between his cornfields. Maya jumped to attention and licked Russell's face. With a helping hand from Spencer, Russell sat upright and wiped Maya's dog kisses from his face.

"Emma warned me not to tilt my chair back. She is probably waving her finger at me, laughing on her cushy cloud. She still makes me laugh even from way up there. Sometimes I think she is directing my thoughts. Spencer, I wouldn't worry so much about scratching old wounds. Wounds heal with exposure. I'm worried about the festering. Nothing heals if the past is left to fester. It's what is hidden that worries me."

"And are you going to tell me about the old problems, or am I going to have to stumble my way through? If you want me to stumble, I will be knee high in dog excrement."

"It all starts and ends with Molly McCain. I'm not saying she caused all the problems—in fact, I think Molly believes that everyone else in the whole valley is the problem. All I can say is that since rediscovering your uncle through my hobby with the ham radio, so many of the issues of old need to be reconsidered. If Molly wasn't involved, she had her tentacles close by."

"What does this have to do with Maria and Monica, or for that matter, the toxins in the soil?"

Russell got up from the table and put his arm around Spencer's shoulder.

"Come with me down to the cellar where I have my ham radio set. I'm expecting to hear from your uncle. You know that he is the senior and you are the junior for a reason."

"I never could figure that one out. My dad's name is Robert, and I had never met my Granduncle Spencer until my dad died."

"It's foolishness naming boys the same as their fathers. Just like the royalty with all their confounded numbers attached to the same name—King Edward VII, Queen Elizabeth III. It confuses everyone, as if people are cookie cutters. In your case, it has more meaning. Your granduncle picked you out, made you like him. He was a fixer, gentle, wise. He was close to his nephew, your father, Robert. Although your father was young when he passed away, he was wise enough to send you to be with your granduncle."

Spencer was mulling this over, and neither spoke as they descended the basement stairs. Russell grabbed the key, but left the light off, and made his way slowly like a hooded slug across the floor and into his radio haven. Spencer let his eyes adjust to the darkness and the musty smell of earth mixed with grease, oil, and age. He rubbed his finger along the wall, feeling decades of grime and living. His own shop was like this. Clean dirt, purposeful, pure, laden with the sweat of love's labor.

As Russell opened the hidden door to the radio room, Spencer snapped out of his melancholic thoughts. The walls, lined with shoreline maps, spoke of the last fifty years. Secured by duct tape, maps yellowed and faded appeared as wallpaper with the fresher aerial photos adjacent. Red pushpins lined the Pacific coastal area, running up the Skagit River and into the streams. Blue pushpins marked the path of the farms, olivine mines, and gravel pits.

"Might as well sit yourself down. Spencer T isn't always punctual, and the time difference between Washington State and Puerto Rico confuses him. When was the last time you two spoke?"

"Usually we call every couple of weeks, but lately he is more anxious, worried. He has always been secretive about his work even though he is supposed to be retired. But since I told him about the birds dying and the toxicity of the vineyard's soil, he is obsessive."

"Did he mention coming back to the vineyard?"

"No."

"Good, I was afraid he would come back now that he knew JoAnne was here. I was afraid he'd start trouble."

Spencer stared at the older maps, noticing the currents, the pathways marked for boat crossings. The maps dated back to World War II, and most of the red pushpins delineated the ship route to Japan. His skin began to crawl, burn with an explosive thought. Could the birds dying have anything to do with radioactive waste from that war?

"Russell, it looks to me that the trouble is already here. Do you want to explain, or should I just make something up? You said that Molly McCain had her claws in everything. All I see here is what appears to be a government mess-up."

Russell fiddled with the dials. There was a crackling of radio waves and then, "This is Mourning Dove, copy."

"Hummingbird here, over."

Chapter 7:
Cast in Stone?

JoAnne pursed her lips, hiding the pain in her arms. No one could see her grimace, yet she felt exposed as she wheeled herself down the tarmac of the Concrete Airport. She had roused herself up early so as to peruse the field, making sure that all details for the onslaught of refurbished airplanes in the coming weeks fell into place. The airport, Mears Field, was a public facility surrounded by private hangars. Most of the tenants loved the fly-in as a way of keeping the past alive, and they volunteered their time setting up, bringing out their own planes, and even housing the pilots who flew in. Passions ran high at the airfield, as most of the pilots were fanatical about their hobby or livelihood. JoAnne didn't relish talking with the one tenant who was the opposite.

Wheeling up to the hangar, JoAnne hit the buzzer. She knew from the open windows and the door left ajar that Frank McCain sat inside downing his stash of moonshine.

Against her better judgment, she called out, "Frank, are you in there? It's me, JoAnne, here to talk about the fly-in."

Not getting an answer, she slowly opened the door the rest of the way and wheeled herself in. Frank had his back to the door and slowly turned his blotchy face toward her.

"Who invited you in here? Can't you see I'm busy?"

JoAnne slowly started to wheel her chair backward, closer to the exit.

"Where do you think you're going? You interrupt me and then leave?"

JoAnne knew that no matter what she said, Frank would react. Usually he was reasonable, or at least not confrontational, but seeing his reddened eyes and the dark stubbles of prickly hair on his chin, she estimated he had been drinking all night and into the morning.

"I just came to ask you if we can have some of the refurbished planes park in front of your hangar at the fly-in next week."

"Why should I?"

"Because it is the neighborly thing to do."

Frank spat into a canister and shook his head. JoAnne continued backing up ever so slowly. The last thing she needed was for Frank to turn belligerent. Off in the corner of the hangar, she eyed a rifle, old oil barrels, and wire cutters; on the other side was a cot with jumbled blankets. The odor emanating from the barrels, mixed with Frank's own odor, told her he was living out of the hangar.

"I'm not feeling real neighborly lately. In fact, I don't like neighbors, and I don't like the banks, and I don't like living in this hangar. And don't you go spouting off that it's against the rules. As my sister is so famous for stating—rules are for others, not us McCains."

"I'll come back another time, Frank. If you need something, let me know. Sorry to hear about your mother and the closing of the sheep farm."

"Who told you about the farm, and what do you know about my mom's death?"

Clearly JoAnne had said the wrong thing. She wondered what was making Frank so volatile. Someone dying in a small town was common knowledge, as was the disrepair of the sheep farm and their absence at markets.

"Times are tough for everyone now, Frank. If you can spare the space in front of your hangar, we can find a way to compensate you.

We need to accommodate all the planes. Although the fly-in is all volunteers and not a moneymaker, if you need anything we can bring you some of the good food from the barbecue or take pictures of your plane or . . ."

"Just leave. I don't need any food from the barbecue. I don't need anyone telling me what to do. Not you, not the Concrete Airport, not my stupid sister. I'm tired of following orders."

JoAnne turned her wheelchair around and left Frank ranting at the air. Her arms tingled as she headed back to the main hangar, where there was a makeshift office. She still had her strength, but lately she was too conscious of her arms, too aware of every muscle. Her wheelchair zipped along the tarmac despite her perceived weakness. Something other than her request had bothered Frank. His defensiveness smelled more than the reeking of his hangar, and JoAnne smelled a lie.

Halfway to the airport office, she spotted Maria running toward her. This was Maria's heavy, determined run, a run JoAnne remembered from the girl's first years living with her. Instead of meeting Maria along the way, JoAnne parked herself on the tarmac, giving her more time to blow off steam.

By the time Maria reached JoAnne, her grandniece's words were already clambering out. "Okay, okay, tell me what is going on. I need you to talk to me about Monica. What have you kept hidden? You order me home to fly to Puerto Rico, and now I find out that Monica lives there."

JoAnne ignored Maria and continued wheeling herself to the office. She held her head and shoulders upright, straining with each roll of the wheels, until she finally paused. "I guess it isn't that good of a morning. Your note said you were off for a run, fishing for answers. I don't think you like what you heard."

"Stop, just for a second, Aunt Jo. Let me look into your eyes."

The two faced one another. JoAnne sat quietly as Maria knelt and removed her aunt's straw hat. Maria's penetrating eyes searched her face to find her tired eyes, the dark circles, the small twitches of her lids. Yet JoAnne met Maria's eyes with an unwavering gaze.

"I once believed I knew truth when I saw it, Maria. Facts, like the altitude of the plane I flew or that the sun always rose in the east. My first inclination that truth wavered was when I did an acrobatic turn flying. With the instruments upside down, I couldn't rely on facts I had to feel where I was in the sky. Up was down, and down was up. In some parts of the world, the sun never rose. Bear with me, Maria. I'm talking to you as a fellow pilot, although an old one. Sometimes when the WASPs flew across the country delivering planes to a military outpost, our gut told us about the how of the planes, told us things the manuals didn't. I have never knowingly lied to you. The truths I once knew aren't cast in stone. Sometimes they shift to the other side."

JoAnne felt Maria's gaze warming her cheeks, searching for more. Her grandniece held both of her hands inside her own, felt the blood flowing through JoAnne's hands, the pulsing of the thumb, a heartbeat straining to make sense of circumstances.

"What is it that has shifted to the other side?" Maria asked.

"I think the last time you flew out here on a visit, before you hitch-hiked here, was when you were eight years old. Your mother sent you here because she was struggling with depression."

"That's what everyone said. My mom drank her sorrows away, but they never left. Before my parents split up, they fought. I think they confused love with anger. Afterward, more men came and went. She was meaner, less loving. Depression was a lie—she had to hurt someone to feel."

JoAnne's eyes welled up. The tears fell onto Maria's hands. It was as if they were back eighteen years reliving the anguish of a child.

"My visits with you, Aunt Jo, were my salvation. After Monica left, I pretended all was well. I ignored the house, the stench, the wine bottles lying empty on the floors. Monica raised me, getting me ready for school, cooking us meals. She left me to save herself. Her last words were a promise that she would send for me. Letters arrived with money, but many didn't have a return address. Sometimes Monica would call, and I lied, telling her I was fine. *Fine* is a silly word that defines nothing."

"Maria, you were a little girl of eight. Now you are a grown woman of twenty-six. You had the strength to hitchhike out here on a memory, a feeling, a sense of love at fourteen. You had gotten yourself into trouble, but you weren't trouble."

JoAnne placed her hands back on her lap. Maria stood up slowly as if letting the kinks of past years dissolve. Stiffening into her present age, Maria kissed her aunt on the top of her head as she took hold of the wheelchair and headed to the office.

"What shifted, Aunt Jo, that suddenly Monica is real again? I waited after my mom died, waited for her to come and get me. She knew that the only place I'd come would be here."

"I think Monica looked for you. I think she sent letters. I think that the truth didn't really change, only that a lie occurred, one not from Monica, not from you, and not from me."

"What are you saying?"

"Remember when they arrested you along Highway 20? You were drunk, incoherent, and they took you to Northern State Hospital."

"Yes, I remember kicking everyone in sight. I remember holding on to the piece of paper with your address. I remember repeating your name over and over."

"I always thought it odd that it took the hospital two weeks to contact me. Especially since you had my address. Only now am I realizing why."

"What does this have to do with my sister?"

"I'm thinking of letters that never arrived. I'm thinking of my own disappointments from another time long ago. All I can give you is a fact, a truth of sorts. Maybe the facts cover a lie. Molly McCain worked at Northern State Hospital when you were admitted."

Maria turned the wheelchair around so she could see her aunt's face.

"What color would this lie be?"

"I don't know if there is a color that describes something so intentional, painful, and mean."

The two stood looking back at the tarmac. A small two-seater plane bounced down onto the runway and taxied its way over to Frank McCain's hangar.

JoAnne and Maria watched as Frank came out, glanced around, and hurried over to the pilot.

Chapter 8:
Waste Not, Want Not

Molly woke to the sounds of crows squawking over the body of a rabbit. She watched as they dove down from her chestnut tree, landed by the remains, and flew off. She thought it curious that they left the spoils.

From her bedroom window, she yelled out, "The rabbit isn't good enough for you? You ungrateful birds! After waking me with all your squawking, the least you could do is clean up the mess."

Molly took the pistol she had under her pillow and shot into the chestnut tree. "I don't need any birds here that will waste good meat. Now I'll have to have someone come bury the remains."

Most of the sheep had been buried down below. First, she had burned the bodies, and then she had a huge pit dug for burial. She tried to salvage the wool, but her brother Frank said the wool was infested with bugs and refused to shear the sheep. She had raised the sheep for meat, not wool, but over the years, their bodies shriveled beneath their curls. Even her favorite sheep, a blob that she named Rock, was all matted curls with little meat. She had finally given in to slaughtering Rock, only to find out that the meat was sinewy and inedible.

Forty years of raising sheep amounted to half her lifetime. She was ready to do something different. Most of the old-timers in the area wanted to sell their land, move closer into town. Molly smiled, thinking of her grand plan, the one she started when she was in her thirties. With little money but cunning ways, she had worked her way into confiscating property along the river. The only hitch now was the regulations about polluting the waters, keeping shorelines open with buffers. If she was lucky, the sale of the old Olivine company would help her cause. No one knew what she and Frank had illegally buried on the property over the years. Frank's call about the bank wanting to foreclose on her sheep farm worried her, but she knew enough of the board members and their vices to put a stop to any problems.

The ringing of the phone startled Molly out of her thoughts. She placed the pistol back under her pillow and turned to answer. She knew it would be Frank. Even before the crows woke her with their squawking, Frank had called in a blubbering stupor. She could barely understand what he said. Now she was ready to listen.

"Molly, the shipment came in. The guy unloaded the canisters and took off again."

"How many canisters?"

"One, two, three—"

"Count to yourself and just tell me how many they delivered."

"Ten, there are ten sitting inside my hangar. We unloaded fast since that stupid JoAnne and her niece were here at the airport."

Molly felt a slight flutter of her heart. A sudden rush of blood made her dizzy, so she sat down. "Why were they at the hangar? You didn't let JoAnne in, did you?"

"Don't worry, she came in earlier before the plane arrived. She left after I shooed her away."

"JoAnne is always messing things up. Don't let her in again. If she smells anything, she'll start investigating. The last thing we need now is for her to snoop around. Being wheelchair bound doesn't stop her—you would think she'd learn from the past. You have to get to the mound before they shut down the site. We have to get that stuff buried."

Molly waited for Frank's answer. She heard a click and then nothing. She yelled into the phone, "Don't you hang up on me, Frank! This is important!"

Distracted, Molly pulled her nightgown off, but got tangled up in the phone line. Hurrying made her clumsy. In frustration, she threw the phone and sat back down on the bed. Taking a deep breath, she visualized the quarry. Thirty-five feet of ground olivine spoils was enough to hide more waste. She needn't worry. This would be the last time. Now all she had to do was get it done before the sale and before the young Spencer got involved.

His arrival last fall had taken her by surprise. Molly thought the property had gone into foreclosure, that the taxes hadn't been paid. Last time she had checked, most of the property along the Skagit was either in the flood zone and the owners couldn't afford to come into compliance, or their businesses had gone belly-up. Molly always checked with the assessor's office each fall after the last of the taxes were due. It made good business sense to help out those who were in trouble.

Molly cackled, "Oh you poor landowners, Molly is here to save you from yourselves."

Abruptly her laughter ceased. The game had changed. She had never before needed to ask for help, but the sheep farm failure placed her in a difficult spot. She blamed her brother. Frank's only job was to attend the sheep and their mother. He failed. Now the community wanted to know her business. JoAnne's dinner party had invaded her privacy. JoAnne was the problem.

Breathing heavily, Molly took her time getting dressed. Already in a sour mood, she knew better than to rush. Her doctor told her not to get stressed, to find something that soothed her. She could hear him now. "Envision an island in the South Pacific, where the ocean waves slowly lap the shore. Let the waves take your stress away." Molly had a better remedy for stress. Ever since she was a child, she collected trinkets, souvenirs that calmed her when she felt out of sorts.

She pulled open the mahogany armoire her mother had so graciously gifted her as an engagement present. Molly still felt slightly bad that she had made up the engagement, but her mother never knew. She even gained sympathy when she told her mother the guy had jilted her. Now that her mother had passed on, Molly had less of a hankering for the piece. It had lost its potency.

The top drawer held her oldest trinkets: a picture of Spencer T, a necklace with a gold heart charm, and the skin of a snake.

Looking into the mirror on the armoire door, Molly held the necklace up to her neck. She used to pretend the necklace was meant for her, but it really belonged to the neighbor girl who used to sleep over. The girl had buckteeth and braids. She was spoiled, and her mother and father had given her the necklace. Molly took it just to see her cry.

The snakeskin was a remnant of tortures she performed on her brother. He was younger and cried all the time. Her mother had ignored the cries, thinking he was fussy. Molly would put the snake in his bed each night, and he would pee from fright.

She held up the picture of Spencer T and marveled at how much he looked like his nephew.

"Good looks aren't everything," she said. "Your nephew will vanish, too. And to think poor JoAnne believed you loved her."

Feeling more relaxed, Molly almost smiled as she opened the next drawer. Letters neatly stacked in piles, letters addressed to JoAnne, letters addressed to Maria, and some even to Russell. She had organized them chronologically by weeks and years. The postmarks from Puerto Rico started in 1945 and continued weekly for ten years. Ah, the hopeless insistence of love. Molly felt the smallest twinge of regret when she counted the letters written to Maria. So many postmarks crossed off as Monica sent letters searching for Maria. Tattered envelopes crisscrossed the ocean to finally rest with Molly. Years ago, she had pored over them, reading about a doomed affair. This morning, she felt the temptation to reread the history she prevented. Molly opened the last letter in the pile addressed to JoAnne.

My dearest JoAnne,

This is my goodbye. I long for you still, but must accept that you have moved on. After all these years of silence, I will wonder no more. I wish you well, I wish you love, I wish I never left you.

Spencer T

Realizing it was already late in the day, Molly mumbled to her reflection, "Sappy hogwash." She'd liked it better when she could steal conversations at the telephone company. Nowadays, people didn't even send letters. She was almost too old to master the new-fangled computers. The younger generation had taken her art of stealing to a new form.

Molly put her binoculars and retractable cane inside her big purse. She grabbed a handful of chocolate caramels, slipped them into her pocket, and headed out to her car. Backing out of the garage was harder as of late. Twice this month, she had backed into other cars in a parking lot, and once she even ran over her own wheelbarrow. Frank had stupidly left it in the driveway out of her vision. Today, she whipped around without a problem, despite the kink in her neck.

Out of habit and caution, Molly pulled the binoculars from her purse and scanned the valley before she headed out of her driveway. From the hilltop, she could see as far as the Concrete Airport, not individuals, but the general activity, the shapes of planes, the runway, and the hangars. Frank had their hangar open, which made Molly nervous.

She could see JoAnne's car still parked at the main office.

Molly hoped that her brother wasn't careless enough to do anything with JoAnne around. Molly made her way down to Highway 20, turned the opposite direction from the airport and headed into the bigger town of Sedro-Woolley. Long ago, she split up her finances between the small towns. The advantage she had in Concrete, Hamilton, and Lyman was that she knew everyone's business. She didn't want them to know hers, so she went the extra miles to distract and cover her transactions.

The banks closest to her home held the money from her social security, the money from the farm, and some savings. All her investments were held in Sedro-Woolley. That way, the banks felt more secure when she took out mortgage loans on land. All you needed to do to get a loan was to have the illusion of assets and the ability to pay. Molly had enough foresight to be co-owner to all of her mother's property on paper, allowing her to leverage her mother's assets as well.

She pulled into her bank's parking lot. The lot was full, which meant it was payday. Wanting to park closer and avoid walking, Molly searched for her handicap tag. Her doctor had been reluctant to give her one, as she had no handicap. He wanted her to walk more, get exercise, and lose weight. With the handicap tag, Molly controlled where and when she parked. Taking her cane from her purse, Molly extended the rod and hobbled into the bank.

Ignoring the lines, she headed to the main desk. She coughed, wobbled, and walked some more. The attendant looked up and smiled.

"May I help you, Ms. McCain?"

Somewhat flattered, Molly molded her lips into a dog grin. "I see from your name tag that you are Kim. Kim, I need to transfer some money."

"I thought you would be in soon, ma'am. I saw the obituary of your mother. I have a few people to see, and then I can attend to your needs.

Would you like to sit awhile and wait?"

Choices, but no choices. Molly didn't remember Kim, but Kim knew who she was and that her mother had died. Her anonymity dissolved, and with it her advantage. Taking a handkerchief from her purse, Molly mopped her forehead and fanned herself.

"I don't have a say, do I? Yes, I will sit and wait. Can I have a cool glass of water? I seem to be parched and overheated."

Molly made her way to the waiting area where a chocolate-colored leather couch with matching chairs surrounded a coffee table with a fruit basket, cookies, hot coffee, and ice tea. Drinking ice tea and eating cookies, she felt agitated. The sign read, "Buy Local." The only local things on the table were the peaches and strawberries. They looked dreary, as if they had been sitting there waiting for the bank patrons to applaud but wilted in anticipation. The basket had to have come from China, and the cookies may have been made at the local bakery, but the wheat came from somewhere else. Molly was smart enough to know the politics of networking. Local was the *in* thing. What about saving money —wasn't that what banks were for, saving and protecting her money?

The tea and cookies disappeared within minutes, and still she waited. Kim talked with three families and didn't look up to see Molly. Reaching into her pocket, Molly popped three chocolate caramels into her mouth. By the time Kim came for her, there was a pile of wrappers next to an empty dessert plate.

"Ms. McCain, sorry to keep you. I had a few scheduled appointments."

Molly rose slowly, using her cane to lift her body. She conveyed her annoyance with waiting by not speaking and overemphasizing the effort of walking. Molly thought the act would gain her sympathy, but Kim kept a thin smile on her face and extended her hand to help her walk, without offering more apologies.

"I need to close my mother's accounts and transfer the money to my own."

Kim nodded as she clicked on the keyboard.

"Which accounts are we closing, Ms. McCain?"

"I just told you, all of them."

Kim looked up from the computer screen and tried to reframe the question. "You're referring to Maggie McCain's accounts. I need to verify. Do you have any of the account numbers with you? Perhaps a recent bank statement. Your mother had quite a few accounts with us. I'll need to verify the accounts, and I'll need the death certificate."

An itching irritation at the stupidity crawled across Molly's face. Her chin quivered, her cheeks flushed, and her eyes stung as she felt her blood pressure rise. This woman must be trying to trip her up. Mentally, Molly went over the various accounts in her mind—the sheep ranch, her mother's house account, the Concrete Airport Hangar account, the savings account for repairs, and the three certificates of deposit. Molly knew exactly how much money the accounts held, over $500,000.

"Kim, why do you need the death certificate? You know my mother died."

Flustered, Kim looked back at Molly. "I'm truly sorry, Ms. McCain, all of this is a formality, protocol to protect our patron's money. I can easily help you with the accounts you share with your mother, but I'll have to see a will and a death certificate for the others."

Something didn't sound right. Molly shared all the accounts with her mother, or at least she thought she did. Her mother couldn't possibly have opened new accounts, not in her late nineties. Molly had been working with her mother's money for the last fifteen years.

"Kim, I have the power of attorney for my mother. Certainly that is enough for me to make these transactions."

Staring at the computer, away from Molly's gaze, Kim shook her head. "Sorry, Ms. McCain, when your mother died, that power dissolved. There are ten accounts. Three are marked trusts, but I can transfer the money for you on the other seven accounts. The CDs don't come due for a while. You might want to wait on those so you don't lose interest."

Molly faked a gasp and choking, making Kim look up from the computer.

"Are you okay? I'll get you a glass of water."

Molly shooed her away, annoyed that others customers, now staring at her, might reveal her schemes. Trying to regain control of the situation, she forced herself to slow her heart rate, to calm the beating of annoyance in her temples. She reached out across the table and clasped Kim's hand.

"Kim, would you be kind enough to make those transfers and just give me the names of the trust accounts? I'll search for the proper paperwork."

Molly knew the cardinal rule of a teller is not to give out too much information. Clearly stalling for time, Kim patted Molly's hand and started typing out the transfers. Eventually she had a stack of forms ready for Molly to sign.

"Ms. McCain, please sign where I have marked the lines with an X, and then the transfers will be placed into your personal accounts."

"And the names of the trusts . . ."

"Oh, really, I do have to wait for the will and death certificate before I can give you that information."

"For goodness sakes, girl—just give me the damn names!" Before Kim could answer, Molly whipped the computer screen around to face herself. She heaved herself out of her seat and walked out of the bank.

Chapter 9:
Missing Pieces

Maria waved at JoAnne as she pulled out of the airport parking lot. Her aunt looked small sitting on the tarmac with her hand up in the air making half circles, her attention split between Maria's leaving and the plane on the runway. Rolling down her window, Maria listened to the plane's motor, heard it revving up to speed. Her aunt sat poised, listening and moving her wheelchair back and forth as if she were making ready to fly. Maria felt the vibrations of readiness for liftoff. Sadness stuck in her throat, stalled her thoughts. She took one last look in her rearview mirror. Just as she pulled onto the road, her aunt craned her neck to watch the plane rise into the sky. She was flying in her mind's eye, flying by memory.

Maria's own memories felt stale. She had buried so much of her past that all of it felt like a lie. She wanted to blame JoAnne for hiding facts, as if facts could fill her voids. Missing Monica was an old wound, one that she kept coming back to, scratching at it so she would bleed. If she bled, then she was alive. Yet instead of bleeding, Maria was drowning in a pool of self-pity. Once JoAnne had taken her in, Maria had chosen to forget Monica. She had given up.

The only remnant Maria still held on to was the silliest of silly habits. Even as tears filled her eyes, she found herself smiling at the thought of why she enjoyed the sky, particularly the night sky. Monica and Maria would sit out on the roof of their apartment on evenings that were unbearably humid, evenings when their mother was either absent because she was out on a date or absent because she was nursing a bottle. The sisters would lie on their backs, looking at the constellations, watching the stars. In the background, Bing Crosby crooned, "Catch a falling star and put in your pocket, save it for a rainy day . . ." Sometimes they were lucky, and a star would literally drop and trickle through the night sky, coasting to some unknown destination. They held their breaths, squeezed each other's hands in delight. For each falling star they saw, they would place a gold stick-on star in an envelope. When Monica left, she told Maria to keep their stars safe.

Just thinking about the stars made Maria feel more whole, more hopeful. Even after all these years, she was still consumed by what was missing, rather than what was present. JoAnne never seemed to dwell on what she had lost; in fact, she seemed to fill her life up by giving. Yet today, her aunt had alluded to her own disappointments from another time. She wondered what Molly McCain had to do with JoAnne's past life.

Maria had an urge to find the star-filled envelope. As soon as she parked her car in her aunt's driveway, she ran upstairs to her old bedroom closet. Standing on tiptoe, she reached the top shelf where she kept a silk scarf that JoAnne had given to her on her sixteenth birthday. Then, hearing a truck pull into the driveway, she looked out the window. To her chagrin, Spencer stood staring up at her window.

Maria couldn't for the life of her think why he would be at their house. Annoyed and panicked, she ran downstairs, holding on to the scarf and rushing to open the door.

"Spencer, whatever are you here for?"

There was no immediate answer, only the sly smile, a slightly reddened face, and a hand extending toward her own. "Maria, I came over to apologize. I upset you this morning."

This morning felt like eons ago. Yet she looked down at her clothes and realized that she hadn't even changed after her morning run. Spencer's hand was still extended, and she reached out with hers to motion him in. As he took her hand in his own, the scarf opened, and out fell her cherished envelope.

Horrified, Maria watched as gold stars sprinkled out onto the floor. She didn't know what to say. So she didn't say anything. They both bent down to gather the stars. Maria held out the envelope and Spencer placed each star inside as if they were jewels. Maria's only thought was to keep the stars safe. When they stood up, she tried to explain.

"The envelope is from when I was a kid, keepsakes."

Spencer nodded his head as if this was important information. "These must be stars of honor. I never earned gold stars when I was a kid."

"I don't believe that. From what I can tell, my aunt and Russell think you are honor-student material."

"Do you accept my apology? I wanted to invite you on a walk. I thought maybe we could talk, share some of our history, and go over the problems with your aunt's property."

Maria didn't stop to think, just nodded and whispered, "Yes."

"Yes you accept my apology, or yes you will take a walk with me?"

Despite the awkwardness, Maria smiled. "I'll need to change my clothes. You can wait in the living room while I get ready. And those stars, they're not for any honors. I just catch falling stars."

As Maria took the stairs two by two, she could hear Spencer humming.

She dressed quickly, throwing on a pair of jeans, a long-sleeved top, and a sweatshirt just in case they ventured upriver or took a long hike. She grabbed a backpack and threw in a flashlight and a bottle of water, allowing herself one quick glance in the mirror. Her reflection came as a

65

surprise. Since her thoughts were still stuck back in time when she had last seen her sister, Maria almost thought she would see her fourteen-year-old self. Instead, the image was that of a lean, petite woman with a determined face, short hair that curled in odd directions, and large eyes that held fast. Maria raced down the stairs, lighter than she had felt on her way up.

Spencer was at the front door, helping her aunt wheel herself up the ramp into their house. With her adapted car, JoAnne maintained her independence, driving herself mainly to the airport and grocery shopping. Her gracious acceptance of Spencer's help surprised Maria. Usually she resisted help, pushing herself up with the grit of determination and the will of her muscles. Her aunt's eyes sparkled brighter than when Maria had left her earlier in the morning, and her smile was one that Maria rarely saw, one that folded in on itself. Maria noticed that her own smile felt deeper. As much as she didn't want to think that Spencer had anything to do with it, she knew that his presence made her aunt happier than she had ever seen her. Perhaps JoAnne felt the presence of Spencer's uncle. Maria wondered if this was yet another missing piece.

"Aunt Jo, did you finish up with all the arrangements for the fly-in?"

"I've done all I can for now. There is only one tenant who will be a problem, Frank and his sister, Molly. I was just telling Spencer that I think something else is going on with their hangar. Did you watch that plane take off when you were leaving?"

"Yes, it seemed like a normal takeoff. Why, what did you see?"

Her aunt took a few seconds to answer. "It isn't what I saw. It's what I didn't see. Usually the pilots take their time when they land at Concrete. They stretch their feet, walk the runway, stop and talk to the people around. The pilot didn't even refuel. He dropped something off, exchanged words with Frank, and headed out. Frank disappeared inside the hangar and then left with his truck bed filled."

JoAnne knew the heartbeat of the airport, the habits of the tenants and the pilots. Since there was no fueling airport nearby, the pilot would have had to go to a larger airport to refuel. Obviously rewinding the scene, JoAnne paused in thought, placing her right hand on her chin, half caressing and half squeezing the tip gently together as if this action could extract a reason. "Maria, when I talked with Frank just before you arrived at the airport, he was in a foul mood, drinking and in no condition to work. I am sure that delivery was something illegal. Why else would the pilot leave in such a hurry and Frank sober up so quickly?"

"You may be right," Maria said. "When I first started flying before I got the job with ATSI Explorations, I would fly clients to destinations on their private planes. I'd be propositioned. Their thinking was that a small plane piloted by a young woman would be able to sneak beneath normal radar."

Spencer made a movement closer, and her aunt's jaw tensed.

"Don't worry. I can take care of myself. The sexual propositions never got anywhere, as I held the takeoff and landing controls. The attempts at carrying illegal product never went anywhere either, as I checked all the luggage and weight, and performed my own maintenance. But I can tell you that the description of what transpired at the airport today seems suspicious."

Spencer's brow furrowed in worry.

Her aunt made a shooing motion. "You two were leaving. Frank and Molly's dirty business can wait. Go have fun."

"We won't be gone long. Spencer invited me on a hike."

Spencer bent over and picked up her backpack. His gaze met hers, his blue eyes twinkling. Maria felt the laughter in the set of his shoulders. "I think I mentioned a walk, but from the likes of what Maria put in her backpack, I think we are going for a hike."

Maria's mouth opened in protest, but quickly closed. "Aunt Jo always taught me to be prepared. I thought we might hike—I mean walk—up toward the Pit. The views are spectacular."

Her aunt's arms stiffened, and her lips tightened. Maria knew immediately the signs of worry, the ones that made no sense, the ones that had always stopped her in the past. "Can't you go somewhere else? You know how dangerous the slopes are."

Spencer looked from Maria to her aunt, his loyalty divided. Usually, no one defied JoAnne. She knew what was best, so why resist, except that Maria was drawn to the Pit precisely because her aunt forbade it. She suspected that this was another missing piece, one that held answers to her aunt's condition.

"I promise to take special care of your grandniece," Spencer offered. "I haven't been up to the Pit myself, and I wanted to see the surrounding area. Much of what is there hovers over my property, and I'm curious to see the vegetation and the conditions above the vineyard."

The sparkle had gone out of her aunt's eyes, and she seemed resigned. Wheeling herself away from the front door and making way for them to leave, she gave them a faint smile. "No one can promise against accidents. If they do, they lie."

Chapter 10:
The Flight of the Hummingbird

JoAnne folded her hands on her lap, squeezed them tightly as she held her tears back. Caution meant nothing in the face of youth. She could no more prevent Maria and Spencer from hiking in the Pit than she could make her legs move. Sighing, she tucked her fear back inside her heart and made for the garden.

Too much had changed in the last few weeks. For so many years, she had accepted her paralysis, accepted the challenges of being a single woman, bound to a wheelchair, raising a grandniece. Never once had she looked backward to the loss of mobility. To do that, she would have to look at the loss of love and question the meaning of her life. Instead, she took comfort in her garden, where life presented itself in full color: the greens of young shoots, leaves unfurling, the dark richness of soil turned with compost and manure. Flowers, fruits, and legumes cycled through, nourishing her body and connecting her to what she couldn't understand. The religious called this connection faith. She called it survival.

Wheeling herself along the path toward the flower beds, JoAnne already heard the hum of the wings. Bird feeders hanging from the house's eaves and bushes with brilliant oranges and red blooms drew the hummingbirds from their migratory paths. Every year, she was blessed to watch their dancing wings. As long as she provided a source of sustenance, they loyally returned from their more southern homes.

Forty-five years. For forty-five years, the hummingbirds flew to her gardens. JoAnne considered this an informal marriage. The anniversary of her fall marked the end to her own flights. It was her old friend Emma, Russell's wife, who had sent Russell over to create the gardens. The distraction helped, as those first weeks and months blurred in her memory. JoAnne to this day had never questioned where Russell and Emma found the money to create the gardens or the money to convert her home into a manageable space for the wheelchair-bound. Every time she had asked Emma about the hospital bill, Emma had shushed her. "You worry about healing your heart and getting strong. There is money coming in to take care of everything." Too proud to continue asking, JoAnne had stopped.

Now, sitting in the middle of wings humming, speeding flutters twenty beats per second, JoAnne held on to her heart. She felt the racing of blood, the rushing of thoughts that could go nowhere. She hovered in thought, perching on a hope from a letter. Youthful love still throbbed through her veins.

She placed her hands on her thighs and slowly massaged her muscles, reaching down to just below her knees. Lately she had begun to feel again, though she knew it was impossible. Sensations in her legs had long since died, while her upper body remained attuned, super-sensitive. With her fingers touching her thighs and legs, the nerves responded only through her outer touch. In the last six months, the layer of nerves from the inside of her legs gave off energy, warming, burning, and then twitching.

JoAnne never tired of watching the courtship practices of the hummingbirds. Today, she held her thighs and her breath as she witnessed the ritual. She identified with their wing power; their feet were useless appendages, not good for walking, only perching. Their wings showed their emotions. She followed the male rufous rising high into the sky and then counted the seconds as it dove and sped downward in flitting flight toward his chosen female, who clung in anticipation to the branch of a vine maple.

Anticipation; JoAnne refused to anticipate or wait. She had done that once before, and while she now sat perched in her garden, near the end of a long life, she was determined to face a different set of truths. A simple letter sent to a professor working on the study of nerve regeneration had ripped open her past. An innocent inquiry was changing her fate, just as the hike she had taken forty-five years ago along the trail to the Pit had propelled her down the slopes and out of the arms of her lover.

JoAnne pulled an envelope from her skirt pocket. Worn on the edges, the letter inside looked abused, folded and refolded, crumbled and smoothed. The second paragraph still caused JoAnne to shake. Skimming through, she reread the professor's words:

I will be visiting your state for a conference this summer in July. I would love to meet with you concerning nerve regeneration. My studies with a tropical vine have shown some success, even with damaged nerves from very old injuries.

The next line is where JoAnne always paused.

It seems that our lives are more connected than one would think. Odd as it may seem, two of my close friends have a connection to your hometown. A man named Spencer T and a woman named Monica. I believe coincidences are not just coincidences.

Shaking, JoAnne sat quietly listening to her own heartbeat. Between the throbbing lubb-dupps, she felt the powerful effect of *coincidences*. She had met Spencer T while flying for the WASPs during World War II. He was an engineer for the bomber planes, and more. The *more* intrigued her, and when she flew her last flight for the program, he invited her to visit him here along the Skagit River in Washington State, his hometown of Concrete.

Long ago she took a chance, followed her heart. She moved permanently to be by his side. JoAnne sighed, thinking that her heart wasn't wrong, but maybe she was destined to be like the hummingbird, more concerned with survival than pairing for life. Calming herself down, JoAnne tucked the letter back into her pocket and focused on what was really worrying her.

Matters of the heart had nothing to do with the illnesses of friends or the dying plants and animals. Since JoAnne had received the letter, Russell had made some inquires for her about Spencer T, Monica, and now the toxicity of the soil. A common thread held all of these mysteries together. She had tried to explain this to Maria, but she knew she had fallen short. Molly McCain loomed like a hawk, waiting to devour all around her. At least the hummingbird kept its loyalty to migration patterns, courted with only the babies' welfare in mind. A hawk, on the other hand, robbed chicks from the unsuspecting, fed on anything susceptible. Molly pounced on any weak link, and her power came from the desire to harm. No, Molly was worse than a hawk. Hawks robbed and killed in order to survive. Molly's survival depended on filling a void, an insatiable dark hole of greed.

JoAnne looked longingly at the pool. As much as she needed to swim to clear her thoughts, she didn't want to expend the energy. She believed that Maria's hiking with Spencer along the very trail where she had fallen was more than coincidental. History had a way of repeating itself. At least this time, Maria would be with Spencer, not alone going to meet him.

Despite JoAnne's determination to focus on the now, she found herself closing her eyes and traveling back to the past. She could hear

Spencer T's voice on the phone, "Congratulations, JoAnne, you received the highest accolades from the Women Air Force Service Pilots program. We should celebrate."

She was so young then, so in love. Her disappointment at the end of the WASP program lessened with his words. They were to meet at the Pit, their favorite spot for a picnic dinner.

JoAnne packed the dinner: buttermilk biscuits, cold elk meat from Russell's yearly hunt, tomatoes from Emma's garden, oatmeal cookies, and a flask with a special blend of moonshine. Since the sun hung high in the sky, she hadn't worried about the nighttime darkness and cool air. Summer days were bonus days, allowing for work, play, and celebrations. JoAnne was floating when she left her home.

Her hike was easy enough from the gravel road, up through the forest to an area that spread out like the flattened bottom of a cauldron, a former limestone quarry now filled with clear blue water. But she hadn't anticipated gunshots or the presence of other people digging. She remembered climbing up along the columnar sides of the Pit, trying to stay hidden. Her footing, made precarious by the flaking chips of basalt, grappled as the earth beneath her crumbled. As she fell, her hands grabbed for the roots of prickly bushes, which gave way with her weight.

The free fall had been nothing like flying. Out of control, her arms hit the sides of the Pit. She landed on her back. Splayed like a possum feigning death, she pretended all was well, still fearful of the gunshots. Unable to move, she waited for her Spencer, her love, to find her. The only voice she heard was the echo of Molly McCain reverberating off the walls of the Pit.

Days later, she woke up in the hospital with Emma and Russell by her side. They had found her with her hand holding on to a chocolate candy wrapper, incoherent after a cold night and a day of lying in the

Pit. Spencer T had vanished. Apparently, the phones had stopped working, and Russell had sent a party out to look for both of them.

JoAnne sighed with the memory. That was the last time she had walked, the last time her feet touched the ground, the last time she felt the romance of love. Molly McCain had played havoc with her life for too long. Knowing now what she always believed, JoAnne understood that her noble pride was a lie. In order to keep harmony, not to experience the pain of rejection, JoAnne had refused to seek answers. She had ignored her instinct, ignored the gunshots, and ignored the voice that echoed in the Pit, afraid that she had misjudged someone she loved. Her pride had cost her years of intimacy and had ironically protected an enemy of truth.

Nerves, sensations, coincidences—JoAnne knew the time had come to face life fully. She touched her pocket, felt the crumbled letter, and let her heart flutter. Thanks to Russell and his ham radio, she knew now that Spencer T had not abandoned her. Her self-doubt had caused her more pain than the loss of her mobility. She realized that doubt works like a lie, coloring life brown with decay. She wondered if she was too old, too late in her life to rise from the decay.

Listening to her intuition, she wheeled herself into the house and called Russell.

"Russell, this is JoAnne. I thought you should know that Spencer and Maria are hiking by the Pit."

Chapter 11:
Screen

Maria sat quietly as Spencer drove along Highway 20. Neither of them had spoken since her aunt's ominous warning about the Pit. She wasn't sure if Spencer knew that this was where her aunt had fallen. Maria knew, not because her aunt had directly told her but more from putting together all of her warnings, objections, and deterring tactics throughout the years. Her disproportionate display of concern today was a clear giveaway.

As they turned off the highway and made their way up along a gravel road, the forest rose around them. They rolled the windows down, letting in the sounds of woodpeckers tapping on tree trunks, the rustling of critters on the forest floor, and the cool breeze inside the truck cab. Maria smelled the spearmint scent of conifers, the musty leaf litter, and the sweetness of honeysuckle, remnants from past logger shacks. Gradually her shoulders relaxed, and she sighed with a sense of release.

Spencer chuckled. "I wasn't sure if you were off in deep thought, somewhere unreachable, or content to be here. Your aunt was adamant in her disapproval. I'm surprised that you pushed so hard."

Maria turned to look at him. His eyes remained on the road, attentive. Even though he was making light of the situation, she could tell he was concerned, and for some reason Maria felt the need to explain. "I don't know if you figured it out, but I'm sure this is where my aunt had the accident that caused her paralysis. She fell on a walk when she was about my age."

Spencer nodded. "I suspected as much. She is a private person carrying lots of history. Your aunt reminds me of my uncle. He never talks about the airplane crash that brought him to Ramey Air Force Base in Puerto Rico. I've only been able to piece together what happened through the Ramey AFB Museum. One of the older guys archives anything written from World War II—people, planes, families, and personal letters. My uncle can expound on the virtues of the Skagit River, the mountains, the soil of his property here, but he keeps silent about his mission forty-five years ago. I used to tease him that it was top secret. He never laughed."

As a pilot, Maria dreaded hearing about crashes. In the forties, planes were still working out all the kinks that technology for the most part had now fixed. She imagined JoAnne testing and ferrying the military aircraft across the county. Her dangers weren't from bombs or artillery fire, but from the lack of engineering advancements.

"Was your uncle a pilot? Was he injured?"

"No to the first question, and no to the second one as well. My granduncle was an engineer, the fix-it guy on the flights. He'd be sent out on secret missions, to scout or make sure the planes were in tip-top shape. He met your aunt in Pratt, Kansas, when she was a WASP. I guess they were close friends."

They were almost at the end of the gravel road, having meandered around the mountainside. Maria's mind raced with questions. Without thinking, she stretched her arm across the space dividing them and brushed her hand on his forearm. His pulse throbbed against her palm. Just then, the truck bounced, vibrating over the washboard ruts. They slid to the left, missing a pothole as the sand and gravel played havoc with the transmission. Spencer shifted down and shrugged, making light of the conditions, but Maria's hand felt his arm tense, felt the strength of his concentration. Maria's shoulders and hip rested close to Spencer's body, having slid with the truck's motion. She removed her hand and inched her way back toward the window.

"You don't have to move all the way back. I won't bite."

She felt a flush come to her cheeks. "If I don't scoot over some, the next rut will put me in your lap."

Spencer kept his eyes on the road, but his smile teased. "I would like that."

Maria turned her head to the window, feigning the need for fresh air, trying to hide her smile. "Do you know what happened between my aunt and your uncle? If she came all this way to be with him, you'd think that he wouldn't have changed his mind. You can't have warm feelings for someone and then freeze those feelings as if they don't exist."

"Are you speaking from experience, or just surmising?"

Maria sat with the question, not having an answer that wouldn't need a lengthy explanation. Hadn't she done that with her sister? She had frozen her feelings into a solid lump of disappointment. Abandoned, Maria had numbed herself from hurt.

"Maria, Maria, come back to me. There I go again, sticking my foot into my mouth."

Abruptly Spencer pulled to the side of the road, yanked the brake, and faced Maria.

"I'd do anything to keep that smile of yours beaming. I have no right to question your past relationships."

Spencer's voice drew Maria back from her thoughts. His sky-blue eyes peered out from under a line of dark lashes, willing her into the present. It finally dawned on her that whatever prickly feelings of attraction she felt toward Spencer might be mutual.

"You were talking about past boyfriend relationships? I was thinking about my sister, Monica."

At this, Spencer started laughing. "I guess I've played my hand for all to see."

"No, just for me to see. Thanks."

Starting up the truck, Spencer continued on the gravel road. Neither of them talked. The original question—what had happened between her aunt and his uncle—remained unanswered.

More curious than ever, Maria ventured another question. "When did your uncle go to Puerto Rico?"

Spencer kept his eyes on the curves of the road, focusing on everything but Maria. The evergreen forest thinned out, and they came to a clearing of sorts. A thick green metal gate ended their journey with a sign: Private No Trespassing.

"I guess this is the end of the road. I think the Pit is just a half a mile's walk inside."

Maria waited in the truck for the answer to her question, but Spencer wasn't talking. When he came to her side to help her down, she said, "I don't need help."

"I know. I wanted to hold your hand, a man's ploy at getting closer."

They gathered their backpacks, and he locked the truck.

"Right near the end of the war, my uncle was called to train on a B-29 Bomber. They called the plane the Superfortress because it could carry 20,000 pounds of bombs over 6,000 miles. The secret training missions left from the Borinquen Field in Puerto Rico. As the head mechanic, his job was to resolve an overheating issue with the four engines. On March 31, 1945, he flew from Pratt, Kansas, to Punta Borinquen. The oil pressure dropped in two of the engines. The pilot declared a forced water landing because the plane couldn't rise high enough to clear the coastline ridge."

"How many on the plane survived?"

"Three of the crew died. My uncle was among the ten survivors. He was able to inflate a five-man life raft for the injured, and he waited in the water for rescue."

They walked, holding hands. Maria let the story sink in. Mentally she counted back the years to JoAnne's accident, spring of 1945. It couldn't be a coincidence that the time frame aligned. And now after all these years of silence between them, JoAnne insisted on going to Puerto Rico.

Maria felt a squeeze, a thumb stroking ever so softly the top of her hand, the physical pull back to the present. They stopped walking, and Spencer directed Maria off the trail. They had been walking up an incline parallel to the road. Now the grade became cumbersome, the trees gone and only a few scattered bushes holding on to crumbling rock.

"Maria, when were you up here last?"

"I have to confess that I have never been here. You were my excuse to come. Up until now, I knew only that the locals used this place as an oasis, a place to swim, picnic, and enjoy nature. I knew my aunt fell here. Curiosity drew me here, but I didn't want to come alone. You caught me in a white lie. Does it matter?"

The look on Spencer's face gave Maria her answer. His jaws tightened, his shoulders stiffened, and he let go of her hand. She could hear JoAnne's voice in her head: *Even white lies have consequences.* Maria wracked her brain for a reason that this should matter so much. She knew that if she failed to say something, purposefully omitted a detail, then it did matter. Her hand felt empty.

Spencer shushed Maria with a warning finger to his lips. His eyes looked beyond her, to the curve across the exposed rock, the ledge of chipping columns. Off in the distance, she heard a motor. Maria pulled binoculars from her backpack, peered through the lenses, and handed them to Spencer.

She whispered, "That's Frank, Molly's brother. The one who left the airport in a hurry after an odd delivery from a small plane."

The only response from Spencer was another shush and a signal to keep climbing. They walked in silence on a nonexistent path. The forest had fallen away and left a scoured mountain wall. Each step broke off fragments of rock, the entire side a sloped avalanche waiting to happen. Maria concentrated on placing her feet one above the other, angling herself, slanting with the lines of the mountainside. For some reason, her insides felt fragile, as if her heart would crumble.

Maria followed Spencer's lead, his steps an urgency of controlled haste. She fell behind, nervous with a fear of falling and failing. Why would her aunt have taken a walk here alone? She imagined the slipping, the crunch of landing. Maria pushed her fear back, but the falling sensation persisted. Spencer seemed so distant. The space between them widened.

He still had her binoculars. Perched at a forty-five degree angle to her left, he scanned the horizon, fixed his gaze toward the motor source. He motioned to Maria with a wave of his hand that she should continue moving up and over to him. She scurried on all fours, keeping her body close to the spurs of rock, hugging the mountainside. Out of breath, she reached upward just as Spencer wrapped his hand, wrist, and arm around her forearm, a secure rope of connection.

He pulled Maria up to share a shelf no wider than her shoes. They stood side by side. His face full of concern, he bent down to brush dirt off her cheek and left a soft kiss. No words, no explanation. Still clasping her forearm, he handed over the binoculars. Focusing, Maria watched Frank as he dug a large hole with a tractor and backhoe. She couldn't make out what he buried within the dirt, but she suspected that his truck would be empty of the recent arrival of canisters.

"Spencer, let's go. I don't feel comfortable."

"Keep your voice down. The scree on the rock face magnifies sound, and we don't want Frank to see us. Either he or his sister owns this property, or Frank is trespassing as well. We should wait until he leaves before we descend."

Maria pulled out the water bottle, took a drink, and then passed it to Spencer.

"Frank will spot your truck by the gate. He'll know you are here."

"Good point. Then let's just continue on our walk and pretend we didn't see anything. Can you muster enough resolve to keep walking?"

"Why did you kiss my cheek?"

Ignoring Maria's question, he grabbed her hand and wrapped his wrist around hers. They walked in tandem, tied by the mountain's outcrop of rubble, holding on to each other with the unstable earth below their feet. Maria found her breath more steady now, her pounding heart slowed. The mountain ridge widened as the slope lessened to a flattened area. Their walk had taken them to the back side and below where Frank had been digging. There they found, out of nowhere, a man-made lake of emerald-green water, the prize of persistence.

"This must be the water hole where the locals swim."

They walked to the lake edge, ready to cool themselves off with a quick dip, when Spencer shook his head. "Do you smell something? That odor seems out of place."

She sniffed the air, then bent down to the water's edge. It smelled rotten, decayed, a sulfury whiff of death. The green water held a sheen, as if it was coated with oil. "This was an old limestone pit, now filled with rainwater. There should be more greenery around the lip, a fresher smell like dewdrops. Something is off."

Spencer bent down to the edge of the lake and peered inside. He took an empty bottle from his backpack and filled it with the lake water. He filled a plastic bag with dirt samples and some of the plants.

"Tomorrow, I'll take the samples into the Agricultural Department for testing. If you look below us, you'll see that all the rains flow downward toward the Skagit River. Take a look through the binoculars, and you'll see my property is that green area to the right of the airport."

"What are you expecting to find?"

"If there is some contamination from whatever Frank is burying, the water will percolate along the fractures of the mountainside. The freezing and thawing of the basalt crumbles the rock but also allows for water, and in this case contaminated water, to flow into the folds of the rock. Eventually if it flows into the Skagit River, the contamination spreads."

Maria shivered with an eerie thought, envisioning JoAnne walking along the scree forty-five years ago. "How long do you think Frank has been burying stuff here?"

Spencer stared into her eyes. "Let's get moving. We should head back before the sun sets. We have just enough time."

They half walked and half ran. They were almost by the trail when they heard the echo of two gunshots.

Spencer paused. "I think Frank found my truck."

Sure enough, when they came to the green gate, they saw Frank heading down the road and Spencer's truck hunkered down with two flat tires.

"I'll call Russell."

Chapter 12:
Skid Road

Frank pressed down on the accelerator, pushing his truck to move as fast as his heart pounded. Fumes leaked from the exhaust, fumes leaked from the truck bed, fumes leaked from Frank's thoughts. Vibrations from the puckered road sent waves of anger and fear through his body.

He turned off the gravel road onto Highway 20, going too fast. Overcorrecting, he barely missed a car before the truck righted itself. Within seconds, he heard sirens and saw red flashing lights. Resigned, Frank clicked his right blinker and veered off to the shoulder. A stream of police cars and an ambulance zipped by him without a glance. Saved by someone else's stupidity.

Frank worried about his own stupidity. Shooting holes into that truck parked near the Pit only brought attention to himself. His hands shook on the steering wheel as he put his own truck back in gear. The shaking had more to do with fear from his sister than the law. He wanted to swig some moonshine and disappear, before facing Molly's wrath.

He wished his mother hadn't passed on. He missed visiting her at the nursing home, where he'd sworn everyone to secrecy. If Molly had known about his daily visits, she would have blocked his admittance. He had felt safe at the nursing home, just like he had felt safe at Northern State Hospital when he worked there. Molly could never understand his affinity for helping. His sister understood meanness, hurting, deceiving, and gaining the upper hand. She couldn't lend a hand or feel compassion. His mother taught him compassion. At the nursing home he'd sit with her, wheel her to the cafeteria, and play cribbage with her and the other patients. He'd forget about the past and the present. He'd ignore Molly's perverse pull.

Worn down by his sister's malice, he felt like the skid roads that dragged logs from the hillside to railroads and logging trucks. Yet muddied with lies and deception, his body cringed, knowing his part in her schemes. He felt the dirt, the deep grooves of humiliation that now skidded across the fat folds of his belly. His mother knew. She acted as his confessional.

Frank drove slowly, calmed with his mother's vision. Her last gift to him was a kiss, a blessing of understanding. That kiss held more power than the scars Molly had inflicted. His mother gave him purpose. "Frank, you have power. Don't let Molly bully you. Your sister won't change. She can't see the truth in her own lies, and that is her weakness."

His cell phone rang. The calm dissolved with Molly's voice. "Frank, what have you been hiding from me? I just left the bank. Mom screwed us."

The word *us* sent an electric shock up his arms, and he felt his heart spasm. He never talked money with his mother and didn't care. She knew better than to include him in the financials, not because she didn't trust him but because she knew her daughter.

"Molly, what are you talking about? I don't have a fuckin' clue about the bank or money. You took care of all that. I don't even have a bank account."

"Mom was a lying cheat. She hoarded money away from us. You have got to do something. There are three trusts that I can't get into. Did she ever mention them to you? As the sole heirs, we can contest the will, say she was insane."

With each word defiling his mother, Frank felt his blood pressure rise. He turned off the highway toward the river and took a back road through the town of Lyman. He found a side road with a secluded lot and pulled off.

"Molly, I've got too much to do with these damn canisters to worry about her will. If you stir things up, you'll bring too much attention toward us. Let me just get rid of the canisters!"

"You're just a lazy good-for-nothing. I sent you to bury the canisters hours ago. What have you been doing, drinking moonshine, messing with the neighbor's dog?"

Unable to lie, Frank found his mother's advice the best. If he told Molly the truth, she wouldn't recognize it among her lies.

"I went to the Pit to bury the canisters, and there were visitors. I popped two holes in their tires as I left."

"Stupid green-loving hikers. Can't they read the sign? That is our property now. Serves them right. I thought I told you to bury them at the Olivine spoils pile."

"I'm headed there now."

"Frank, one of the trusts has the initials WASP. What do you think it means?"

Frank kept looking for a truth that would make sense, that would make Molly leave him alone. "You're the smart one," he said. "You figure it out."

With Molly's abrupt click, Frank pulled back onto the road. The old Olivine processing plant sat next to a gravel access road near the concrete ready-mix plant. He followed parallel to the Skagit River, dipping in and out with the winding curves of the river until he arrived at the 130-foot mound. For many years, Olivine maintained the overflow of storm water and the filtration system in sites nearby. No one bothered to check the sites, having deemed the chemicals stable, nontoxic to the environment. Frank knew the guards, shared moonshine with them, so it had been easy to distract them when he had left his loads on previous visits.

The river, however, meandered, nibbling on the site's edge. Frank didn't need a degree in biology or engineering to know that the power of flowing water eroded unpredictably, and what was stable could easily become unstable, nontoxic changed to toxic. The mayor of Hamilton didn't want this site even as a gift. With the Department of Ecology breathing down his neck, the mayor threw up his hands. Everyone worried about the pile spoiling the salmon runs. Frank figured the salmon would just go with the flow of the river, find another spot to spawn. Nature, in his opinion, could outsmart most humans.

He didn't know if nature could outsmart his sister. Years ago, Molly had found a great source of income, hijacking toxic waste and making it disappear. She'd been doing it since the end of World War II, when she worked at the telephone company and the composite factory. All the industries had waste, all needed to get rid of messes. Only Molly knew the ins and outs, from listening in on private conversations. She'd jot down information, then counterbid at a much lower price. No one ever checked the sites. Like the old saying, "Out of sight, out of mind," once the waste disappeared, the companies failed to verify.

The first order came from Puerto Rico, the disposal of hazardous waste from a top-secret way station of bombers and a United States nuclear maintenance facility. Even then, Frank thought it odd that someone would be calling from Puerto Rico. He learned later that there were no such things as accidents when his sister was involved. Molly had overheard a call from Spencer T, who had disappeared on the night JoAnne fell. Molly claimed that Spencer T had called her, but Frank's own recollection of the romantic heat between Spencer T and JoAnne led him to believe otherwise.

Molly always found someone else to blame for all her troubles: JoAnne, or this new guy who was at the vineyard for interfering with soil tests, or Frank for the sheep that died on their land. Now she'd find a way to blame their mother for her financial problems.

Frank knew why the fish were dying, why rodents, birds, and the bigger game didn't thrive. He had toxic canisters buried in so many sites throughout the valley and hills that he sometimes dreamed he'd wake up to see an iridescent glow.

He pulled his shovel from the rear of his pickup truck and walked to the back of the soil heap. Gold-colored sticks melded into the landscape, markers that shone with his flashlight. He counted twenty-five holes. With the ten canisters just delivered and the ten he had retrieved from the Pit, and the removal of these twenty-five, there would be enough to fill the truck bed. He dug for over two hours, carefully removing old canisters that he had previously buried. Dusk acted as a camouflage.

Tired and satisfied that no one had seen him digging, he filled his truck bed with landscape debris—tree limbs and root balls from a recent clearing—completely covering the canisters. If his luck held, Frank would be able to sneak into the waste yard of the local composite manufacturer and place his cache on their truck.

As he drove, Frank focused on the ruts in the gravel road. The town of Hamilton had once been vibrant, but now it was an outcast like him. When the factory closed, the high school shut its doors. A town without a high school meant everyone would leave. Sooner or later, the mayor would have to deal with the new status of the Olivine pile. Sooner or later, Frank would have to deal with his sister.

Frank drove in a trance. Back on Highway 20, he passed the local diner, the hungry hub where the townsfolk wiled away their days. He expected to see the parking lot filled with trucks and campers, summertime visitors, but three of the police vehicles and the ambulance he'd seen earlier in the day lined the parking stalls, blocking the diner entrance. Patterns, he liked patterns, the predictable. He gripped the steering wheel tighter, as if this could control the knot forming inside his stomach. In the distance, he saw the smoke, the black billows of chemicals floating up into the sky. His nightmare became real as he realized that his more recent dumps of unstable chemicals had not yet been shipped out.

By the time he arrived at the manufacturing plant, the last of the fire trucks had dispersed. Spotting an old friend, he rolled down his window. "Bob, what happened?"

The fireman shrugged. "We got it under control. Some of the chemicals from the composites built up, caused an explosion. Looks like the cleanup will keep the plant closed for a few weeks. We were damn lucky that there wasn't anything out here that was toxic."

Frank nodded, gave a wave of his hand, and circled behind the plant. He didn't dare leave his cache, even though the waste yard gate lay wide open. He could hear his sister's voice, "Opportunity only knocks once. Take advantage whenever you can." Indecision. For most of his life, decisions belonged outside of him. He did what he was told. He had no compass.

He felt the pounding of his heart in his head. The blood beat with the force of knives, stabbing at the back of his eyes. Frank held his head between his hands, pressing inward, shrinking the space, confining his thoughts. Trying to follow his mother's wishes to make things right, was feeling wrong, now as one right created more wrong. He took the worn path, letting his truck glide along the course of least resistance.

He knew, as he dumped the canisters in the waste yard, that he had no other choice. Bad led to bad. You couldn't clean up your past when you couldn't see the future. He missed his mother. He didn't trust Molly, and he didn't trust himself. Getting rid of one problem created another. There really wasn't any truth to be found in a lie. He needed some moonshine and the peace of the meandering river.

Chapter 13:
Two-Way Communication

Silence, the sound of nothing—that was what Russell craved. By his feet, Maya moved with the kinks of age, half lifting a paw, bending down for a long stretch, and then popping up to see what was going on. Russell had just come up from the basement after listening to chatter on the radio. He shook his head as he patted Maya.

"Girl, at eighty-eight, I'm too old for the goings-on around here." He'd wished he could snooze like her, dreaming of finding buried bones. His own bones ached from climbing those damn stairs, and listening to the ham radio had gotten him riled. Firemen were down by the composite factory putting out a chemical fire, and the town was lucky that there wasn't any real damage. "I suppose I know more about what's going on in the valley than most. I don't need TV to keep me informed."

Russell caught himself. Talking to the dog had become a habit, and he wondered if people thought he was going crazy. He filled the house with his own voice to make a conversation, as if a thought would remain just a thought unless he said it out loud.

Silence couldn't keep his thoughts from becoming real. He wished Emma had not died, that she could still listen and offer her opinion. He patted Maya, his loyal companion. He'd gone downstairs to await Mourning Dove's call. Russell sighed, the sigh of an old man who knew too much and not enough. Spencer T kept sending Russell more disturbing information. Gone for forty-five years, yet his life connected too snugly into the present, making a leap from across the ocean, affecting the future. Mourning Dove seemed to travel the airwaves, honing in on home.

Russell went into the kitchen for a cup of coffee. He poured thickened mud from the pot and added milk. The red light from the answering machine blinked. Messages—no one left messages unless they needed or wanted something.

Hitting the button, the first message beeped, "Hello, Russell, this is JoAnne. I thought you should know that Spencer and my grandniece are hiking at the Pit. If you get this message, please call me back. I have a bad feeling."

Pausing, Russell scratched his head and looked at his watch. The call had come in four hours earlier.

The next message beeped, "Russell, this is Maria. Spencer and I are at the Pit. Our truck has two flat tires. Frank shot them as he left in his truck. I'm not sure why. We are okay, but we need a ride."

Russell glanced quickly around the kitchen, making sure all the burners were turned off, then grabbed his keys and turned off the lights. Maya wagged her tail, thinking that they were going on an adventure. "Why not, girl? You can come, but once I pick up the kids, you have to sit in the back of the pickup. If something bad happens, I want you with me."

The two headed outside, and Russell scanned the back of his pickup for supplies. Throwing in two tires, a shovel, an extra flashlight, a rope, and a blanket, he calculated the time it would take to get to the Pit. The sky still held light and no rain clouds. He realized that rescuing had nothing to do with age or strength, more the willingness to help and the availability. Old age gave him free time; friendships made him willing.

Maya sat curled up by the half-open window, letting her nose stick out. Russell let the silence settle into the truck. He ignored Maya's panting and concentrated on coincidences, or as JoAnne put it, "a bad feeling." Russell kept to the facts, and the most interesting was Frank. Coupled with the stupidity of shooting tires and the fact that the younger versions of JoAnne and Spencer T were present at what was now Frank and Molly's property, Russell saw a connection: stupidity and greed.

Instead of heading straight for the Pit, Russell drove to JoAnne's house. He'd forgotten to call her back and knew she'd be worried. As if on cue, he spotted her sitting on the front porch. Rolling down his window, he hollered, "Thought I'd mosey over to the Pit and have a look. Got your call."

JoAnne wheeled her chair down the ramp and up to Russell's truck.

"You can't fool me, you old goat. What took you so long? You can tell me as soon as I'm sitting next to Maya. I'm not waiting around for trouble."

Once on the road, Russell let the silence settle in again. He didn't want JoAnne to ask him anything. Russell didn't mess with memories popping up as "déjà vu" and didn't like small talk. He glanced over at JoAnne out of the corner of his eye.

She sat with her head turned toward the window, holding Maya's head in her lap, petting her as his Emma had always done with their dogs. JoAnne emanated strength. Her neck and arms revealed muscles that he knew came from her constant swimming, lifting, switching arms for legs whenever possible. Her face held a different kind of strength, lines around the eyes of worry, but also determination, defying age.

Despite his resolve not to talk, Russell said, "I got a call from Maria. They have two flat tires."

JoAnne slowly turned her face toward Russell. "I assume Spencer didn't have two spares and that the flats weren't from nails. Do you want to tell me anything else?"

Russell kept his eyes on the road and shrugged. "There isn't much else to say except that the flats came from Frank shooting bullets into the tires. The kids are okay. Frank shot the tires, not them."

Russell waited as JoAnne petted Maya, rolled down the window for air, and let her tears flow along her cheeks. Russell waited for the past to dissolve, for JoAnne to be back in the pickup, not in the ambulance of forty-five years ago.

JoAnne finally said in a forced whisper, "The kids are okay, but things aren't right. Frank is an idiot, an idiot with a gun. He was an idiot years ago. I guess not much has changed."

Russell thought back to his latest contact with Mourning Dove, Spencer T, the man who left JoAnne with a broken heart. Russell couldn't keep up the two-way communication when it should be three-way. His ham radio hobby had morphed to something more subversive, and Russell felt like a coward, yellow with truths not told.

"Years ago, the phone system failed us. I got your message today, and Maria's. Change happens with technology. Molly McCain hasn't changed, but we have."

JoAnne nodded. The two of them rode in silence along Highway 20 past the Concrete Airport, past the local diner.

"Have we changed, Russell? I keep so much to myself. I wonder if I'm not being stoic, the martyr who can take care of herself. Worrying about Maria, seeing the young version of my Spencer, makes me wonder if I am being honest. I put so much stock in telling the truth, but I have lied to myself for so many years just so I can keep going—small distortions, white lies of protection."

Russell reached across Maya's furry body and patted JoAnne's hand. He didn't have a witty response, one that would ease the conversation, keep up the façade they both had worked out since the fall, since

Emma's death. "Sometimes we just keep the peace with ourselves. But when peace concerns others, we have to speak up. Look down the way. Frank is parked along the side of the road, and Molly is ragging on him over that phone. They aren't keeping any peace that I can see. Their life is one lie after another."

JoAnne followed Russell's gaze as they passed Frank in his truck. Her voice sounded calm, but the message was firm: "Time we start setting the record straight. Clean up the mud pies, brown dirt fabricated to appear like dessert. There is nothing sweet about their deception."

Russell turned off the highway and headed into the forest. The lush canopy of summer brought darkness early here. The sun was still up, heating the river, but it hid behind leaves, cooling the air. JoAnne shivered.

"If you're cold, you can use my old sweater. That is, if Maya will move her body."

"No, I'm not cold, just shivering from memories. I know now that Spencer never abandoned me. I just can't reconcile the why of the lies afterward from Molly and Frank. The Pit is where my world, as I envisioned it, literally slipped away."

"You can't go backward," he said. "That has always been your motto."

JoAnne reached over to Russell's arm, squeezed it, and slowly turned her face toward him, letting him see both her smile and one tear making its way to the corner of her mouth. "You know you can have two emotions at once. I love my life here in Skagit County. I came because I met a man, Spencer, and wanted to pass my life with him. That dream disappeared, but I made friends, you and Emma, and most blessedly I was able to raise my orphaned grandniece. All that is true, but the parallel truth is that I am still wary of what I feel toward Spencer. Knowing that he left years ago because of a special mission doesn't make it okay."

Russell fidgeted with the gears, mumbled under his breath about the upkeep of a public road. He didn't want to hear JoAnne's private thoughts, although he had been listening to her since Emma died. He thought about Spencer's call this morning. If he thought of him as Mourning Dove, it didn't seem as intimate.

"You're fussing again, Russell. My feelings make you squirm. We could talk about Molly and Frank if it makes it easier on you. I can still muster up some anger."

"Well, I was going to rant about the DNR not maintaining the roads, anything to not have you cry. But since you brought it up, tell me again how you knew that Molly saw your fall and left you out on the scree slopes."

JoAnne shook her head and gave a half laugh. She adjusted herself, pushing down on the seat and lifting her bottom up so she could sit straighter. She carefully folded one limp leg over the other. Maya, awakened from her dog dreams, repositioned herself, curling between Russell and JoAnne.

"I've been keeping that secret for years, partly because I didn't want to believe it, but now to have the power of knowing. Power is something Molly craves."

Russell nodded and shivered. "From the looks of her, she craves more than just power."

"Yes, ultimately her cravings gave her away. When I first woke up in the hospital, I couldn't remember anything. The hospital had saved all my belongings—my bloody peddle-pushers, a red scarf, a blue sweater, and my sneakers. They even found the picnic basket with elk sandwiches and my flask of moonshine. Among the pile was a candy wrapper. Apparently, they had to pry my hand open to take it out."

Although Russell had heard the story before, he settled back to imagining JoAnne, not the physically damaged JoAnne but the one putting the pieces back together.

"I remember that. The doctors drilled you on sequences, pushing to see if you had all your faculties. You stared at the candy wrapper as if a creature from outer space had entered the room."

Russell watched as JoAnne's eyes lit up, glowing with a fiery intensity.

"That candy wrapper was like a light illuminating my way out of darkness. Funny how something so simple became sinister and also gave me strength. The figure behind the wrapper was Molly. Even though I remember hearing her voice, seeing her running as I fell, my mind wouldn't go there. I didn't tell the doctors or anyone why I was fixated on the candy. No one who visited me ate chocolate candy. No one would have a reason to see me harmed. Only when I was out of the hospital, healing at your house, did I know."

Russell realized that they were almost at the gravel road leading to the Pit. He couldn't wait for JoAnne to continue. Impatient that she would clam up as soon as she saw Maria, he interrupted. "You were with us for almost two months. Emma sat by you, and I worked at getting your house adapted to a wheelchair. I remember walking in one after-noon when Emma was telling you she had bumped into Molly at the grocery store. Emma said she was pumping her for information, asked if you remembered the fall."

Joanne nodded. "I asked Emma what Molly was buying at the store. She said, 'Oh, you know, Molly is always eating chocolate candy.' I knew then that my fall was an accident, but not my abandonment."

"You must still have your reasons for keeping quiet. Or have things changed?"

"We are almost at the Pit. I don't want to discuss this in front of Maria and Spencer quite yet. Years ago, something bad was happening that wasn't about me. I got caught in the wrong place, but now I'm in the right place trying to use that light of awareness. I don't want the glare of Molly to obscure the facts. No matter what the outcome, I have to know."

Russell nodded. He wondered if that included knowing about Spencer T's involvement.

"Is that why you are going to Puerto Rico?"

JoAnne adjusted her bottom and legs, moving her hands up and down the calves and thighs.

"Yes and no. I'm meeting with a specialist, a healer of sorts, named Rosie. She lives in Puerto Rico and is coming to give a presentation at the university. This information isn't new to you. What do you want me to say?"

"I just don't want you to be hurt by the truth."

"Then will you tell me where you and Emma got the money to pay for the hospital, fix up my house, and start my home farming business?"

Russell purposefully hit a pothole, making JoAnne bounce up and down. He pulled up next to Spencer's truck.

Chapter 14:
Baa, Baa, Black Sheep, Have You Any Wool?

Molly wished she were home, wished she didn't have to corral the world. She turned the volume of the car radio up to drown out the singsong in her brain. The old childhood rhyme, "Baa, baa, black sheep, have you any wool," taunted her. She corrected the verse as she sang, "No sir, no sir, now that they're all dead . . ." She hated the song for its simplistic, sweet sentiment. Molly knew better. When she was a kid growing up, the sheep were her salvation. Docile, they'd follow her wherever she went. Her favorite sheep, the black one, ruled the mob. It led the others to safety, was the first to feed, the first to see danger, the first to find a mating partner. Molly watched as her favorite sheep took charge, protecting them all. The dominance served the flock well, countered the idea that no one wanted a black sheep. Molly patterned herself after the black sheep, pushing, maneuvering, and leading others to where she wanted them to be.

She mumbled to herself, "You have to fence everyone in, or they will run loose, take more than their share."

Her face flushed as she felt her blood running hot, even as the cool dusk of night settled in. Molly rolled down the window, hoping to find a breeze. Gone since early morning, she'd intended to be back at the ranch hours ago, with a bank account steeping with cash. She had run around to all the banks in the valley hoping to find out more information. Frank had been no help identifying the three mysterious trust accounts. Their mother died lying. Molly pushed the gas pedal down, infuriated at the idea. "Baa, baa, black sheep, I'll show you that no one can pull the wool over my eyes."

Molly drove, studying the highway, searching as if the key to her mother's defection were in plain sight. She fumed, popped a chocolate caramel into her mouth, and let the chewy candy work its magic. Her teeth and tongue played with the flavors, earthy, sugary, and a touch of bitterness. The caramel stuck on her molars, between her teeth. She used her tongue to pry the gooey delight out, and then she swallowed, feeling the candy slide down her throat.

If only she could, Molly would swallow JoAnne and the entire valley. She wouldn't even spare her brother, not after his irritating behavior. Devouring another candy, Molly tried to soften her thoughts. Frank was an idiot, misaligned momentarily, but JoAnne and her grandniece, they deserved restraint. JoAnne was an outsider who'd invaded Molly's territory.

The pressure between her ribs moved upward. Molly belched, feeling indignant with indigestion from the past. Again she heard her physician: "Your thoughts affect your health. Bad thoughts raise your blood pressure, cause you to overeat. First control your thoughts, and then you will feel better." She shook her head. What an idiot, clueless to what gave her pleasure.

Molly found herself driving past the old, defunct Northern State Hospital. The closed gates didn't deter her. She drove to the back, toward the cemetery, closer to the roar of water from wild, uncontrollable Hansen Creek. Years ago, this was where Molly came when the patients bothered her. She'd frighten them with the soggy smell of death, the oozing of the cemetery. This had been her spot of choice, a place to bury the deliveries of waste. A closed cemetery gave ample opportunity for stowing away that which needed burying. The secret underground tunnels between buildings also gave Molly more power, knowing all the mischief between staff and patients.

The more recent damming of Hansen Creek, the new interest in the hospital, left her without a burial site. Frank warned her that he could no longer enter. Molly stopped the car, rolled down the window, and took out a flashlight. She scanned the grounds. Hole after hole, black markers of graves and bottomless pits, were all that remained of her stash. She stared in disbelief. Why had Frank removed the waste?

No one stopped Molly. JoAnne didn't stop her years ago; she became a casualty of being in the wrong place at the wrong time. Molly had no choice but to leave her at the bottom of the Pit. Business came before pleasure, and by leaving JoAnne at the bottom of the scree, Molly protected her secret business deal and eliminated a romantic rival, as well. And fortune found its way to her doorstep again when Maria, JoAnne's grandniece, arrived drunk at Northern State Hospital. The poor girl blubbered about family, having a grandaunt named JoAnne. Oh, how the pleasure and pain of that combination thrilled Molly! Maria suffered under Molly's hand for two weeks before JoAnne came to the hospital.

Turning off the flashlight, Molly felt deviled. She didn't believe in coincidences or the haunting of the past. The cemetery had been ravaged, her pleasures of long ago raped by an outside intervention. Molly felt a twinge, more of a spasm of awareness, a horrible thought that prickled close to her heart under her ribs. She couldn't move, was paralyzed by a foreboding loss of control at what she had just seen. The grave sites were empty, as were her waste burial sites. The new interest in the Northern State Hospital grounds had ruined her business and pleasure. Molly had to find the source of money, the directors of the

Foundation for the Northern State Hospital Restoration.

Her ribs ached, and her arms tingled. Fury fueled her. Molly reached for her cell phone, her hands fumbling as she hit the keypad with Frank's number. No rings, just the voice piping, "I can't answer your call now. If you would like to leave a message, wait for the beep."

"Frank, why did you turn your phone off? You know I despise leaving messages. Did you know the cemetery stashes have been robbed? Something is going on, and if I find out you are behind this or know anything, I'll do what I had you do to the sheep. If I can't trust my brother, who can I trust? I hate liars! Remember the sheep, remember the smell of sickness rotting."

Molly rested her head against the steering wheel. Her breath came in spurts, her arm tingling. She tried to remember her doctor's words. "If your arm starts tingling, take this pill, and call 911." She grabbed her purse and found the pills. Closing her eyes, she counted black sheep.

Chapter 15:
The Moon Is Made of Green Cheese

Perched on a rock, Maria listened for Russell's truck. She contemplated Spencer and her attempt at picnicking with cheese, crackers, and a bottle of Pinot Noir. Most of the snacks remained, but she wasn't sure for how long as she stared at the ants carrying off cracker crumbs. The line of black specks moved as an army focused on a mission. A few stray ants sipped spilled wine. They teetered on another path and eventually fell in line. Maria put her ear to the ground, wondering if she could hear their tune, know the direction to take. She never followed a linear path, except when flying, and wondered what it would be like to not question, only accept someone else's call.

She rarely drank anymore, and only when she felt secure. Visions of her deceased mother lying drunk on the bathroom floor, or herself at Northern State Hospital, captured like an animal and too wasted to know her rights, held Maria in check. Despite the gunshots, the foreboding sense of history repeating itself, she felt the strength of sharing. Spencer's brief touch as they drove into the Pit remained on her thumb. She pondered the intensity of his gaze, where she saw warmth and caring. With few words, Spencer's presence gave her comfort under stress, the voice of reason and understanding. He was muttering to himself now as he gathered samples. She chose to be the sentinel, watching over the truck, watching for trouble. Her ears heard more than she could see as the tree canopy darkened the sky, bringing in night.

After what seemed like hours, Maria recognized the low hum and rattle of Russell's truck. "I hear Russell coming up the road," she said.

Spencer came up behind her, dumped his backpack on the rock, and squeezed her shoulders. "Good thing we aren't trying to be quiet, just hiding in plain sight. Russell's muffler needs fixing. I'll try to get to it next week."

Maria shook her head, smiling despite herself. Again she felt Spencer's ease, his comfort, relaxed under his straightforwardness, allowing her body to succumb to the attraction.

"You really can think about ten things at once. Collecting specimens of contaminated soil and water, worrying about your vineyard, dealing with gunshots, making me feel comfortable, and now how you will help Russell with his truck. What else can you do?"

"Well, making you feel comfortable is a first for me. The other stuff comes more naturally. Did I ever tell you what the *T* in my uncle's name stands for?

"Let me guess. Thoughtful, or maybe torturous. No, I think I have it: Tender, Tempter, Tinkerer."

"Be forewarned if I take you up on one of those. The real name might not be as interesting. My granduncle never forgot his roots. As a young kid, he would often come to school with no shoes. His parents were poor and never really cared until the kids taunted him. They would ask him to show his heels. Tar Heel in their minds meant his heels would be black and sticky."

"Did your granduncle get into fights when he realized that they were bullying him?"

"No, even as a kid, he knew ignorance when he saw it. He would smear tar on his heels after football games and run in the fields, leaving footprints. He was the quarterback, the hero of the team, and the fans would go wild. My granduncle taught me never to get even, just to get smarter, and to laugh more."

As Maria picked up their picnic remains, Spencer took off his shoe. He lifted up his heel, showing a black stain. Maria almost laughed until she saw his sock.

"What did you step in? You weren't just sharing a family story, were you? Is it even true?"

"Maria, how could you think I made that story up? I share with you my inner secrets, and you doubt me?"

Maria thought at first that she had offended him, but his ear-to-ear grin made her laugh. "Seriously, what is that stain?"

Spencer's face transformed from playful to serious. "Without a lab at my disposal, I can only guess that something buried here years ago has come to the surface. The smell is sulfuric, and the consistency could be from a decomposed fuel or another petroleum-based product. Whatever it is, I don't trust it. By the smell and the residue left behind, it appears to be affecting what grows in the pond, or more likely, what does not grow."

Behind Spencer's voice, Maria heard the clinking of a muffler dragging along the bend in the gravel road and then smelled smoke and burning gas. Their rescuer, Russell, pulled up alongside Spencer's truck.

"Looks like we saved you two from an embarrassing moment. You just putting your clothes on or taking them off?"

Maria's jaw dropped at Russell's insinuation. She ran over to the passenger's side of the truck and pulled open the door to greet JoAnne. They embraced with a hug of knowing, a hug of fears averted.

Finally JoAnne pulled away. "You didn't expect me to sit calmly waiting for your return? I promise not to lecture you, but you—"

"Aunt Jo, you and I both know that the 'but' is the start of a sermon. You can see for yourself that Spencer and I are fine."

Maria looked over at Russell and Spencer. Spencer's body was half under the cab of his truck with his feet hanging out. Maya circled the truck, sniffing the ground and growling. Russell bent down on one knee, shook his head. No lectures, just immediate action. While she and her aunt were hugging, they had popped off the wounded tires and were examining the damage. Spencer scooted out from under the truck with his jaw set and his eyes darkened. Maria squeezed her aunt's shoulder and whispered, "Fine doesn't describe that look."

Russell stood with his arms folded across his chest, his right hand cupping his cheek. "If you two don't mind me stating the obvious, Frank's shots not only put holes in the tires, but one of the bullets also nicked your gas line. I'm glad Spencer told me he smelled gas. Frank only meant to stop you, but that gas leak really could have hurt you if the car ignited the spilled fuel."

Maria let Russell's words sink in.

JoAnne was the first to speak. Still seated in the truck, she leaned out the door, agitated, and called out, "Get all of your gear inside Russell's truck. Just leave everything as it is. We have to stop thinking there is a man in the moon watching out for us. The moon isn't made of green cheese, and this is not a fairy tale. Real facts, real danger, real action."

When JoAnne took on the leader role, people jumped. Within minutes, Spencer had collected his tools and thrown the tires in the back of Russell's pickup. Maria gathered the food from their picnic and watched the ants scatter as she shook the makeshift blanket. She pictured heads flying like the ants. Would Frank be decapitated by her aunt, or by his sister, Molly?

Maria slipped in behind the front seat, squished in with Maya on her lap. Spencer sat sideways so that his legs extended over hers. Even as the adrenaline rushed through her blood, she felt the comfort of being with family. As Russell patted JoAnne's arm, Spencer reached for her own hand.

Russell spoke first, as he pulled out. "All this craziness started years ago. I'm an old coot, and I give people the benefit of the doubt. I'm a doer and helper. I listen, have listened, to the gossip of everyone along the river, and I apologize to all of you for what I'm going to say. I usually mind my own business, but the business of greed is ugly, and I am angry. JoAnne, you and I talked about setting the record straight. That means you have to tell me what you suspected years ago. It means I have to share with you what I have found out, and it means that you, Spencer, need to stand up for your family name."

Maria had never heard Russell say so many words in a string, or for that matter, raise his voice in anger. "Russell, you didn't mention me. What am I supposed to do while all of you delve into the past and reveal secrets? Why don't we just call the police?"

Russell looked at her in his rearview mirror. "You will do what you do the best. You will keep us calm, focused, and accountable. You'll help your aunt be honest with her feelings, you'll pry my forgotten thoughts from my brain, and you'll trust your new friend Spencer. As far as the cops are concerned, you two were trespassing on the McCain property. Your complaint will go nowhere."

Maria felt Maya gently licking her hand. She stared out the window, watching the darkened forest close down. The ghosts of lies lurked behind the trees, black shadows running for cover as the truck lights passed by. Confused, Maria tried to pry answers from her aunt. "Aunt Jo, I came to fly you to Puerto Rico. I came to help with some emergency."

Her aunt reached from the front seat for Maria's hand, her fingers dipping inside the cupped palm. This was their wordless signal, a time-out of sorts where they could show love without demands.

Finally her aunt spoke. Her voice softened, the tone controlled, the words chosen with care. "I brought you all together for dinner because of the recent discovery of plants and animals dying on lands above and below Concrete. The path of odd deaths follows along the lands near the Skagit River. I suspected that Molly would know something because her sheep farm sat in the middle of all the lands. Also, she was actively buying up property across Skagit County. I had ulterior motives as well. I made a separate discovery concerning Monica's whereabouts, as well as that of Spencer T, when I was researching medical treatments for my legs. These coincidences seem to have caused an emotional reaction."

Russell motioned to slow down, breaking in. "I'm going to interrupt because my brain can't hold on to the emotional part. I won't drive with emotions, or tears, or anger, or even fear. Let's look at this logically. Frank shot Spencer's tires out and hit a gas line. He did this because you guys were prying or spying on something he was doing. I'm not saying you were prying. It doesn't matter. Frank was paranoid and scared you would find something. Forty-some years ago, JoAnne was up here, and she heard gunshots and fell. No one came to her rescue. My conclusion is that the innocent picnics you all wanted interfered with Frank and Molly's plans. It isn't a stretch to believe their plans caused and are still causing problems downriver with the land."

Maria plunged in. "So, you are saying that Aunt Jo was to meet her friend, Spencer's granduncle, up here, and the gunshots were a scare tactic to keep her away? Her fall was an accident, but a sinister one?"

Her aunt found her voice. "Yes, I was walking along the scree, heard a shot, and later I remembered seeing Molly looking down at me. I never said anything because I didn't want to believe a so-called friend would want to hurt me."

At this point, Maria couldn't hold her tongue or her thoughts. She felt like an elephant was in the truck, but no one wanted to acknowledge its presence. "I have a question. Bear with me, Russell—even though I'm a woman, I can think rationally. Everyone leaves Spencer T out of the story. I'm not saying he was at fault, but he never showed, and even after the accident, he disappeared. I don't know the connection, but if you all still believe him an honorable, kind person, why the absence, why the failure to find an answer? According to his grandnephew, he only ever talks about the wonders of Skagit Valley. If Spencer T loves his old home so much, why abandon his vineyard, his friends, and my aunt?"

Maria waited while the silence deepened. She feared she had alienated everyone in the truck except Maya, who continued licking her hand. Maria knew the pain her aunt felt. Abandonment went deep inside her veins and heart. Monica was all she had, and when she left, the promise of their reunion eventually died. Maria had watched her aunt fill her life after the loss of mobility and the loss of love. Maria couldn't understand the loyalty from everyone concerning the idolized persona of Spencer T, and her doubts stung like her unshed tears.

Russell smiled in the front mirror and winked at Maria, a sign that she had pushed the right button. Maria felt her stomach flip, a sense she had when she flew her plane upside down. She hoped that her outburst would turn their thinking around, steer them to a safe landing.

She looked over at Spencer, waited for a sign that he understood her questioning. He adjusted his legs over hers, ignored her glance, and cleared his throat. She waited for words. None came.

They had left the forest cover and were back on Highway 20. Just to break the silence, Maria asked, "Where are we going?"

With her question, the spell of glumness broke. Everyone talked over one another, making suggestions. Russell ignored all of them.

"Quiet. We are heading up to my place. I don't have much in my refrigerator, but between the canned goods and the garden vegetables, we can make a decent meal. After we eat, I'll offer more food for thought."

Chapter 16:
Mourning Dove

After wolfing down Russell's makeshift spaghetti dinner, Maria stared out his kitchen window, the perfect spot to gaze as she washed dishes. The sun had finally set, and the dusk left silhouettes of the garden stakes. Rows of cultivated earth laden with rising buds surrounded the house. Maria let JoAnne and Russell's reminiscing fade behind her, contenting herself with the comfort of a full belly. Washing dishes kept her hands occupied, but left her mind free to wander. Her thoughts drifted back to the Pit and then fast-forwarded to flying to Puerto Rico where her sister lived, where the mysterious Spencer T lived. She avoided thinking about his nephew, who had gone silent since Russell had come to their rescue.

"I think you have washed that pot three times."

Startled, Maria dropped the pot back into the dishwater.

"Now you'll have to wash it again," Spencer said. "You'd think there was magic water in the sink to keep you so spellbound."

Maria took her time rinsing the pot and placed it on the drain to dry before she turned to face Spencer. "Aunt Jo always set me to washing dishes when I was perplexed or out of sorts. She claimed the warm water warmed the heart, softened the brain muscles to open wider."

Spencer took the dishrag from her hands and placed it back on the hook where Russell had three others hanging to dry. He faced Maria, moving closer. She lifted her chin so that their eyes met.

"If your aunt is correct, then your heart would be warming toward me by now and your thoughts a little gentler toward my namesake."

She studied his eyes, so wide and blue. Maria wanted more than anything to put aside her fears. She closed her eyes and started to back away, but his hand took hers. Maria squeezed his fingers and then felt Spencer's arms encircle her. Their hug overrode Maria's doubting thoughts, letting words disappear as the simplicity of caring took hold.

"Thank you for this afternoon," she said. "Not just the picnic and walk, but for helping my aunt get into the house. She used to come to visit Russell and Emma. Back then, there was a long ramp for her to ride in on her wheelchair. I hadn't realized that it had rotted."

"Russell is getting older, and I try to help him out with the chores. Your aunt prefers that Russell visit her at her own house, so there was no need to fix the ramp. I don't know of anyone else who uses a wheelchair, and we all know that Russell will outlive the house. He stays here for the memories and because he is bound to the land."

"Are you bound to the land as well?"

"Owning land is complicated. Some people love it for the view, for the smells, for what it gives them. I love it for what I can give the land. Raising grapes makes me pay attention. Any crop tells you so much about the soil, the weather, the insects, the birds. In Puerto Rico, they say, '*La tierra sabe todo*,' the earth knows it all. Farmers know their land. They are true ecologists, stewards of the land. That is why Russell, your aunt, and I are so upset. We feel responsible."

Despite herself, Maria bristled. "Feeling responsible isn't always the same as being accountable. Somehow those words just cover up the truth. I know I'm not making sense. Being responsible is the same as saying that one is to blame, that they are at fault. My ideas get twisted unless I feel like there is a way to act, to change an outcome, not just to passively discover. I need to fix things."

"Are you talking about the land right now, or your aunt's fall, or your sister, Monica?"

A gasp escaped her lips.

Before she could answer, her aunt called from the living room, "Maria, Spencer, no more talking in the kitchen. Russell disappeared, and I'm not going to sit in here alone."

Maria turned off the kitchen light, and they made their way to the living room. JoAnne sat on the sofa near the unlit fireplace. With her wheelchair folded off in the corner of the room, she was stranded. One of JoAnne's house rules had been breached: always have a means to become mobile.

"Russell said he was expecting a call and went down to the basement. I almost scooted down with him. Spencer, I want you to carry me down the stairs so I can hear what is going on. Don't look so surprised—I've known about the ham radio calls for years. Emma told me."

Maria looked from her aunt to Spencer and back again. The two were on a page in a book that she didn't even know existed.

"Don't tell me that Russell's ham radio calls are covert, that they aren't just innocent hobbyists having a good time?"

JoAnne's face crumbled as if she had been slapped. "Maria, this isn't about your life. Emma died years ago. All of this was before you arrived here. Remember that I lived here after my accident. I saw and heard things. Emma shared with me that Russell received calls during the war. I never asked about them."

Maria's ears rang. She knew now why Russell wanted them to come back to his house. He was expecting this call. He wanted her to ask questions.

"Aunt Jo, you told me never to apologize for my actions, only to make amends. I think that is exactly why Russell wanted us all here. He wants to make amends. He knew he would get a call tonight. This is part of his plan for all of us to face the truths we have failed to see. Do either of you know who he is talking to?"

She expected silence again, but both Spencer and her aunt simultaneously blurted out, "Mourning Dove."

"And Mourning Dove is the call name for whom?"

And this was the million-dollar question. For over forty-odd years, Russell had been speaking to someone with no identity. The pieces began to fall together ever so slowly. Maria could see the lines of history as a timetable of events. Mourning Dove stood at the beginning, the middle, and now the end of the line.

Spencer scooped JoAnne up in his arms, lifting her as if she were a child. Her aunt wrapped her arms around his neck, making her weight lighter, and they headed to the basement, slowly descending into Russell's secret world. Maria could hear voices as they made their way to a small door only visible by the stream of light coming through the holes of pegboard.

As a way of warning Russell that they were entering his domain, Spencer coughed.

JoAnne called out, "Russell, you've got visitors."

Russell looked up briefly and made an "okay" signal with his hand.

Three chairs encircled his. The closest held a soft cushion that acted as a nameplate for JoAnne. Spencer eased her onto the cushion. Maria sat next to her aunt, and Spencer found his spot next to Russell. Cramped into a space twice the size of a cockpit, Maria studied the walls. She expected that Spencer would be just as curious, but by the way he kept his eyes on her aunt and avoided hers, she could tell he'd been down here before. Maria wondered what separated a surprise from a lie.

The older maps showed currents, shipping routes. Yellowed and frayed, the markings were of a history from before Maria's time. JoAnne stared at the lines that marked plane routes, so old that Maria could barely discern the flight patterns except for the fact that Russell had written the names of planes on little pushpins. The XB-29 and XB-32 Bombers marked flights that spanned over 5,000 miles. Washington State seemed so far away from Japan, but Maria remembered hearing that during World War II, ships patrolled the Pacific coastal waters, fearing an attack from Japan. Her aunt's eyes fixated on the route from Kansas, where she had once been stationed, to Puerto Rico. Judging from her wide eyes and opened mouth, Maria realized that her aunt's surprise revealed a new truth.

Maria moved away from the older maps and studied a smaller map of the Skagit River. She noted Spencer's vineyard, the Concrete Airport, the Pit, JoAnne's property, Russell's land, and then the old Olivine plant, and the town of Hamilton. All had markings of skulls, Russell's tagging of dying fauna.

Just as she visualized Frank at the Concrete Airport hurrying to leave after a plane left a delivery, and then Frank's violent behavior toward the truck, Spencer looked her way. A film covered his eyes, a shield of sorts, as if he wanted to run for cover. No one here had done anything wrong, yet they all felt responsible. Truths are layered and easily become lies. Maria still wasn't sure of the layers of deception, but she knew that Mourning Dove held a place in the mound.

Russell's voice broke through the confusion. "I've got them all gathered here. I'm tired of just our two-way communication. Too much is at stake. I don't work for anyone, and you don't either. You've been retired from the agency for years. We are both free agents. Over."

"Hello, this is Mourning Dove from across the airwaves. Could you all say hello so I can hear your voices? Over."

At this point, Maria couldn't tell if there was static. The scraggly voice on the other end of the mike waited for their reply. Her aunt's eyes teared up, and she held her hand to her throat. Russell handed the mike over to her. Despite the shaking of her hand, JoAnne visibly pushed through her feelings.

"Mourning Dove, this is Jo, from across the airwaves. Where have you been all my life? Over."

The room closed in on them. Her aunt had heard the voice of her past and only asked the obvious. Maria's heart pounded against her ribs while her aunt's face remained calm, as if all was normal. Spencer stared at Maria. And then Mourning Dove came back on the radio. His voice came through stronger, more hopeful. "Jo, I've been mourning since the day I left. Over."

Spencer quickly scooped up the mike. "This is Spencer, and I'm handing the mike over to—"

"Me, the only one you haven't met. Maria, Jo's grandniece. Over."

Maria held on to JoAnne's hand, and her aunt squeezed tightly, releasing all her pent-up emotions. Already Maria could see the transformation of her aunt into the woman she had been with Mourning Dove, her old lover, Spencer T. Maria noted that her aunt called herself Jo, the name she used for strength, the one she piloted with. The room shook with memories.

When Mourning Dove spoke again, Maria noted the absence of emotion. His voice held a sense of urgency, as if they all were under his command.

"Hello, Jo, Spencer, and Maria. I'm talking to you all now to solve a noxious problem that spans more than just your private lands and that of the Skagit River. It started forty-five years ago, and I unwittingly created a monster without knowing the scope. I need you all to trust me."

Past conversations filtered through Maria's brain—Spencer telling her about his uncle working under pressure, secret projects, his devotion to his land in the Skagit Valley, and the lack of any substance concerning his initial trip or present work in Puerto Rico. Spencer T had never really left. He had maintained a connection with Russell and sent his nephew to live in a place he longed for. This was a man who left the woman he loved and, after forty-five years of absence, was calling on her and her grandniece to help. Bonds, loyalty, forgiveness . . .

Maria took hold of the mike. "Mourning Dove, I have one question. Is this a matter of national defense, or is it your defense?"

"Maria, you have your aunt's sharp mind. It is both. When you are caught between two truths and you can't choose, both seem like lies. For me, the safest place was to remain in the gray space, a place I thought would give me perspective, while I waited for more information. By playing possum, I tried to find the source of misunderstanding. I believed I had put the needs of my country first, my personal needs last. I was wrong. By waiting too long, I served no one, and my silence played into a sick mind. Molly McCain was and still is a toxic player. She is the wild card that can tumble us all."

Russell grabbed the mike. He looked tired, his age catching up with the day. His eyes held the worry of half a century, and Maria understood that this call was a drain on him.

"Mourning Dove, this is Hummingbird again. I'll try to fill everyone in on your discovery. Personal matters will sort themselves out. Let's keep our schedule, over and out."

And that was it. Russell had maneuvered them all into this room to push them into action. Maria rose from her chair just as Spencer rose from his. Russell held JoAnne's hand, not saying anything.

As Russell went to turn off the ham radio, a static message came through. "Ambulance on the way to the old Northern State Hospital. Looks like Molly McCain is in a ditch."

Chapter 17:
Flying Without a Compass

JoAnne sat immobile as a statue, frozen in contemplation: back straight, chin and head level, looking out at the lines of the airport runway meeting the grass edge rising up toward the Skagit Valley and Sauk Mountain. The clouds wisped in, red hues mixed with gray, giving way to waves of light. Her sun hat blocked the rays, but still she used her hand to filter out the brightness of the greens of the morning valley. She had slept fitfully after leaving Russell's house, mind tangling with a sense of urgency and purpose, her heart fluttering with pangs of buried emotions. Without sleep, her vision blurred so that it felt like the rising heat caused the pavement to buckle, illusions wafting up to meet the sky.

No, the pavement stood still. The movement came from waves of air, particles of dirt moving with the wind. She remembered flying in the desert where windstorms and heat whipped up odd visions. Mirages were real only in the sense that they occurred, changing perceptions to meet the mind's need. Science trumped vision, letting the instruments tell the story of where to land. Her days as a WASP kept her to facts. She didn't trust her emotions, especially after hearing Spencer T's voice. The facts trumped her imagined excuses of absence, made her feel less sure of the meaning of her existence.

Although it was a Sunday morning, the airport hummed with the sound of engines. Most of the hangar doors stood open. At this private airport, nearly all the pilots flew for fun. That was why the Concrete Fly-

In existed, why the main hangar housed a museum telling the story of flight from an old-timers' perspective.

JoAnne pushed her arms and hands swiftly along the wheels of her chair, propelling herself down the tarmac. Even after her morning swim, she couldn't seem to find the peace she needed to take care of the final details before the fly-in. Only through exertion could she feel. Her arms trembled, and her legs prickled as if a porcupine had attacked with pins and needles, the sensation of awakening. Were these sensations lies, taunting her? After so many years of numbness, dead weight dragging her down, these nerve endings pinged, popped with pain. Somehow her legs were remapping the connections, bypassing nerves, reconnecting to her spinal cord and brain. Either that or she now had phantom legs that lied to her senses, confused her everyday reality. Sweat beaded along her brow, and her arm's efforts showed through to her armpits, where dark stains like the moon shadowed her dress. Dead weight. Dead like a possum.

She replayed Spencer T's words in her mind: "By playing possum . . ." While she waited, languishing with pain and fear, her lover had played dead. She wanted to throw a tantrum, scream at the paradox of her situation. What did she know about truth? Old age had given her wisdom, patience. Youth had robbed her of love. Now her heart confused the lies with truth, and she had no clear path.

Tracking the runway, JoAnne wheeled herself up and down until she felt calm. Slipping back into her office, the museum hangar, she viewed the walls. History lied, but the photos on the wall didn't. JoAnne knew a truth that had to be told, one fact of history shadowed by the glory of male veterans. As a WASP, JoAnne felt compelled to revitalize the heroism of a small group of women who took to the skies during World War II, instead of staying home to take care of their families.

Usually, the Concrete Fly-In celebrated old planes, refurbished to fly again. This year, JoAnne had enlisted the help of the few remaining WASPs and had petitioned to have the legislature award Congressional Gold Medals.

Alongside the photos of old bomber planes, JoAnne had mounted prints of thirty-eight women pilots who had sacrificed their lives in support of World War II. JoAnne wheeled herself up to each photo, remembering them from training classes, from episodes where they had been rejected from continued work at the very bases where they had flown. She felt the irony of prejudices from the male pilots of old and now: with the pending legislation, many in their nineties were declaring that if the WASPS received medals, they would return their own medals. As if the skies belonged only to men. So much for progress.

As JoAnne looked into these women's eyes, she imagined herself in uniform, short hair cropped so that the headgear and goggles fit. She was wearing her first oversized issued coveralls when she met Spencer T. His deep laughter had caused her to turn around in the hangar.

"Bravery doesn't care about how you look, but you are swimming in those coveralls," he said.

JoAnne stood at five feet and two inches, just making the cutoff for height to be eligible to join the WASPs. Instead of taking offense at his remark, she had walked over to him and asked what he was doing. As the head mechanic and unofficial designer, Spencer T began explaining the nuances of the engines, the propellers, the small idiosyncrasies of each plane.

The feelings of the past still held power over her heart. Sighing, JoAnne felt a tear descend along her cheek. Falling in love with him had been easy. Whenever she had time after her flight training, she'd slip back into the hangar for lessons, and ultimately found herself learning more about life. Long days consisted of rising at six o'clock for reveille, five hours of ground school, and then four hours on flight line. The need for sleep pulled, as did the need to see Spencer T. He made her laugh. Comingling with the men on base had been discouraged, but JoAnne and Spencer T justified their actions with learning preparedness. JoAnne once flew a solo cross-country flight, and on landing saw smoke coming out of the right exhaust stack. Spencer T had been in the tower when she called in her emergency landing, and his voice held her steady.

JoAnne wheeled herself to her desk, looking to fill out the last of the paperwork for planes registering for the fly-in. Her concentration wavered once again as she remembered Spencer T's words, "His story or her story, our story." That had been his proposal, her push to move so far across the country once the WASP program had been dismantled.

So far, forty planes had registered for the fly-in, and a stack of papers awaited JoAnne. Sifting through the mail, she found one envelope addressed to WASP, in care of the Concrete Fly-In. Odder things had happened, and since this was an aero museum as well as an airport, the address seemed plausible. Slitting the envelope open, JoAnne pulled out a check for $20,000 and a note.

Dear Ms. JoAnne,

Please use this money to further the health and education of women pilots. Veteran women pilots needed support, but they were never recognized. Your work did not go unnoticed. Continue on. You will receive a check each year for the next five years.

WASP Trust Fund

Turning the note over, JoAnne searched for a return address, a phone number, or name. She stared at the check, made out from the local bank. Her mind raced, thinking about the money used to help her recover from her fall. After all these years, Russell still kept its source from her. Money falling from the heavens did not feel like God's work. Although JoAnne appreciated the help, she felt indebted. *Your work did not go unnoticed.* The question of who and why left JoAnne feeling spied upon.

Rolling her wheelchair backward, JoAnne moved closer to the door, studying her home away from home. Too old to fly, she passed two or three days a week at the airport museum as an unpaid volunteer. Age was her excuse for not flying, when really her wings had been clipped after the accident. No legs, no wings, a handicap that she had not surmounted. From the hangar door, JoAnne admired the simplicity of the airport. They averaged a hundred and some flights a week, mostly single-engine planes. Although the runway was 2,600 feet long, the unmanned tower and lack of instruments kept the traffic down.

JoAnne shrugged her shoulders. Concrete was an isolated community, the airport even more isolated. Who would even know of JoAnne, know about her work? Proud of her past, she kept thinking of "her story" and wondered if this check was a sign from another woman. Perhaps some famous person wanted the legacy of the WASP revealed, wanted lies corrected, wanted history to reflect another truth. If all this were true, there would be no need for anonymity. This check went deeper, more personal.

Needing fresh air to clear her brain, JoAnne sat by the edge of the hangar, ignoring her piles of work, admiring the landing of two small planes, listening to the chatter of families out for a stroll. The third ring from her cell phone woke her out of her contemplation.

"Aunt JoAnne, it's Maria. I'll be by to pick you up in a half hour."

"There is no hurry. I've a lot to do still. Take your time."

"You sound like you were far away. Are you okay?"

"Yes, I'm fine."

"Sure you are. Tell me what is going on. You didn't sleep last night, and Russell dropped you off at the airport early."

"Nothing new has happened, just coincidences. Don't worry, unless you think receiving unsolicited money in the mail for the WASP foundation is strange. Twenty thousand dollars!"

"That's bad? I would go out and celebrate! Why are you worried?"

"Someone knows too much about me."

Chapter 18:
Walking on Eggshells

The room smelled rotten, medicinal with a touch of alcohol and sweet syrup. The sulfury aroma of bodily discharges lingered by Molly's bedside. Wires and tubes hung from machines with digital markings, and the tubes wormed their way over the hospital bed and into the veins of the puffy left arm protruding from the white sheets.

Molly's eyes fluttered. From far back in a dark tunnel, she felt the heat of a shining light. Her lids remained shut, though she tried to pry them open. Exhausted from the effort, she lay still, letting small sounds enter her tunnel. She listened to a dripping, wondered if the roof had a leak, wondered if she was drowning. From a distance, she discerned a voice. She tried speaking, tried to make herself heard. Feeling claustrophobic, she clawed at the tunnel, screamed through sealed lips, "Let me loose. I'm drowning! What idiot has me trapped?" Her words went unheard except in her own brain. She pulled at the sides of her bed.

Two nurses rushed into the room and held Molly's thrashing arms down as they administered a shot. The older one tried soothing her. "No need to fuss, Ms. McCain. You aren't going anywhere. You're at Skagit Valley Hospital, and you're safe. What you need is sleep. Rest your heart, and let us take care of you."

"She has been fussing like this for over an hour, coming in and out of consciousness. When the ambulance brought her in, they treated her for a heart attack, but after the blood work, the doctor wanted to do other tests. I'm glad you're on with me this shift. Ms. McCain has a foul mouth. Right now, we just need to keep her sedated until the doctors advise us otherwise."

"Has she had any visitors? Have they notified her brother? He is the only next of kin listed on the records."

"No one has come to visit her. When they called her brother, the receptionist said he yelled some nonsense about waste and then the phone went dead. There is something odd about this one. I overheard the doctors say that the Health Department might need to be notified."

"The way the room smells, the Health Department would close us down."

Lifting up the blankets, they checked to see if the bed was wet or if Molly had soiled her gown.

"I checked her clothes and underthings. She hasn't soiled her bed. The smell is coming from her skin."

Molly lay still, resting until she could gather enough energy to explode. The fog in her brain had lifted, and now she realized that she was out of the tunnel, on a hospital bed, and constrained so tightly within the sheets that it felt like a straitjacket. Her mind shifted sideways, to the patients at Northern State Hospital, when they acted out, and how she had contained them. The doctors and nurses didn't care how she got them to behave, just that she did, especially her favorite patients. She wasn't their nurse but helped with dispensing the little cups with pills in them if she had finished working in the office. Many times, she would switch the medications, giving the meanest patients a double dosage so they would be lethargic and just follow her demands. To keep them loyal, she would steal food for them, and they in turn acted like puppy dogs.

Now Molly concentrated on remembering methods to break loose from the tightened belts. All she needed to do was listen until the stupid nurses left her in peace. If she counted slowly to sixty, the nurses would think she was asleep. Tricking the hospital staff had always been easy. Tell them what they wanted to hear, show them sleep, and they would think you slept.

Molly slowly rolled her head from side to side. Her eyelids refused to open. She suspected that the nurses had glued them shut. Breaking out would be harder than she anticipated. Cursing inwardly, she tried another tactic.

"You can't hold me here. I know people at this hospital. I'll get you all fired. Someone come here immediately and remove these restraints."

To her surprise, Molly didn't get a reaction. No movement, no hustling, just the absence even of the wavering of the air. She was alone, without the ability to be heard. Her threats lay between her lips, her voice caught in some tunnel of misconnection. The nurses were poisoning her with their injections. Slowly her body let go, and she tumbled back toward sleep. They may have won this round, but Molly would be ready for the nurses when she woke.

Falling into unconsciousness, her mind drifted back in time to when she worked at Northern State hospital and then to when she had just fainted at the hospital cemetery. She floated over a dark hole, one hole after another lined in a series. Her dream left her lost in the Northern State Hospital Cemetery. The cemetery held buried truths. Molly floated above each hole, peering inside to see faces of patients who failed her tests of loyalty. At Northern State Hospital, every patient had worked as part of their healing process, and Molly had assigned her patients to the cemetery just to dig. Some uncooperative ones fell in. Most recovered, climbed out more obedient to Molly's whims. Floating above the graves, Molly felt regret at the emptiness of the holes. Control. Everything she worked for had disappeared over time. Was death the only way these people had gotten free from her grasp? Had her secrets died with them? Drifting inside the holes, she saw the oozing earth, the sheen of oil, the bubbling of gases rising to the heavens. Panic set in as the gases engulfed her, and she couldn't breathe, her lungs seized with sticky caramel. Out of the holes, she rose, drifting above the cemetery.

And then she fell from the skies and landed back on the hospital bed. A plastic mask planted over her mouth let in oxygen, and she felt her lungs loosening, her arms and legs tingling.

Her lids flashed open to the bright lights of a headlamp. She recognized the man hovering above her as a doctor.

"Ms. McCain, take it slow. You have been in a fitful sleep after a mild heart attack. We were worried about you. Can you talk?"

Molly's mind raced. Of course she could talk. "Would you please remove the snakes from my bed?"

The doctor moved closer to Molly's head. Bent down to look at her face and gently lifted up her blankets. His face took on a stern look.

"Ms. McCain, can you repeat your request? I thought you asked me to remove the snakes from your bed."

"You are dumber than I thought. Can't you see the shedding skin, the small pricks on my legs, and the tracks of the snakes? Don't deny it—you are torturing me."

The doctor pulled the chart from the end of Molly's bed. He pored over the information, turning the pages over and over as if the snake would jump from the pages. Molly watched as he wrote some notes.

"Ms. McCain, how long have you had the sensation of a snake crawling over your legs?"

"You tell me how long you have been putting the snakes in my bed.

That will give you your answer. You can't scare me with snakes. I won't pee the bed like my brother did."

"Unfortunately you did wet your bed, but the nurses can change your sheets and gown. I'm Dr. Knobs, the attending physician. I have a call into your regular physician, Dr. Green. You are one lucky lady. Your heart attack was very mild, but we detected some inconsistencies in your blood sample. Your white and red blood cell count seemed low. We started you on iodine injections, so perhaps the sensation of tingling comes from the new medication."

Molly pulled her lips into her mouth, sighed so loudly that the sheets by her chin flapped. She needed information, needed to tend to her affairs, needed to close the holes at Northern State Hospital. Frank had better get her out of here. He'd created a nightmare worse than the ones from his youth. Her face softened, and she let moisture fill her eyes. "Dr. Knobs, what does iodine have to do with my heart? Can you explain why I need this?"

Doctor Knobs noticed the patient's mood swing, aggressive to saccharine, and marked the change on her chart. Intuitively he questioned the exchange as a symptom versus a state of being. He wondered if this patient had different masks for different purposes.

"I think that is best left up to your regular doctor. He will be here tomorrow."

Molly gave him a cold stare, throwing icy darts even as she smiled and let a tear drop. "I used to work at a hospital. You have to give patients information about their medications."

Her tone of voice made Dr. Knobs flinch. The chart said to treat the patient with kid gloves. The nurses wrote that they had to walk on eggshells, being careful not to trigger an aggressive response. He decided to ask Molly questions to find a way to break through her masks.

"Ms. McCain, the ambulance found you at the back end of the defunct Northern State Hospital. Is that where you used to work?"

Molly smiled. "You aren't from around here, are you? There is nothing defunct about that hospital. The gardens and revenue were huge. The hospital was a state-of-the-art facility with funding from all different sources. They closed it down and just left it there vacant."

Dr. Knobs nodded his head as if Molly had answered his question. He guessed that her answer was a truth covering a lie, omitting any fact that was a direct answer. He tried again. "You wanted to know about iodine injections and pills. Did you tell the patients at Northern State Hospital about their drugs?"

"I don't know anything about medications. I worked in the office dealing with the financial situation of patients."

He paused, absorbing Molly's words. On the one hand, she alluded to working at a hospital, insinuating she knew all the rules. She was clearly angered by the closure of Northern State Hospital. Then she denied knowing anything about medications but stated she worked in the office. The doctor felt like she was playing a game of chess. Each move became a maneuver to reveal or conceal something. He decided that the facts as he knew them would be his best move.

"Ms. McCain, I am not sure why you were out at Northern State Hospital, but they discovered a series of holes, old graves, that appeared to have held chemical toxins. Your blood tests showed evidence of decay usually attributed to a toxic exposure, either radiation or a chemical or biological cocktail of substances. Your blood count can no longer fight the foreign substances, and your thyroid has been compromised.

The iodine will act as a sponge, absorbing the toxins."

The patient made no comment, but her eyes went to her purse.

"Ms. McCain, you aren't listening to me. We have to discover what caused such severe decay in your body. Have you changed your eating behaviors or gone anywhere that could expose your system to a large quantity of reactive material?"

"Hand me my purse, please. I need to call my brother."

Dr. Knobs moved slowly, observing a stoic expression that closed off Molly's face. She had stopped listening to his words. He wondered if she understood or if she even cared. He handed Molly the purse and watched as she took out a chocolate caramel and popped it in her mouth. She fished through the bag and pulled out her phone. After pushing buttons, she threw it down.

"Dr. Green put me on a protein diet. I ate eggs and meat from my farm and my neighbor's. I'm organic. Do you have a problem with that?"

"How long have you been on this diet?"

Molly smiled. "Long enough to lose ten pounds, but you can't even tell."

At this the doctor snapped her chart shut. His pen dropped on the floor, and as he bent down to retrieve it, he saw the nurses waiting at the entrance. The look on their faces confirmed his conclusion. He picked up the pen and wrote in her chart: *Ms. McCain appears to suffer from a narcissistic personality disorder. Her present physical illness is a combination of her psychological makeup: caustic, paranoid, and what appears to be a contamination from locally grown food. The Health Department needs to investigate the origin of her diet.*

"Ms. McCain, did you notice anything odd about the eggs you ate?"

"Why should you care about my eggs? If you must know, they were delicious. I eat five or six deviled eggs daily. The shells were so soft, it made them easier to prepare. Are you questioning Dr. Green's advice?"

"No, Ms. McCain. Soft eggshells indicate a bioaccumulation of chemicals. You have poisoned your system, and maybe others, too."

Molly closed her eyes. "Can you have the nurses come by with some food? I'm hungry."

Dr. Knobs left the room and closed the door. The nurses scattered.

Standing at the reception station, he asked for the numbers of the Department of Health, the EPA, and the Agency for Toxic Substance and Disease Registry.

Chapter 19:
Citizens of a Community

Spencer grabbed his red cutters and slipped them in his back pocket. His worn jeans accommodated the cutters with a small hole where the sharp point poked out. He took the gravel path from behind his house, stopping first to get his wheelbarrow, twine, and gloves. Almost without his guidance, the wheelbarrow rolled down the winding slope to the newest planting of grapes.

Habits made his life easier, allowed him a certain amount of freedom. Each morning after fishing, he inspected his grapes. To ensure the purity of the fruit, he trained the vines so that no cane touched the ground. Keeping the vines at a particular aspect and separated allowed the sunrays to reach each cluster of grapes. Equal opportunity in the plant world meant he checked each vine, smelled the flowers, studied the grape's skin, and monitored the soil and water.

As he snipped stray vines, selectively thinning the grape clusters, he listened to the morning sounds. Swooping wings of the stellar jays, the chatter of the squirrels, and the buzzing of the bees assured him of flower pollination. Nature combined the forces of fauna to create a haven of fecundity. Fine-tuning was Spencer's only job, or so he had thought. Now he worried about leaching soils, contaminated water, and the silent, unseen, deadly attackers from unknown sources that made the survival of the fittest not necessarily a desired outcome. He toiled to ensure his grape's survival, but the grapes needed the right combination of sugar, alcohol, and acidity for him to produce a fine vintage. His worst fear, now that he understood the dilemma, was that the grapes from his garden that survived might not be healthy for human libation.

Since his arrival two years ago, Spencer had spent more time and money on revitalizing the vineyards than he had anticipated. His uncle had warned him that the job would not be easy, since the vineyard had not been maintained for forty-five years. His uncle had not known about the change in soil, the dying birds, or the pollution of surrounding groundwater. Despite the challenges, Spencer felt he had the ability to create the best pinot noir in Washington State.

This town of Concrete was a far cry from the tropics of Puerto Rico, but his uncle knew about good land and weather. Here the weather came from the southwest, warm air currents bringing lots of rain and creating a wet, mild winter. In the summer and fall, the hills of Lyman and Cultis kept the rain in abeyance. Long summer days of sunshine slightly stressed the grapes, allowing for the sugary sweetness needed in a good pinot noir.

The south sun on his back warmed Spencer through his skin, down to his core. He snipped another cane, touched the skin of the grape, and thought of Maria's skin—smooth, soft, succulent. Involuntarily, his lips parted with a sigh, and his face reddened.

Embarrassed, he laughed out loud. In less than a week, his thoughts toward the future had shifted. He had always seen himself as a loner, one who loved people but preferred the solitude and dependability of nature's ways. Now nature had its way with him not only in the very physical sense, but he also found his thought patterns altered. Each decision incorporated Maria's anticipated reaction. He understood the normal biological attraction, the hormones that drew two people together, but something more was at work to create that mental connection. His attraction to Maria was meant to share during a lifetime. He shook his head, mumbling the only word he could think of to express this infatuation: "Dang."

Spencer Senior once told him, "Trust the heart to discover the essence. Be smitten not by what you see but by how your attraction endures during tough times." Spencer trusted his instincts, felt comfortable with Maria as he watched her thrown into the politics of a small town, unknown dangers, and the rise of past demons. He liked that he could see her emotions, that she did not hide herself.

Lost in the maze of vines, Spencer forced himself to think about the results from the toxicology report. So far, the normal culprits of fecal matter and pesticides showed in all of the ditches and runoff in the county, but he knew that the newest samples from the Pit were of another ilk. His gut told him that the problem was widespread. Russell had alluded to shipments of hazardous waste gone missing from Puerto Rico. Not one or two, but a series since the 1950s. Mourning Dove had finally figured out the puzzle.

Spencer finished pruning the last of the vines and paused on his knees to watch the erratic path of a worm.

"Good morning. I didn't know you prayed out here."

He looked up, startled to see Maria looking over the vines at him. He smiled. "Praying isn't my thing, but if you are the answer to my prayers, I'll take it."

With a smile and a shake of her head, Maria bent down next to him. "Tell me what holds your interest on the ground, if it isn't prayer."

"Just a worm. But I'm watching the head lead the tail and the tail lead the head. Each part has feelers of sorts and can sense what is next to it. The poor worm can't figure out which way to go. Its head leads and part of its body follows, and then for some reason, the tail lifts up off the ground, and the movement forward ceases."

Maria crouched in closer, almost touching Spencer's shoulder. He reached over and squeezed her hand. The two watched the worm make no progress, tiring itself out and finally curling itself up into a ball. Spencer stood and put out his hand to help Maria up.

Neither spoke as they made their way up the hill toward Spencer's house. Maria stood off to the side waiting while Spencer discarded the old vines in the compost pile and stowed the wheelbarrow.

"This is a beautiful spot for a home. Your uncle chose wisely."

Spencer nodded, looking out over the valley and the Skagit River. "The scenery is magnificent. I never tire looking at the mountains and the river. But I'm leery of the runoff from above. I don't know the scope of pollution and toxicity of what Frank buried. My uncle sounded the alarm to us, but now the discovery of disposal sites seems too daunting. It's almost like I'm the worm. If I find one source, I can fix it. Just as I begin to work, another area of concern pops up, and I move off in that direction. I might as well not fix anything until I know all the sources."

Maria took Spencer's hand, cupped hers in his, and continued walking.

"I doubt you will curl up in a ball and do nothing. But I agree with you that until we know all of the areas that have some buried waste, we will not make a dent. I see two things that need to happen. The first is to identify all the areas where Molly and Frank made their fortunes burying waste, and the second is to detoxify these sites. I have an idea on how to achieve the first, but am clueless on the second."

"Here I am up early, worrying, and you have an answer. JoAnne told me you'd have answers to questions not asked. I'm glad she called you back to Concrete, to take time from your work. How do you propose we find all the sites?"

Maria smiled, faced Spencer and looked up at the sky.

"I'm a pilot, I take the high road, the wide-angle perspective. One of my many jobs as a pilot is mapping areas. Not mapping roads, but terrain, rivers, soil. All I need is laser equipment to see below the surface. I'll create something like a TOXMAP."

Spencer didn't want to deflate Maria's enthusiasm, but he thought of the money and resources needed to achieve a good result and felt defeated.

"First, you'll need laser equipment, a plane, and more help. Maybe we should go straight to the EPA."

"Do I hear skepticism? I have connections for the laser equipment through the Division of Specialized Information Services of the National Library of Medicine. And I know where there will be many planes and capable pilots to do the reconnaissance."

Spencer's grin stretched from ear to ear, and his eyes crinkled as he laughed. "Of course, the Concrete Fly-In will have all those veteran pilots looking to be useful again! I have to kiss you for that."

Spencer took aim directly on her lips. His intention was to be quick, amusing, but Maria's lips lingered, as did her fragrance. He backed away just enough to restrain himself. The word, *dang*, popped back into his head.

Taking a breath, he switched back to finding a solution. "Once we find the sources, I think I know of a way to decontaminate the areas."

Maria touched her lips with her fingertips, as if testing. Finally, she moved them into a grin. "Don't tell me, you were a mad scientist in another lifetime."

"Now you're the skeptic. Truth be known, I did dally in the sciences, but the real scientist is my uncle. About five years ago, he made a discovery at one of his jobs. Apparently, the United States created a nuclear weapons plant in a remote area on the island of Puerto Rico. It was one of many maintenance facilities located throughout the Atlantic and the Pacific Ocean to strategically defend the country."

Even as he spoke, he realized that what he knew as common knowledge might strike Maria as a public deception. She raised her hand. "Which part of this is my aunt's history, and which part is your uncle's past, or an answer to our current problem? Remember, I have only been in the loop for the last few days and know nothing about Puerto Rico or your uncle."

Spencer stared out over the valley and rocked back on his heels as if to change his perspective, add another angle to his view. He reached into his pocket, took out a half-chewed cigar, and absently lit the tip.

Silence hung in the air, like the cigar smoke.

"There are so many things I don't know about you," Maria finally said. "I would have thought you would despise smoking, yet you lit the cigar as if it were an old friend."

Spencer shrugged. "I like a cigar for its richness. My uncle smoked them when he felt perplexed or wanted to think. He gifts me a stash each year for my birthday. Does the smoke bother you?"

Maria shook her head. "No, I have fond memories of cigar smoke for some reason, maybe from my father before he left my mother. Did I upset you? I ask questions because it's my nature to discover truths. There were so many lies in my life that I keep looking for fullness, not snippets of facts."

"Snippets! That is exactly what I was feeling. All these years, I never questioned my uncle's actions or reasons for doing things. I accepted each fact he gave me. I just never put them together. Now I see that his engineering work may have created a serious problem. I only hope that his new discovery can fix it."

Spencer reached for Maria's hand, holding it gently in his right palm. Maria had turned her head, releasing him from her probing stare. Content to look out over the valley, Spencer let his hand convey a touch of trust, a sense that words couldn't communicate. Unconsciously, his thumb moved gently over hers. They held hands, communicating a willingness to share. Then with an extra squeeze and a slight separating of space, they moved away from the view and began walking back down the hill.

"I still want to hear about your uncle's discovery."

Spencer's smile returned. "Without going into the history of the Secret Weapon of Undersea Surveillance program or the thermonuclear facility at Ramey, I can piece together some of the snippets to make sense. My uncle worked on the SWUS program tracking Soviet submarines. He knew more about WWII and the Cold War than most people. It wasn't just the policies but the technology. I think that is what he loved, using what he knew to discover more. When that program ended, he moved on to helping with the nuclear facility that housed bombers ready to launch if deemed necessary. I don't know the whole story, but he was doing a final assembly test on a thermonuclear weapon that was 180 times the capability of the Nagasaki bomb, when there was a malfunction."

"How does this relate to fixing our toxicity problem?"

"The more I think about all the stories my uncle told me, the more I realize that this was his quest. He grew disillusioned with the program. Apparently, his job dealt with 'the fallout,' the errors, like the one in the 1960s. He had to get rid of the waste, the radioactive material from his research."

The more Spencer talked, the more distant Maria seemed. He sensed her disbelief in the holes of his explanation.

She nodded slowly. "My skin is crawling with all the connections.

Somehow the waste has made its way across the ocean to Concrete, to the soil, the waterways, and into the food chain. Gone from one place to another, out of view, forgotten."

She shook her head. "This doesn't make sense. You are saying your uncle made a discovery—that the waste was hijacked or that he created risks for other people, just to protect his immediate area. Talk about a moral hazard. His actions created a chain of misinformation and harm."

Spencer stiffened, raised his chin. "Don't say another word. I refuse to trash my uncle. He made a discovery that had him holed up for years. Now I know what he was, and is, trying to do."

Maria closed her eyes, but Spencer saw her tears. "Why are you crying?"

"There has to be more to the story, more to explain your uncle's silence for forty-five years. These tears belong to another time, to my aunt, to your uncle. I see an old man who looks like you, burdened with knowledge, spreading a risk to others, feeling like a contaminant. My tears are for Aunt Jo, who was forsaken over this. How could your uncle have been duped by Molly? What other secrets lie behind her control? No wonder he hasn't returned to Concrete."

Spencer's face contorted with all of his uncle's pain as he watched Maria's tears roll down her cheeks.

"I'm sorry," she said. "I won't think anymore. I'll leave judgment out of this conversation. Please tell me what you—I mean, *we*—can do once I gather the old veterans to find the toxic waste. How can we make this right?"

"My uncle has his own lab. When he retired from his last job, he told me that he had a mission to complete. Last time I talked with him, he said he had accomplished his mission."

"What makes you so sure that you know his mission? And if it is to decontaminate toxic waste, wouldn't the general science community be working on it? This smells of secrecy."

Spencer sighed, wishing Maria would filter her thoughts sometimes before she spoke. He believed in his uncle, but she had a point. Spencer had never asked his uncle where he got funding for all his projects, his tinkering. His focus on waste projects didn't end when he retired, but he had become more reclusive, more haunted. Spencer realized now that he felt relieved to leave the island and come to Concrete. The irony of his leaving now felt contrived. Perhaps his uncle knew all along about the soil contaminations of the vineyards and the Skagit Valley.

Spencer opened Maria's car door and eased her inside. She held her hand over her mouth, letting him know she wished she could take back her accusations. He didn't want her to think him angry. He bent down and kissed her hand.

"Go to the airport. Tell JoAnne about your plan. I'll try to contact my uncle."

As Maria drove off, Spencer looked at the grapevines, neatly lined on trellises. He saw order where there was none. He saw the fragile fruits hanging, trusting in nature. Spencer worried that the nature of man was unpredictable. His heart hurt, wanting to blame someone for the unseen messes, the buried lies of old. He wanted to believe that only Molly McCain was at fault for the woes of Concrete. He knew better. How could he free his uncle from his prison?

He put the butt of his cigar in his mouth. Tasted the bitterness of the leaves. Without the smoke, the cigar tasted stale. The allure of flavor altered so easily, dependent on smell as well as texture. He chose to think of Maria's kiss, letting her taste linger. Her fragrance, her texture more bold than simplistic. Maria might be the courageous one in the group. Russell rightly gave her the role of doubting, questioning, so that no one could continue to turn a blind eye. Avoiding conflict gave everyone the excuse to spread guilt.

Chapter 20:
Diablo: The Devil Made Me Do It

Maria rolled down her window and waved goodbye to Spencer, as if this morning and all of the days since she had returned home were normal. *Normal* would be jogging, flying daily for a few hours, having a glass of wine with one of the other pilots, eating dinner with a friend, and curling up in her cozy bed to sleep a few winks before she woke to do it again. Normal would mean that she didn't have to think or feel about anyone. She was good at that. Maria wore the uniform of a pilot as a title. Instead of designer clothes, she fit herself into a role that demanded focused awareness and responsibility, not the expression of feeling.

Despite her bewilderment, Maria couldn't help but hear her aunt's voice from when she was in high school: "Oh, go chew a stick of gum. By the time your jaws are tired, you'll know what to do." Maria fumbled in her right pocket and pulled out a stick of spearmint gum. The silver wrapper had split open, and the remnants of her last snack of almonds were stuck to the gum. So much for her healthy habits.

Knowing what to do was easy, what to feel was much more difficult. Maria knew her confusion had nothing to do with the present. She liked Spencer, wanted to pass more time with him. What bothered her was the blurring of history. So much of what she knew or thought she knew about her aunt, about her life, and the goings-on of her old home were wrong. Concrete seemed to be filled with evil, poisoned with lies. She needed to see beyond the lies, past the hills and the idyllic version she had created in her mind.

Clouds appeared from behind Cultis Mountain, but the sun held its ground. As Maria neared the Concrete Airport, a full rainbow arched from the river over the runway. She was in a foul mood when all she could see was a rainbow of lies, each color fooling her into believing that the pot of gold would be just around the corner. But she never wanted gold. JoAnne taught her that honesty was worth more than riches, and her aunt's nightly ritual was to make sure that Maria felt like she could "sleep with a free heart, open to the skies."

The promise of gold seemed like a temptation, removing the simple beauty of the rainbow. Wasn't the arc of colors good enough?

Maria's jaws ached as she chewed on being angry with a rainbow. If she squinted, the rainbow morphed and all the colors blended to black. If she wasn't careful, she would become noxious with her own anger. As she pulled up by the airport museum, she spit her gum into the wrapper. No answers, but at least she could smile.

The hangar door was wide open as Maria approached. Papers lay strewn on the floor. The air was stagnant, no breeze to cause the ruffling of files. Soft music from her aunt's favorite jazz station, KNKX, played softly from the back of her office.

"Hello, Hello! Aunt Jo, I'm here. Are you ready to go?"

Maria only waited to take a breath of air before she ran through the museum to her aunt's office. Too many thoughts crossed her mind as the adrenaline propelled her forward. In their last conversation, JoAnne was "fine" but irritated by a stupid letter with money. Maria regretted stopping off to visit Spencer. What would she do if her aunt were injured again?

Beyond the doorway, she heard murmurs. From the corner of

her eye, she noted her aunt's empty wheelchair and someone's brown muddy footprints. Someone else was here. It was too late to keep quiet, so she made the noise of an army, banging her way through the hangar.

"Aunt Jo, hold on. I'm here." She burst through the doorway.

Frank stood looming over her aunt. Maria smelled the sweet-sour aroma of a drunk, and something more metallic, like the insides of a flask. He paid Maria no attention as she came up from behind. Frank held her aunt's hand and kept whispering. Slowly Maria's racing heart resumed a normal beat. Her aunt, conscious and breathing, kept her gaze fixed on Frank's eyes. Maria motioned with her hand to see if JoAnne wanted her to interrupt, using their old code for yes or no. Maria put up one finger to indicate that one blink of the eye meant yes, two no. Her aunt blinked twice.

No meant no, and Maria kept her place off to the side, out of Frank's view, but tiptoed closer in an attempt to hear Frank's whispers.

"I never meant for you to be hurt. I never meant for you to fall, not then, not now. I tell you, it was the devil that made me do it. I never meant for you to be hurt."

Frank kept repeating himself, stroking her aunt's hand. He kneeled close to her face, pleading, "Ms. JoAnne, I'll fix it. I promise. My mother hated Diablo. The devil changed her life. I tried, but I failed. I never meant for you to be hurt."

Her aunt cooed as if she understood. Her legs were splayed to the side, her head propped up with books, but she looked intact, not in pain, only bewildered. Maria's own bewilderment settled in behind the anger. She'd seen Frank drunk before, but never apologetic. Certainly not gentle. His blubbering reminded Maria of a child, lost, fallen from grace. He didn't act like a retired seventy-year-old who once held a position in the Concrete Public Works Department.

Finally, he seemed to sober up. Maria listened as her aunt began to talk to him.

"Frank, the Diablo incident occurred before I ever arrived here in Concrete. Tragedies happen. The building of the dam helped create this whole area, and you should be proud that your father was on the crew. What does his death have to do with me?"

Frank's stare bored into her aunt's face, and his body stiffened. Abruptly he pulled his hand from hers. Maria could see that he felt caught like a rabbit in a trap meant for a bear. Caught dredging up his past, he didn't know what to do with what he knew.

JoAnne put her hand out further, reaching for his. "Frank, it doesn't matter. You came in here to tell me something. It can wait. Can you help an old lady back up? Maria is standing behind you to take me home."

Gracefully JoAnne had given Frank his exit, restored him to some semblance of normal. The next move belonged to Maria.

"I'll just run and get your wheelchair. I'll be back in a second."

By the time Maria returned, Frank had scooped her aunt up in his arms. He gave Maria the evil eye, as if she had put her on the floor. Gently he placed JoAnne in the chair.

"Tell your aunt to stay put. She can't walk."

Maria nodded her head and stared at JoAnne. Frank walked past Maria as if he were a king making sure that those in his fiefdom were cared for.

Her aunt stared back at Maria, her eyes wide in disbelief, her hand over her mouth stifling a laugh.

"Aunt Jo, do you want to tell me what that was all about?"

"Just Frank being Frank. He was drunk, upset about his mother's death. He ranted on and on about Molly being in the hospital, wasting. He kept repeating 'waste' over and over. I couldn't tell if he was using the word as an adjective, verb, or noun."

"I meant, why were you on the floor and your wheelchair in the other room? I want to know why Frank told me to tell you that you can't walk."

At this, her aunt looked away. Maria knew the signs of a yellow lie about to be told, or an explanation for a white lie. For her aunt, there was always a pause, a sigh, or a look in another direction, as if this would give more credence to a statement. Her aunt said that these were Maria's own giveaways, "tells" that kept her honest, at least to JoAnne.

"Aunt Jo, we can talk about Frank later. How did you fall?" Maria knelt so that her eyes were level with that of her aunt's.

Joanne had no choice but to answer. "It wasn't Frank's fault, if that is what you are asking. He came in and startled me while I was trying to stand."

"You haven't been able to stand since I have known you. Why would you think you could stand now after all these years? Did you forget?"

"Well, something like that. I told you that I've been working with this woman doctor named Rosie, from Puerto Rico. She specializes in natural medicines that work on the nerves in our body. I read an article of hers and . . ."

Maria shook her head as her stomach flipped over. The last thing she needed was for her aunt to be working with a shaman, trying to create a miracle.

"What have you been taking? Have you gone to a real doctor? Are you losing your mind?"

Maria regretted that last statement just as it left her mouth. Questioning her own sanity years ago at Northern State Hospital, Maria knew that this is the worst fear an individual can have, not to be believed. Tears fell from her aunt's eyes, making tracks down her cheeks.

Maria bent down and kissed her wet cheeks. "I'm calm now. I can listen without making assumptions. Please tell me what is going on with you."

JoAnne patted her hands and gave her a feeble smile, keeping her dignity, and ignoring her tears. She placed her hand on the wheels of her chair and moved through her office, out through the museum toward the open door of the hangar.

"Fresh air and sun always clear the air, just as rain or a good cry does. I'm not angry with you, Maria, just not sure you will be able to understand what I have to say."

"Aunt Jo, I'll try. I'll listen. I'll hold my tongue."

At this, her aunt smiled, watching Maria wrap her thumb and forefinger around her tongue.

"I haven't forgotten that I can't walk, just the opposite. My mind knows all that, but the nerves in my legs seem to be remembering. It's as if they took a forty-five-year siesta and woke up from a nightmare. I feel pings, pressure, almost like electrical shocks trying to start motion. It may sound like a crazy idea, but I thought I would try to see if I could stand up. Just as I was holding on to the furniture, I knocked the files off and saw Frank at the hangar entrance. Seeing me upright scared him and startled my brain. The nerves in my legs fell back to their deadened state. I'm not sure if I took a step or just collapsed."

"I don't know what to say. Now I'm beginning to understand your urgency in going to Puerto Rico. "

"Rosie will be flying in to give a presentation at Western Washington University, and a friend of hers is flying up to attend the Concrete Fly-In. I thought I'd meet with her and perhaps work with her."

There was logic to all that her aunt said. Maria looked for the holes, the part that didn't fit. It seemed too coincidental that while JoAnne had pursued an article in a medical magazine, she found the one doctor who knew both Maria's sister and her aunt's old lover. Maybe Maria shouldn't be thinking logically but let nature unfold along its own course. Although her thumb no longer held her tongue, she kept her thoughts to herself.

Her aunt sat with the sun on her face. She looked so elegant, even without her white linen dress. Maria couldn't imagine her any other way. Her beauty flowed through her eyes. Her broad shoulders softly opened so her heart filled her chest, and each breath she took released energy, as if the sun kissed the breath and released it back.

Maria let her doubts recede. "Aunt Jo, why don't I help you pick up all the files on the floor? Then we can go home and have some lunch."

"Thanks, can we make copies? Just before Frank came in, I wanted to document information about the deliveries at the McCain hangar."

Maria gathered the yellowed files off the floor. They smelled like dust mites had made a permanent home inside. She scanned the penciled ledgers, noting dates from the 1950s to the 1990s. She assumed newer information would be stored on the airport's computer.

Maria felt like a girl scout sneaking a cookie from the boxes she was supposed to sell. "Aunt Jo, do you have authorization to look through these files and make copies?"

Feigning innocence, JoAnne cocked her head and winked. "I have been volunteering here for years, and I can't help it if I suddenly decided to reorganize old files. The manager wants to digitize everything. You have to see what is there to do that."

"In that case, can you also reorganize the files that contain information on what veteran pilots have planes that can accommodate laser equipment and might want to search for buried contaminants?"

Her aunt's eyes widened as she rolled her wheelchair toward the file cabinets. With closed lips, the tiniest of smiles reached the tip of her cheeks. Her aunt's brain worked quicker than Maria's, and she pulled out a thick file from the W's. The label on the file cover simply stated "WASPs."

"I'll copy the flight journals of the McCain's hangar and the list of pilots coming to the Concrete Fly-In. I'll see if any of my old friends would be willing to help with the project. My only question to you, Maria, is what do we do if we find the buried waste?"

Maria marveled at her aunt's quick analytical skills.

"Spencer says that your old friend Spencer T has been working on a solution for years. Apparently his uncle collaborated with a biologist and found a way to cleanse and eliminate toxic waste. If we find the areas, hopefully we can return the land back to a more natural condition."

JoAnne nodded as if all this made sense, but her eyes narrowed, reading between lines of history, lines that connected to today. She stared at a photo on the wall, all the women with whom she had worked. Looking at the stack of files, she sighed.

"Maria, make sure your Spencer contacts Rosie before she leaves Puerto Rico. Maybe she can have the substance shipped up to Concrete. Who knows, Rosie might be the biologist working with Spencer T."

"You can't fool me, Aunt Jo. Maybe the companion traveling with Rosie is Spencer's uncle."

The thought sent trembles through them both. A friend could mean anything: male, female, old, young. It would make sense if Spencer T came along with Rosie, but her sister, Monica, could be Rosie's friend as well.

Her aunt gave Maria the look, the one that said, *Let's not discuss this.* "What-ifs don't count. We have to focus on the task at hand. I'll get a list of places that made shipments to the hangar, coordinate dates, and call the veterans and the WASPs. This year, at the Concrete Fly-In, will be a reunion and meeting of many minds."

"Did you mean minds or mines? This situation is explosive. Don't forget Molly and Frank—if they get wind of our plans, we could have problems. Frank may have appeared friendly today, but he did shoot our tires out, and he was the guard at the Pit the night you fell. Frank keeps talking about the devil making him do things. He may be psychotic."

Looking over the ledgers and files, her aunt gave Maria a half smile. "The devil Frank talks about isn't the devil of evil. It's the dam, Diablo. His father was working on the scaffolding and fell into the concrete. Still wet, the concrete buried him alive. His mother was never the same after the accident. They were so in love. When it happened, Molly was eight years old, and Frank was just two. Their father was one of the original homesteaders of this area—wealthy, smart, a worker. Money was never an issue, as they had property and the owners of Diablo paid out a pension. No, money was not the problem, just loss of love."

Maria's stomach growled. "Aunt Jo, I think we should work on this from our house. I'm hungry, and we don't want to get caught."

"Okay, I can give you more history of Molly and Frank later. Let's get out of here."

As they drove off, Maria spotted another rainbow, smaller with less of an arc. She wondered at their stretching the truth. She wondered if their actions fell on the lighter or darker spectrum of the rainbow.

Chapter 21:
Squaring a Circle

The bench swing rocked back and forth. Russell dozed, lulled by the warm breeze, sun, and gentle sway. His after-lunch ritual now stretched from a short break to an event. His own snores startled him awake, jerking his head backward, and he opened his eyes to a red-tailed hawk flying circles around his house.

Russell shook his head clear; the circling meant the hawk had spotted a prey in his fields. Instead of celebrating the natural cycle of the hunt, Russell worried about the hawk's dinner. Eating could be fatal for the hawk if the weakened prey had consumed contaminated water or other sick animals. Molly and Frank took stewardship to another level. Instead of valuing the homestead left to them, they had degraded the land. Russell should have seen the signs sooner. He had been too caught up in his own omissions, the loss of his Emma, and keeping an eye on JoAnne to realize the harm over the years.

Looking up into the heavens, Russell found a cloud with curls and saw in it the face of Emma. She was up there, waiting for him patiently while he stumbled through the rest of his life. He waved to make sure she was paying attention. He needed her counsel, her sense of justice.

"Emma, I should have put two and two together. Remember when Molly's mom came to us fearful of her own kids? She had the saddest look about her. Not like the woman you went to school with and everyone loved. She said her homestead, the legacy of her husband, had turned to poison. You were wise enough to believe her. I just followed your lead. Now what do I do to set it right?"

The answer Russell received was a shift in the wind. The cloud's curls gradually blew away, and his Emma's spirit flew off on an adventure, floating across the sky. He hoped she would drift over the river, up in the hills. Maybe she'd protect what he couldn't.

He stayed rooted to the bench, rocking and watching. The hawk flew off without its dinner—a gentle nudge from his Emma, or just a hawk's sense of an odor too pungent to consume.

Just as Russell was pushing himself up from the bench swing, Maya barked. Lying by his feet, she had felt the vibrations of what Russell identified as the engine from Spencer's truck.

"Good dog, you are my warning bell. My ears still work. I'm just slower."

By the time Spencer had walked over to the porch, Russell had pulled himself off the bench and stood upright.

"You didn't need to get up, Russell, seeing that I am going to sit down next to you."

Russell gave Spencer a crooked smile and slowly lowered his butt again. He held on to the swing chain, determined to keep his balance. "Oh, getting up and down helps me oil the bones. I was just thinking that Maya in dog years is my age, but her hearing and agility outshine mine. I wonder who will outlast whom."

"Why, Russell, do you have any plans that I need to know about? Seriously, are you feeling okay?"

"Feeling better than Molly McCain. I heard on the ham radio that they've called in the Health Department and all kinds of government agencies because her blood tests showed evidence of toxins. "

Spencer nodded, letting this information sink in. "We can talk about Molly in a minute. You didn't answer my question. How are you feeling?"

Russell swayed back and forth on the bench swing, contemplating an answer. "I feel old. Besides the creaking of bones, my heart feels heavy and beats slower. It takes a longer time for the blood to circulate through my body. My ears hear inside me the ticking pulse of the body and my too-full brain. I know too much and not enough. I can't claim that I'm wise. I know a multitude of facts, but wisdom only comes if you know how to put to them to good use, a use that makes a difference."

"And what is it that you know, Russell? What do you want to do?"

"I know that it's useless to call in all these environmental agencies. You and I have gone to them reporting what we have seen. They issue a warning, a penalty, and then they leave. Violations of ditching wetlands and farms and polluting creeks that flow into salmon-bearing streams continue without so much as a fine. They don't have a backbone, and they don't have resources to enforce any of their rules. For all we know, Molly and Frank pulled strings through Molly's intimidation or Frank's past position as a public works official. Unless these departments have proof of the sources of contaminants, Molly and Frank will be seen as victims. Worse yet, your uncle could go to jail."

Spencer acknowledged Russell's comment by digging his heels into the ground and slowing the bench swing to a standstill. "Maria and I came up with a plan. She is going to get laser equipment and planes to search for the toxic spots throughout the Concrete area. She thinks many of the veteran pilots from the Concrete Fly-In could help. Once we find the sites, we can detoxify them with a high-tech soap and gel that my uncle developed. He has dedicated the last twenty years to researching a way to eliminate noxious contaminants."

Russell searched Spencer's face to see if the young man believed in his own words. "Tell me how this high-tech soap works. I believe in Spencer T, but miracle soap seems far-fetched. Have you ever seen it used?"

Spencer swallowed and shook his head. "My uncle is not a criminal, and I won't let him go to jail. All this time, I thought he would be the hero, not the villain. It never occurred to me to question why he's passed so many years sequestered in Puerto Rico, experimenting and researching. He isn't to blame."

"You didn't answer my question. How does his invention work?"

"I don't have the specifics, but late at night when my uncle had a few shots of rum under his belt, he would talk out loud. These weren't conversations, just his thoughts streaming through his head and out to the walls. I remember some of his rants talked about the soaps acting like a magnetic mop. Elements in the substance adhere to the oil, and then magnetic-equipped machinery would suck up the contaminants."

"Have you ever seen the soap work?"

Spencer smiled. "I'll get there, just let me tell you about the chewing gum substance and the blue goop. These were for radioactive runoff. The blue liquid would be sprayed or painted onto the area, oozing into the microscopic pores, bonding with the loose radioactive material. From what I remember, the blue goop shrinks when it hardens and sucks up the particles, encapsulating them in its folds. I've never seen this in action, but I did use some of the soap."

"On your property?"

"Right. When I came to Concrete, my uncle sent some of the soap with me. He thought it might help make the soil respond after remaining unused for so many years."

Russell witnessed a moment of self-doubt in Spencer's reasoning, a hiccup. Sending the soap with Spencer meant that Mourning Dove must have known something was wrong with the soil.

"Spencer, don't try to do the impossible. You can't square the circle. If your uncle made an error, he can't change that. I don't think he ever intended that the contaminants from his work in Puerto Rico would be buried unsafely here in his own hometown, or anywhere. Befouling the planet happened because of his work as an engineer with the Department of Defense. Molly and Frank are guilty of intention, of misleading, of greed, and of breaking the law. They have to be punished for their efforts. Your uncle must remain in the circle to spin the cycle back. We just have to make sure we can draw the square inside the circle, so that we box Molly and Frank inside."

Spencer lifted his heels off the ground and let the swing sway. "And how to you propose we box them in?"

"I was talking to the clouds before you came by. Don't look at me like I've gone off my rocker—I often see my Emma up there. I realized that Molly's mother tried to warn us years ago that something was poisoning her land. I wonder, if we take the information from what Maria and the other pilots discover and match it up to their homestead papers, can we show a pattern? All we have to do then is prove that what they did was done without permits."

"This is just like hunting to you, isn't it"

"Hunting is easier. Animals are predictable. They use their senses to make sense of their environment. Elk and deer stay together, protecting their young until they have skills to survive on their own. Scents brought by the wind warn them of trouble. Cold pushes them to warmer areas where there is food. They follow an understandable cycle, eating, resting, and mating. It isn't the same with Molly. She has no boundaries and isn't interested in propagating her species. And let's hope she never does."

At that, Spencer slapped his knee and laughed. "At least you have a sense of humor."

"That was not humor," Russell responded. "It's biology. Gluttons eventually implode. In this case, weight isn't Molly's only problem. It's greed. We have to corral her by letting her fat lies do the work nature can't seem to do. Layered upon one another, her lies create a greasy brown mess."

"I've never seen you this ornery, Russell. In fact, I'd almost say you have disgust in your voice. No sympathy for an old woman lying in the hospital?"

Russell looked up to the skies in search of a cloud, in search of an answer. "My Emma showed me how to love and be compassionate. But Emma was smarter than Molly could ever be. She knew that when a seed went bad, that you could only nurture it for a while, and then you had to protect the rest of the crop. Molly is a bad seed."

"And what would be the rest of the crop?"

"Oh, your uncle's good name, all the inhabitants that live and eat off the land near Concrete, not to mention JoAnne. Molly's role in all of this drastically altered JoAnne's life."

With that statement, Russell's face suddenly went hot, and he gasped for breath. Maya jumped up from the ground and started licking his hand. Russell looked down at Maya and let her nudge him back to a calmer state.

Spencer waited for the flush to leave Russell's face. "You are all riled. Good thing Maya is attuned to your vital signs."

"Maya may only be a dog, but she took over my welfare when Emma died. I think Emma left some of herself in Maya."

"And from what you are saying, Emma had a sixth sense about Molly."

"More than a sixth sense. Emma listened to Molly's mother, and the two tried to compensate for Molly's greed. That's another story. Molly's mom just passed away, and Molly is now our problem."

"Back to herding Molly into the square. I'm not sure how a pattern of contamination around Molly's father's homestead is going to prove anything. We need other neighbors to come forward. We need to show that their practices haven't created this situation. We need information from the inside, proof of violations served, and information from the outside showing Molly and Frank's intent. I'm not sure that this is sexy enough for those in the government. The public needs to be riled and the health dangers broadcasted."

Russell let the swing cradle his thoughts. He swayed back and forth, thinking back to what already occurred and thinking forward to what needed to happen.

"I could use a good swig of 'apple pie' right about now. It's a shame I'm all out. I'll have to make some calls upriver to find out where I can get some."

"Just the other day you showed me a half-filled jug of it. You couldn't seriously be needing a drink of moonshine. Something else is on your mind. What do you hope to find out in the hills?"

"Oh, I still have lots of friends from my equipment-sales days. My bootleg friends not only supply me with 'apple pie' for their past indiscretions with the 'talkie tooter,' but they are also my oral history. If Molly and Frank coerced any of my moonshiner friends to keep their mouths shut about anything, I can loosen their tongues."

Spencer looked at Russell. "Hmm, Russell, please don't make me revise my opinion of you. I can peel back the years and envision you making the rounds upriver and downriver, schmoozing your way into everyone's life. You weren't a hustler, were you?"

Russell snorted. "All I can say is I wasn't, and I am not an angel. In those days, I was more of a dandy, dressed in a suit and tie. Emma always said I made an impression on all the women and men. She wasn't jealous, because my heart was only for her. Wandering eyes never hurt, but I never sold my soul."

Spencer gave Russell a slow smile. "Okay, enough with my doubts concerning my uncle and now you. I came here to grow grapes and make wine. I never intended to get involved in more than just living my life."

"This isn't just about what is right and what is wrong. If we go down that road, we'll become righteous and bullheaded. Being a goody two-shoes has no real value. As my Emma always said, 'Life isn't about being good. It's about being good for something.' I guess that something has to do with saving our land, making our home safe."

"So if we box Molly and Frank in, you think we can make our homes safe?"

"I think that Molly has over the years intimidated the folks upriver and used the system to hurt people. I think we can expose her and give some power back to your Tar Heel relatives, maybe even wake up the bureaucrats. I don't blame the government for their rules, only the fact that they can't see with fairy dust in their eyes."

Spencer stood up from the swing and offered his hand to Russell. The two of them brushed their hands along their pant legs.

"Do you want to drive or should I?" Spencer asked. "I haven't been upriver for a while. It will do me good to see the old haunts."

"I'll drive. I'd rather not have to give you directions. All my friends recognize my truck, and they'll welcome me, even if half the old-timers are long gone. My reputation precedes me."

"And what is your reputation?"

Russell's eyes sparkled. He shrugged. "Only that I'm fair. Many of the old-timers had trouble with their paperwork when they were home-steading. If they came to me, I'd represent them at the courthouse. Molly's dad was one of the people I helped when the power company tried to trick him out of his property, and he wound up owning huge chunks of land throughout the county. Too bad Molly wasn't like her father."

"What else has she done?"

"I hear through the grapevine that Molly tried to swindle many of the landowners out of their land by telling them it was polluted. Some have already sold to her at rock-bottom prices."

"Ah, now I see the square within the circle. This is where the outrage begins, a groundswell of sorts. Angry landowners who have lost property rights, a scandal of misrepresentation, loss of money, and then the proof of illegal toxic burial, and the laws broken will be just icing on the cake."

Russell gave Spencer his bullish look. "Add to that a few calls on my ham radio to my old friends from the Planning Department to see if we can get information on permits, licenses to operate business—any kind—and maybe even property tax exemptions. Who knows how far this will go? We might as well keep the circle outside of the box spinning."

Russell led the way to his truck. "Come on, Maya, we're heading upriver to visit some old friends."

Chapter 22:
Hinges and Handles

Frank walked slowly through the hospital halls, tucking in his shirt, using his spit to smooth his hair down. His rubber soles squeaked along the tiles, his face reddening as he remembered his mother's gentle reminder to lift his feet up as he walked. A worse memory came to him, a taunt from his sister. Frank could still hear Molly yell, "Quit dragging your feet. Mom thinks you're Frankenstein!"

Blocking out the old voices of childhood, Frank concentrated on finding Molly's hospital room. Three calls from the hospital—one from the nurse, one from the doctor, and one from Molly—had brought him here. The messages from the medical staff held concern for his health. They wanted to test him for toxins. Molly's message berated him for leaving holes at the Northern State Hospital Cemetery.

The only hole Frank cared about was the hole in his heart. With his mother gone, Molly's rants of rage no longer caused him alarm. Her caustic nature had contaminated his life for too long. Now he only wanted to fill the holes, finish what his mother had started.

Smells of ammonia, medicine, and illness permeated the hallways. Frank sniffed his way along until he smelled the odor of poison. Opening the doorway slightly, he peered in to see his sister, asleep with tubes inserted in her arms. Knowing Molly's devious nature, he waited, counting the seconds between her breaths, watching her chest rise and fall and her eyes moving under the lids. Assured that she was in a sedated sleep, he ventured inside and sat down by her bedside.

Frank kept his eyes fixed on Molly's face, unwilling to chance her awakening. Carefully he withdrew from his pants pocket a small black box with hinges on one side and a metal handle on the other. His mother had saved the box for him, had his initials *FM* engraved on the back. That last week of her life she unburdened herself, handing him knowledge. In a raspy voice, barely audible, she had whispered. "I knew, Frank, about the torture. I knew and couldn't save you from Molly. I found snakeskins and saved them. Proof, so I wouldn't forget. Knowledge saves you from distorted lies. It stops the insanity."

That was all that Frank wanted, Molly's insanity stopped. Carefully he opened the hinge, removed the thin casing of a discarded snakeskin, and placed it under the bedcovers near her feet. Frank wasn't cruel. He had no need or desire to hurt his sister. Hurting Molly was like giving oxygen to a fire. Molly loved the challenge, retaliating behind the scenes, "innocently" setting up scenarios to harm. She hurt others because she could. The snakeskin wasn't fuel to inflame Molly, only Frank's attempt to expose his sister to her own self. He thought that looking at truth could crack her façade, that this might cause her pause.

Frank backed his way out the door, keeping his eyes on Molly's face. He could hear her breathing, saw her nostrils flaring as she tried to suck in a breath and her lips parting as she exhaled. He imagined a dragon expelling flames into the air. Remembering the explosion at the manufacturing site, he felt the heat of all the buried canisters fanning out to consume him. The dragon spewed guilt, pulling him back into its lair.

Bells bleeped, and red lights flashed on the machine by Molly's bed. Feeling trapped, Frank stumbled into the hallway and pretended he had just arrived. It didn't matter. He was invisible to the nurses as they rushed into Molly's room.

"Just when we thought this lady had stabilized. Quick, find the on-call doctor. Her heart rate is too fast, and her blood pressure is shooting up."

Frank listened by the doorway and peered in through the door's window. His sister looked angelic, oblivious to the attention except for her lips. They quivered slightly and parted into a sneer. His skin felt cold, clammy, and he knew then that Molly still controlled the situation. The sneer belonged to her trickery. Even if she still slept, the sneer meant conniving, dreams of ruin. Molly never was an angel, and never would be.

Frank felt the pull, the long lasso of guilt encircling his neck. He coughed and choked his way to the nursing station. The nurses noticed him now, offering him a glass of water, a seat. He sat and watched as a tray of medicine and a doctor rushed into Molly's room.

"Excuse me, sir, what is your name?"

"Don't worry about me. I'll be okay. Just here to visit a relative. Looks like there is a problem with the patient in room 246."

"Yes, the doctor just went in. The older woman arrived yesterday, and chaos came with her." Suddenly realizing what she'd said, the nurse put her hand over her mouth and buried her head in paperwork.

Frank took the opportunity to head back to Molly's hallway. Leaning on a medicine cart, he parked himself outside Molly's opened door. Once again, he became invisible, blending into the walls.

Dr. Knobs shook his head, staring at the machines. He addressed two of the attending nurses. "Something must have irritated Ms. McCain.

Her heart rate soared as if she were angry, annoyed. The medicine should help lower her blood pressure. Did you notice anything different? A rise in temperature, sweating, or—"

Before the nurses could answer, Molly yelled from her bed, "My temperature is just fine! I don't want any of your medicine. Just let me leave this hospital."

Dr. Knobs spun himself away from the nurses and faced Molly. Before he answered, he studied her complexion, her demeanor. He realized quickly that she was wide awake and had been for a period of time.

"You seem alert, Ms. McCain. We all thought you were asleep, but there is no fogginess in your eyes or voice. Can you tell us why your heart rate suddenly rose?"

"Can you tell me where my regular doctor is? I want to see my brother, Frank. I have business matters to attend."

Dr. Knobs noticed the machine blips change as she mentioned her brother's name and business. He felt the same disconnect that occurred on his last visit to her room. Molly's health created dis-ease in all around her, as if she was the malady.

"Dr. Green is on vacation. I have the honor of attending to your health while he is gone. I need you to trust me and tell me what caused you to get upset."

Molly snorted, turned her head, and then spat on the floor. The nurses quickly cleaned up the mess and wiped her face. Before Dr. Knobs could respond, his cell phone rang. He turned away from Molly and walked toward the door.

"*Hola*, Rosie, or should I call you doctor? Congratulations are in order on your findings. Yes, I'm at the hospital, but I'll talk with you. The time difference in Puerto Rico makes it hard to communicate. Can you speak up?"

Through the airwaves came musical laughter. The tension melted away as Dr. Knobs felt a smile form across his face. Rosie had been one of his fellow students years back when he was at Western Washington University studying biology on a fellowship in Central America. Rosie was the one person everyone gravitated toward. Even now, across thousands of miles, and years, she could create warmth and understanding.

"Dr. Knobs, you can still call me Rosie if I can call you Roger. I'm calling to let you know that I'm coming to Concrete to visit JoAnne Kraft, and I thought I could see you and talk about some of my latest work on nerve regeneration and toxins. I will also be attending a meeting at the university to explain my dissertation."

"Of course, we can talk. JoAnne Kraft. Is she the former WASP who is paralyzed? Everyone in Concrete admires her. "

From behind the doctor, the machines attached to Molly went off. Dr. Knobs turned to see Molly's face turn red as her heart rate increased.

"I have to hang up, Rosie. My patient is having a heart attack."

Rosie's voice hardened. "Roger, be careful. Your patient's behavior can be deceiving. You make fun of my intuition, but a caustic nature breeds illness. I'll call you when I arrive."

One of the lessons Dr. Knobs had learned earlier in his life was to listen to Rosie. She had a rule about intuition. Despite what science and data showed, doctors shouldn't base their responses on just facts. Handling situations with difficult patients involved the psyche as well as the physical state. They called Rosie the shaman of biology, and today she sent her healing advice long-distance.

By the time the doctor hung up and turned to administer care, Molly's red face had returned to normal, and the machines marked a steady heartbeat. Dr. Knobs motioned for the nurses to leave. He walked around both sides of Molly's bed, looking at the electronic hookups, pretending to fiddle with the connections.

"Ms. McCain, this is the second time within fifteen minutes that these machines have indicated a problem with your heart. What is going on in your head to cause such a response?"

Molly pushed the button on the side of her bed to raise her head up slightly. Her eyes locked onto the doctor's face, and she frowned at his question. "Fear. I'm old and frail, and I fear this place. I need attention so I can get out and attend to my business. I'm really okay, nothing that the quiet of my home won't cure. When can I leave? If my doctor is on vacation, I can wait for treatment. It sounds like you have a friend coming to visit. When would that be?"

Again Dr. Knobs noted the saccharine shift in Molly's tone. First the spitting with hostility, and now the attempt to sweet-talk the doctor. He sensed that this was the clue, the hinge. If he could find out Molly's motivation, then he could handle her with the care she needed.

"I don't think you understand your situation, or maybe you do. The property surrounding your house showed evidence of contaminants. The Health Department took samples of the soil, revealing unexplained high levels of radiation. You and your neighbors are at risk. Your heart attack brought you to the hospital, but the constituents in your blood tell another story. You have been poisoned by waste products from the Cold War era. Uncommon, to say the least. We don't know what they are or why they are inside you."

Molly smiled.

Dr. Knobs saw the smile, the malice instead of worry. Somewhere in that smile held a truth.

"Why don't you find my brother, Frank? He is the devious one. Sneaking around, burying things. He took care of our farm. I just managed the finances. I worry about his mental state."

And here it was, the deflection, the bouncing of words to blame. Dr. Knobs felt the knots of lies tied up in a ball, landing inside his stomach. This patient, Molly McCain, had years of practice pulling strings and creating havoc with the natural balance. He listened between the words, watched for what his colleague Rosie called intuition. He saw that Molly's truths were lies, and her lies were truths. She believed in her fabrications, having lied so long to the world that it made sense. To understand Molly, the doctor needed to study what she feared.

At a knock on the door behind him, Dr. Knobs turned slightly but kept his eyes on Molly. A tall man with slicked-down hair made his way into the room, dragging his feet along the floor. The man clenched his hands and stood awkwardly in the center of the room.

"Molly, I came as quick as I could. I've been sick."

Again Dr. Knobs witnessed Molly's sneer. He wondered how a smile could be so unwelcoming.

"Dr. Knobs, this is my brother, Frank."

Frank held out his hand and squeezed the doctor's hand. Intuition told Dr. Knobs that this squeeze was a sign for help. He shook Frank's hand and told him to take a chair. Molly fidgeted with buttons on her bed. Slowly she let the back down and closed her eyes. Pretense.

The doctor kept up the façade and wondered how he could break the spell. "Frank, we'd like to test your blood. I'll have a nurse bring you down to the lab. Then we can talk."

Chapter 23:
Nerve to Feel

JoAnne perched her reading glasses on the top of her head, dismissing the stack of manifests strewn across the kitchen table. Tired, she wheeled her chair away from the history of deliveries to the Concrete Airport. For the last two hours, she and Maria had been studying records, JoAnne concentrating on cargo for the Concrete Airport, and Maria researching and calling former WASPs and veteran pilots.

"Maria, I'm numb from poring over these reports, and I've got a headache from straining to read the fading ink. If only I had paid more attention years ago. I found at least a hundred deliveries from across the nation and Puerto Rico to the McCain hangar. Most of the shipping companies have acronyms for names, RAS and TWD. They could mean anything. Some of the cargo originates from hospitals, but most are from plants that make weapons. Finally, I can see a pattern of activity. Any luck with your calls?"

"Tracking down former veteran pilots isn't easy. They tend to fall between the cracks, especially the WASPs who married and changed their names. Thank goodness for computers. I found a website that gave me some history. Many of your colleagues live back East, no longer fly, or are too ill to answer the calls. I've tracked down sons and daughters who have followed in their parents' footsteps to become pilots. Once I mentioned your name, many agreed to help. You have a reputation! I bet you miss the flying."

JoAnne stared out at the garden, pretending not to hear Maria's last sentiment. Acceptance had been her motto for so long that the idea of piloting her own airplane made her weary. She rubbed her eyes, surprised to find tears.

"Take the list, Maria, and make the arrangements at the airport for their arrival. Most of the hangars have already committed their spaces for the fly-in, but there should be room. Just in case, notify the Skagit and Anacortes airports that we may need accommodations."

Maria nodded her agreement, but her aunt had already turned her head. "Aunt Jo, take a break. I'll go into the den and make arrangements. I know you don't like me pampering you, as if you need care, but at least take a swim."

JoAnne fell back on an old joke from when Maria used words incorrectly. "Are you *incinerating* that I'm in a foul mood?"

Maria smiled. "I'm insinuating that you need a break. You may not want to talk, but I see through you."

JoAnne shooed Maria away. "Go on and finish making the arrangements. I might get in a real foul mood and tell you how much I missed having you around."

Not waiting for an answer, JoAnne slid the glass door open and headed into the garden, taking the worn path toward the pool. The world slipped away as JoAnne entered into the privacy of her mind. No one could see her hoist herself down the rubber ramp, sliding into the emerald waters of the swimming pool. Her tears melded and swirled as she began her laps.

Ten laps without a stop. She swam until her heart pounded against her chest. JoAnne let herself sink to below the water's edge, submerging her head and letting the weight of her legs pull her down. Breathing out her nose, she exhaled so that her diaphragm emptied. Anchored on the bottom, she felt the pressure of constricting air, the feeling a pilot gets when oxygen runs low. This was her mental test, her will and strength against the elements. Ignoring the demanding cry of her lungs, JoAnne pushed off from the pool bottom with the force of two hands and her muscled arms. Within seconds she popped up, ears ringing, appreciative of each life-giving breath.

The word *appreciative* caught in her throat. For so many years she had been substituting ingenuity and physical strength to compensate for her losses, and had made a point of recognizing all the good in her life. Still the tears came. Who was she fooling? The intense pain in her legs was worse than paralysis. Was the pain imagined, or a lie masking itself as a symptom, a phantom excuse? Was her heart empty or full? Did she trust her senses?

Swimming to the pool's edge, she reached for a flotation pillow. Slipping the device between her thighs, she willed her mind to trigger her nerves to squeeze. Buoyancy became another trick, a metaphor in her life. But today she almost felt the connection jump-start. The flotation pillow held its place, and JoAnne flew across the length of the pool, just skimming the water surface.

Connections. Ever since she read the article, "*Curare*: Phantoms in the Brain," by Rosie Nazario, JoAnne's life had become intricately linked to Puerto Rico. The world of Concrete, Washington, had nothing in common with the island, and yet it seemed that they shared a history as well as a link to specific people. JoAnne had read Rosie's article, fascinated with the concept of remapping the cortical nerves. Using a drug derived from the *curare linea* vine, Rosie had experimented with numb areas in the body. She found that the brain could easily be confused and that phantom pains resulted.

JoAnne paused for a breath. Her thoughts seemed random, yet the trickery, the essence of the brain's potential, distracted her from probing deeper. Since her accident, since Spencer T's leaving, had she merely found ways to be complacent, engage physically without healing inside?

Her reading of Rosie's article triggered a deeper pain. It promised, "The possibility of movement is not only physical . . . We must understand that the body and mind connection, the brain's plasticity to change patterns and to regenerate nerves, works the same way in social and psychological relationships."

Another three laps with her legs extended, her arms pulling her body along. Speed and power—without her legs connecting to her body—felt empty. JoAnne had created a resiliency that camouflaged anything below the surface. Tiring, she thought of the other links to Puerto Rico that numbed her heart. She was skimming the surface with connections, avoiding thinking about Spencer as a person, alive, real, and one whom she had once loved. The path of doubting Spencer's character—his absence, his actions with the toxic waste—protected her. Worse yet, she avoided pursuing the link to Maria's sister, Monica, for fear of hurting and losing the person closest to her. Had she deprived Maria of the chance to heal as well?

After another ten laps, JoAnne's arms ached and her chest pounded. Her breath constricted so tightly that she swallowed water and struggled, reaching for the pool's edge. The tears came from a crack in her heart. She felt the rip, the breaking away of a shield, every nerve exposed. Then the laughter, the joy of hurting, crying, feeling, and understanding flooded her heart.

Rosie's article stated, "Nothing changes unless you remap your thoughts, rewire assumptions. You must have the nerve to feel." JoAnne realized that nerves of steel, her own tenacity, had removed her suppleness, the ability to bend and inch in closer. Her powerful arms had pushed away all that she really valued.

She pulled herself up to the ramp. Placing a harness around her hips, she pressed the button to the automatic pulley. Slowly she rose and turned herself into position over her wheelchair. Grabbing a terrycloth towel, JoAnne settled in and made her way back through the garden.

Listening, JoAnne noted the absence of the hummingbirds' fluttering wings, the abandoned feeders. She kept still, relishing her permanence, admiring the hummers' migratory journey, their shift from mating to nesting. Her home acted as a flyway for these birds, a temporary home. JoAnne saw the wisdom in nature, the adaptations, the understanding of survival. Weak legs meant that the hummingbird's strong wings, speed, and hovering kept them fit, ready to venture forth. Hummingbirds felt no regret.

Regret meant that a pathway could be different. The hummingbird took flight because weather, food, and the winds called. JoAnne realized that her anger and sense of loss came from an old pathway. In "rising above" blaming anyone for her condition, she had failed to recognize inconsistencies in Molly's character. By focusing on spinning everything into the positive, refusing to acknowledge Molly's manipulations, JoAnne had fooled herself. She had also failed to consider the open hearts of others. She had misjudged her Spencer, afraid of what she would discover. The numbness in her legs paled to the numbness she had carried in her heart all these years.

JoAnne felt the power of fear ruling her entire body, holding a lie so powerful that nothing moved. Her stubbornness had blocked the road to healing. Now that her legs hurt, could she use this pain as a key to unlock her fear?

Newly invigorated, she approached the house in a lighter mood, just as Maria had insinuated she would. As she entered the kitchen, she heard her niece on the phone. "Rosie, I will let my aunt know you called. And yes, I look forward to meeting you, too."

Just as Maria hung up the phone, she turned to see JoAnne bundled in a towel, smiling.

"I was just talking with your new medical advisor, Rosie."

JoAnne noted the acceptance in Maria's voice. "I wish we could have talked. Rosie's voice soothes. She seems to sense a person's inner wishes, the quiet thoughts they haven't yet discovered. What did she say?"

Maria cocked her head and shrugged. "I'm not really sure. Whatever she said made me feel as if my world wasn't spinning out of control. She gave the time of her arrival. Her conference at the university is the day of the fly-in, so she won't be there for that part. Not that it matters."

JoAnne sighed, realizing all that was to happen in the next week. "Did you ask Rosie about her guest?"

Maria shook her head. "For some reason, I was afraid to. She said, 'You have the same voice as your sister, Monica. I feel like I already know you.' I didn't feel the need to ask after that. Don't get me wrong—I do want to know if Monica is coming. And I'm sure you want to know if the guest will be your Spencer. Maybe I'm not ready to be rejected by Monica."

JoAnne looked at the manifests piled on the kitchen table. She thought of the next steps, the reworking of the past. "After reading Rosie's articles and speaking with her, I feel more confident about my legs. I'm not so much worried about their pain, as what to do with to-day. What I mean is that I had no idea of how much I had lied to myself, and even to you, in order to keep going. Lies are funny that way. They creep up on you even as you value the truth."

"Are you talking about your Spencer, or the money that was sent to you by the anonymous donor, or the new white silky dress I found hanging in the den closet?"

JoAnne tilted her wheelchair back, lifting the front wheels up, dancing in place. "Let's go to the den."

"I'm right behind you. Promise me you won't answer my questions with more questions."

"I'll tell you what I know. Better yet, I'll tell you what I feel."

JoAnne entered the den, heading to the closet. Maria followed, gently pushing the wheelchair along.

"This dress was to be my wedding dress. Spencer T bought it for me the week before I fell, the week before he disappeared. I found the box much later, after my return from the hospital. I thought it a cruel joke at first. Emma insisted I open the box. Such a long time ago, and I never even put it on. Funny, Spencer knew I liked the swish of a dress. My uniform was anything but sexy. I blush now, thinking of our innocent intimacy. The linen dress I wear now is a poor substitute."

Maria held the dress in her arms and did a twirl. The skirt puckered and flew wide with each turn. JoAnne laughed as Maria laid it on top of her lap.

"I'm surprised that you saw it as painful and cruel instead of a sign of commitment."

"Pain is relative. It was easier for me to punish myself, than to hope. I realize now that I tried thinking the best of people but failed to see Molly's warped charades of civility, and instead instilled that blindness unjustly into the person I loved. Fear that I would be wrong about Spencer T kept me from acting. Emma urged me to search him out, write more letters to the government, but I had no energy. Now I think I created a lie within a lie. Nothing I believed all those years existed."

"Not true. I exist, and all that you taught me exists. You gave me the love of flying and paid my way through aviation school."

JoAnne squeezed Maria's hand. "I taught you to be strong and resilient, to question. Did I teach you to laugh, love, feel?"

"Of course, you did. Not to say that I don't have my own hang-ups with abandonment and loss. You are still teaching me. I'm so glad you called me back to help. For so long, I wanted to know more about your life before the accident. I don't dwell on my life before I arrived here, my mom's death, the sadness of another lifetime. I'm just as guilty as you. Just like you chose not to hunt for Spencer T, I chose not to look for Monica. Instead of blaming them, we took the path of least resistance."

JoAnne handed the white dress back to Maria. "Here, hang it up for now. Who knows, you might wear it someday!"

Maria blushed as she smoothed the dress and returned it to the closet.

"One more question," Maria said, "before we start back on the manifests and calls to the pilots. Tell me your theory on the trust money that you were given. You seemed upset when you opened the letters."

"Upset, yes, and I felt confused and spied upon. See, I'm talking about my feelings! Rosie, in her therapy for nerve regeneration, says to look at the pathways, restructure them. After swimming this afternoon, I realized that I had cut off the pathway to my heart, tried to explain everything logically, which didn't let me feel. If I step back just a little bit, I realize that someone has been watching out for me since the fall. Whatever is important to me has been important to this person. My theory now is that I see the trust fund as the act of a guardian angel versus a manipulator. Emma and Russell were always there for me, and they had no reason to hide behind a trust. If it had been my Spencer, I would wonder why the secrecy. I think whoever created the trust wanted to correct a lie. I don't know."

Maria was listening intently. "Aunt Jo, it might be Frank. He seemed so upset. I'm thinking of Frank's apology, pitiful as it was, and his care in holding you after he found you on the floor at the hangar."

"I doubt if he would be able to pull that off. Not with Molly bossing him all these years. He is a follower, not a leader."

"Speaking about leading, I am worried about those past deliveries of toxic material to the McCain hangar. What is to stop other deliveries from arriving? We need to discover not only where they went but also how the McCains got involved. How did Molly do this?"

JoAnne nodded in agreement. "I remember Molly working for the telephone company. She was an operator listening in on calls, spying. We know how much trouble she caused you at Northern State Hospital, delaying you from communicating with me. I wonder if when she worked at the composite factory, she found a source for waste disposal. Knowing her, she bribed or threatened someone to cross wires in a computer, to change their address or cell phone. We are going to have to think like Molly to stop the deliveries."

JoAnne shivered, realizing she still had on a wet bathing suit.

"Maria, there is an irony in all of this. Molly is not a decent person. I'm not sure of her intent, but her whole life seems to be bent on destroying connections. And now she is sitting alone in the hospital, sick and at the mercy of others. I never thought of her as anything but a lost soul, but now I see her as evil. Her indecent behavior exposed the entire community to toxic contaminants. It puts a new definition to 'indecent exposure.'"

Neither one of them laughed.

Chapter 24:
Neighbors

Russell drove slowly along Highway 20 and then meandered up into the hills overlooking the Skagit and Baker Rivers. Spencer stared out his open window as if this were his first time seeing the sights. The highway signs notifying local tourists of camping parks, milkshakes, and fishing gear disappeared, and the roads narrowed to one lane. They drove through Concrete proper on Main Street, where all the stores waited for the rush of one or two patrons. Outside the central business district, with its lone restaurant, city hall, and the library, Russell's truck passed through the quiet town's small residential center, missed the nonexistent suburb, crossed the old Concrete Bridge, and circled up toward Baker Dam.

"Hmm," Russell said. "Did you ever stop to think about the names of the mountain ranges surrounding our small slice of heaven? Mt. Despair, Mt. Fury, Diablo Peak, Phantom Pass, and Mt. Terror. We have a good life here now, compared to the early 1900s. But all of Molly's shenanigans started back then, even before she was born."

Spencer turned his face from the scenery. "I don't buy that. Don't tell me that you believe Molly is just a victim of circumstance, that history set her up."

"Be patient with me while I try to unwind the story behind it all."

Russell drove further up the road through a more forested area, pointing out small cabins tucked behind trees, camouflaged from view so they blended into the landscape.

"Some of these cabins have been here since the early 1900s when everyone staked a claim through the Homestead Act. Now we have state parks for the public to enjoy, but back then the homesteaders and the Forest Service were at odds. Although the Forest Service stated that they wanted the land to be used for the benefit of the largest number of people, they often acted on the side of large-scale development. People like Molly's father got caught in the conflict."

"So Molly's motive is revenge because she felt cheated from the wrong done to her father?"

"Oh no, just the contrary, Molly's father was able to keep his land intact. He understood business and was able to create easements and negotiate with both the Forest Service and the railroad companies. He came from an educated family but chose to use his body and mind to work on the dams. Molly was just the opposite of both her father and mother."

"Russell, you aren't telling me anything new. Nothing has changed over time. The railroad always wanted the rights to bring out timber and ore from mining. Even today, the rules are so strict that although the railroads have been here for over a century, they can't bring through the cargo they want. The coal controversy is the latest—property rights versus the environment, private versus public, old battles continuing. People who understood the system could negotiate through some of the red tape."

Russell nodded. "I'm just saying that Mr. McCain earned his way legally for all that he acquired."

They fell silent as they watched the circling of three vultures, wings spread wide. The dark feathers and naked red heads flashed as they soared over an open space between trees.

Russell drove on a short distance and parked his truck. "Time to walk in a bit and talk with my friend Ralph. His home is along this road, tucked back a ways. He has a couple acres of cleared land adjacent to the forest. Ralph gave up logging when Scott Paper Company sold and left the area. Now he farms as well as brews an occasional batch of moonshine. He might be able to shed some light on those vultures."

Russell led the way as Spencer studied the trees, plants, and smells of the area.

"Phew," he said. "Something big is rotting out in the field." Vultures searched with their keen sense of smell. They didn't usually kill their prey, but fed on decaying carcasses. "Either your friend Ralph killed an animal, or it died on its own."

Russell barely acknowledged Spencer's observation. He followed a narrow, leaf-covered trail to the clearing, then he waved his hands up in the air and made the sound of a raven: "Cakaw, cakaw."

Within seconds, a tall man wearing stained canvas coveralls and carrying a shovel stepped out onto their path. "Russell, I miss that greeting. It's been a while. What brings you out here for a visit?"

"Ralph, this is my good friend Spencer. We're here because we suspect that the McCains are up to no good."

Spencer reached out to shake Ralph's hand, but Ralph studied his face before he offered his own hand.

"Are you related to the older Spencer who owned land around here? You have that same look of determination."

Russell grabbed Ralph's hand and gave him a bear hug. "Yep, the two are related. This version is more philosophical, but just as determined. He came back to have a go at revitalizing the vineyard."

"Ah, you are my competition. I'll trade you a bottle of wine for my moonshine—that is, if you are man enough."

Spencer grinned, not sure of Ralph's intentions. Ralph's belly laugh and pat on the back let him know that the comments were not a challenge.

"I take it you knew my great-uncle from work."

"I'm not that old. It was my father who worked with him. Your great-uncle encouraged my father to become an engineer. Best advice ever. My father passed away a few years ago still wondering where his good friend went. Last he knew was that the government had requested your uncle for a special mission."

Russell cleared his throat. "Looks like you buried something with a stench. What did the vultures discover?"

Ralph motioned for them to follow up the path, toward where his portion of land met the driveway. "I found three baby ewes in a trash bag by the easement on my land. The neighbor across the way found some dead calves in a ditch near his easement the week before. Neither of us believes it was an accidental drop."

Russell shook his head in disgust.

Spencer walked over to the garbage bag and peered inside. "Before you bury the animals I'd have the Health Department take a look. I'd even have them come out and check your soil and other animals for contamination. Even though these babies were dumped, whatever killed them could still cause you harm."

Ralph took his shovel and tossed some dirt over the bag. He threw down his shovel and kicked a stump. "That's what we thought. A few of us with farms and land out here suspected the McCains of foul play. They've been buying up land surrounding their homestead for years. A lot of the neighbors who farm couldn't grow enough crops to make a living, and others have lost their jobs due to the damn economy. As soon as they missed a payment on their property taxes, Molly McCain appeared with offers to buy them out. Talk about vultures. Molly smells the prey, and Frank makes the kill."

Russell walked past the stench and closer to Ralph's home. He stared at the small cabin with its manicured gravel parking area, the stack of cut wood lining the edges of the lean-to for his tractor, and the cultivated land behind the cabin.

"Looks like you and your wife aren't going anywhere. Why stay?"

Ralph shrugged his shoulders.

"What my wife and I want is to stay here on the family land, keep a low profile, go fishing, hunt, garden, can our food, enjoy our life. We have our slice of heaven, with no need for us to go anywhere. Molly sent Frank out here to intimidate those of us who won't bend to her greed. Knowing something was wrong, we tried going to the officials, but we had no proof."

Spencer followed Russell up to the house and into the spacious gardens. He noted the care of each of the raised beds, meticulously labeled, weeded, and organized. Beds of cabbage with curled leaves cupping the heads, tomatoes pinned along green poles, bush beans covered with green pods, and the lettuces of red leaf, romaine, and iceberg in alternating rows, as if a tribute to the American flag.

"The only crop missing is corn," Russell said. "You have to have corn to make your moonshine."

"I went to growing all our vegetables in raised beds over ten years ago when my wife starting complaining of stomach pains. She said the soil made the food taste weird. I brought in loads of river bottom soil to fill the beds. You can't grow enough corn in raised beds, and I didn't want to chance us getting sick. I barter for corn with a farmer across the valley."

It was the simple wisdom and adaptability of those who knew nature. Living on the land meant just that. You sensed the texture, smell, and taste of the soil. You noticed the smallest of differences and adjusted.

No amount of schooling or tests replaced centuries of observation. Spencer watched another vulture pass overhead and wondered how far the fallout of Molly's greed had spread.

"I battled the same problem with the soil down at the vineyard," Spencer said. "I had it tested and worked with the Agricultural Extension Agency to get it into balance. I finally resorted to using a special cleanser my great-uncle sent with me from Puerto Rico. From your description, I think we are talking something more drastic. Using raised beds probably saved you and your wife's lives. Did you hear that Molly just fell ill? The Health Department's investigation showed a higher-than-healthy level of radiation in her bloodstream. Her exposure means that the whole valley is at risk. Have you or your neighbors seen Frank digging ditches or bringing in canisters?"

"I can't say for sure. Not everyone shares stories about the McCains. Years ago, a house was built way up by Baker Lake. Some bigwig in the government built a vacation home, and the security fences and guards had everyone on edge. Even Molly and Frank kept their distance. The man retired recently, the former secretary of defense. Even so, folks around here fear Molly more than they do the military surveillance. She knows their personal weaknesses, preys on their secrets. I'd say she is a wolf in sheep's clothing. She pretends to help you, buy your land, but really she pounces on opportunities. From what you're saying, Molly and Frank created a problem we have to solve. That is the worst kind of neighbor to have—righteous protectors, and destroyers of what they protect."

Russell fidgeted with his collar, unbuttoning the first three buttons on his shirt. Sweat dripped down from his forehead to his neck. "Ralph, can I bother you for a glass of water and maybe a seat on the porch? The heat just got to me."

The three moved to the porch, and Spencer handed Russell his handkerchief. Ralph returned with three glasses of lemonade.

"Sharon made a fresh pitcher of lemonade before she went into town. Not too sweet, just the right amount of pucker."

Russell drank till his lemonade disappeared. He motioned for Ralph and Spencer to move in closer. "Ralph, I know that most of your neighbors have enough gumption to protect their homes. They put up a fight when the timber industry closed in the early 1990s because of overlogging and the fear of wiping out the spotted owl. Many of their jobs were lost, and then Skagit Manufacturing's closing put more people on the hunt for work. Molly saw an opportunity there, and all of us know a piece of what went wrong. Let's gather information from each of the property owners surrounding the original McCain homestead."

Ralph disappeared into his cabin and returned with a map of his property and the abutting land. He circled his home and those of his neighbors. He marked the lands sold to the McCains and the original McCain homestead. He put the sign of a skull next to where the land failed to produce or neighbors found dead carcasses. The last symbol was that of a chainsaw, marking virgin forests and pristine areas for wildlife.

"What I can't understand is why," he said. "Money can't be the only motivator in this. Molly's family inherited so much money after her father died in that horrible accident at Diablo Dam. Molly's mother made it a point to keep the original homestead together, and she helped everyone around who needed anything. Molly's mother wouldn't knowingly let anything happen to the land or the people upriver."

Spencer studied the map. He looked at connecting roads and trails, searching for access to burial spots. "Molly isn't her mother. I don't care why she did what she did, only that we find the burial sites and contain the contamination. We need to alert your neighbors and then visit the places you marked to find anything Frank buried there. Everyone needs to go to the Health Department and get tested. No one wants to be in the position Molly is in, hospitalized and dying of radiation poisoning and who knows what else. Do you know of anyone who can rally the forces?"

Ralph pointed to a spot on the map. "Rocky lives on this hillside. He used to be friends with Frank in the days when they worked in the mill, then in the Public Works Department, and then in the assessor's office. Rocky told stories of how Frank knew so much about real estate and costs that Rocky felt he was trading information for personal gain. Rocky retired, and now he makes wood carvings with his chainsaw. Most of his bears and old scenes of loggers decorate the Sedro-Woolley's downtown area. Rocky still has his wits about him, and he can convince the neighbors to rally."

Russell rose slowly and shook Ralph's hand. Ralph embraced him and then turned to Spencer. "Thanks for coming up with Russell. Seeing your face is like seeing your great-uncle. Spencer T worked hard for the community. He understood the value of land. Maybe his Tar Heel upbringing made a difference. He inspired people to work hard, use their brains. My dad missed him, never really replaced him as a friend . . . Wait, I just remembered something. I found a packet in my dad's belongings when he died. It has Spencer T's name on it. Hold on before you leave, and I'll go get it."

Spencer watched as Russell headed for the truck, moving carefully, as if each step was an effort. Instead of getting into the driver's seat, Russell entered on the passenger side.

"Here's the envelope." Ralph caught up and handed it to Spencer. "If I remember correctly there are pictures of your uncle with JoAnne and my father. Also a sealed letter."

"Thanks, I'll get hold of you tomorrow."

After a quick handshake, Spencer headed for the truck. Russell sat quietly with his hands over his chest, his eyes distant.

"Russell, do you need anything? Another drink?"

"No, I'm just worn out. Drive me home. I've got phone calls and an appointment with the ham radio to talk with Mourning Dove."

"Do me a favor. Open this packet up, and read the letter inside. Ralph's dad saved it."

Russell sat up, fumbled with the packet. A picture of JoAnne dancing with Spencer T fell out, along with three yellowed ledger sheets. One came from the old Skagit River Telephone Company, another from Northern State Hospital, and the last had the words *Homestead Deeds* at the top. He opened the envelope and read.

I'm heading out on a special mission for the US government. If I don't come back, it is because I failed. The work I'm doing involves the new era of nuclear weapons. No one can know of this, as we will use what we learn against the Japanese. Hopefully I'll be back in a couple of weeks. Please watch out for Molly McCain. I found evidence of embezzlement with two of the companies she worked with. Her motives are worse than greed. There is a deeper malice in all that she does. Unfortunately, I can't pursue that now. Be careful.

Spencer T

Russell folded the letter and replaced it in the envelope. He stared at the ledgers and sighed. "This is where we start boxing Molly in."

Chapter 25:
Trust and the Future

Maria let the cold water from the shower douse her hair, drip off her chest and buttocks. Her run along the river freed her from too much thinking. Her heart still pounded as the cold water cooled down the fiery emotions sparked by Molly's lies that had bound her and her aunt's lives.

She wanted to look in some manual for the procedures to solve yesterday, today, and tomorrow. As if there were instructions written down on how to defuse a bully, how to recover a loved one, how to save the world, and more disconcerting, how to move forward without answers.

Just feeling alive had to be enough. Drying off from the shower, she focused on dressing. She decided against jeans and stepped into a flowered skirt, donned a sleeveless white blouse. Maria envisioned her aunt's white silk wedding dress waiting in a closet for almost half a century. Was that an act of faith?

In a skirt, she felt freer, less confined than in pants or a uniform. Her uniform for work left little room for frivolity, as piloting demanded planning, precision, preparation for quick consequences. Now Maria had no real plan, except to go over to Spencer's house. And this, too, seemed like an act of faith, as Spencer had walked into her life with ease and now figured so prominently. Arms and legs exposed, Maria wondered about her heart.

As she pulled up to Spencer's house, the porch light magically shone onto the driveway. The motion detector seemed to fit Spencer's character; like a pilot, he thought out his actions, worked purposefully, and left her with a sense of assurance.

Armed with a stack of reports on delivery times and names of companies from the Concrete Airport manifests, Maria couldn't knock on the door without a free hand. Just as she hit the doorbell with her hip, Spencer swung the door open. A smile a mile wide greeted her. His eyes took all of her in. Feeling vulnerable, Maria smiled back and laughed at the awkwardness.

"I like that hip action," he said.

Maria felt the heat rise into her face as she hurried inside. Windows from an attached greenhouse extended the visual space of the dining and living area, bringing the outside into the house. Afraid of scratching the wood, she decided against setting her bundle on the red oak table.

Spencer gestured. "Welcome to my humble abode. My uncle designed the house years ago with a family in mind, but none materialized. And as we all know, he vanished as well."

Maria scanned the dining area and noted watercolors of vineyards, Steller's jays, a bald eagle, and an odd picture of large orange coconuts hanging from a palm tree. Spencer reached for the pile of papers, and Maria placed her research into his competent hands.

"I like the sense of space without barriers in your home. Did you bring the coconut painting from Puerto Rico?"

Spencer stared at the coconuts for a long time before answering. "I brought part of what I loved there back here to Concrete. My uncle's taste is similar to mine, and the vineyard and birds date back to when he lived here."

"He left a future behind. Building a house for a family and creating a vineyard as an occupation meant he intended to live here. His disappearance must have destroyed part of his visions."

"Up until now, I never questioned him about the why of not returning. He was and is obsessed with research. My uncle is a man of integrity. He does not leave ends dangling."

The resolve in Spencer's voice warned Maria that she should tread lightly.

"So." He set the papers on the red oak table. "Let's get to work. But first, a drink?"

"Could I get a tall glass of water with ice? And maybe some of your new vintage?"

Spencer headed off to the kitchen and came back with a tray holding water and wine for two and an assortment of cheeses surrounded by strawberries. Maria's shoulders relaxed as her stomach growled.

She drank half the water and then raised her glass of wine for a toast.

He clinked his glass against hers. "Here is to this moment and forever."

She thought about the word *forever* and wondered if Spencer's uncle had said the same thing to JoAnne half a century ago. Maria shied away from the word and offered a different toast. "Here is to more time like the present."

Spencer sniffed at his glass and then drank the smallest of sips. He let the wine swish inside his mouth. Satisfied with the taste, he took another drink. "Wines age—they taste better not in the present but in the future. Just like my uncle building this house for a family, wines equal a commitment. Love is just a feeling, unless the trust for the future is there."

Maria fidgeted with the mounds of paper she had brought, not sure if Spencer's words were meant for her or if they were just thoughts working their way through his brain. "I won't drink too much wine, then, as we have lots of work ahead of us. Let me fill you in on what Aunt JoAnne and I discovered."

Spencer sat next to Maria, pulling his chair in close so that their shoulders touched. She could smell the familiar fragrance of Ivory soap. Distracted, she pulled out the lists JoAnne had prepared with dates and company names.

"This list goes back to 1945 and continues to the present. There have been over a hundred deliveries. More disturbing to Aunt JoAnne were those that originated in Puerto Rico. Since you lived there, you might recognize the sources."

Spencer studied the list. JoAnne had highlighted with orange all the entries from the island, and he moved his finger down the pages, mumbling Spanish to himself. Maria sensed his agitation, a leap into a place she had never been. He flipped the pages, focusing on one and then back to the other.

"I can't be sure, but some of the deliveries came from towns near the pharmaceutical plants. Humacao, Arecibo, and Mayagüez aren't far from where my uncle and I lived. A while back, Puerto Rico attracted the pharmaceutical industry with IRS tax breaks and very low wages for a skilled labor force. Then the incentives disappeared, and now only a few factories remain. The waste from those factories would be poisonous in the sense that you wouldn't want it in your water or soil, and Puerto Rico demanded that all toxic waste be removed before they signed contracts. Many of the plants closed down because of lack of oversight, resulting in inferior products and recalls. Now the move is more toward biotechnology and developing chemotherapeutics."

"Why would the pharmaceutical plants send the waste to Concrete, of all places? The connection must be politically motivated."

Spencer stood and paced. He circled around the dining table, through to the kitchen, and along the greenhouse windows, repeating the cycle four times. Maria studied the floor and noted the worn areas, shiny oiled marks revealing Spencer's patterns of contemplation.

"I think I can make the connection," he finally said. "This afternoon, Russell and I traveled upriver to visit his friend Ralph and search for more waste burial sites or any information concerning Molly and Frank. Ralph's dad knew my uncle from childhood. When his dad passed away, Ralph discovered an envelope from my uncle with a letter, warning that Molly McCain embezzled money from two companies, and ledger sheets as evidence." He took a sip of wine and sat back down. "He also said in his letter that he was coming back in two weeks unless something went wrong."

Maria tried to leap past the embezzlement idea. "The question is, how deep is Molly's corruption? No one willingly does business with her. What were the names of the two companies on the ledger?"

"Skagit River Telephone Company and Northern State Hospital."

At the mention of the hospital, chills went up Maria's spine. The hair stood up along her arms, and adrenaline pumped *danger, danger* through her veins. Her memory at fourteen of Northern State Hospital filled her with loathing. Two weeks there had left her with a nightmare of confusion and fear. She took another swallow of wine and stood up to follow Spencer's pacing route.

"Spencer, when I was fourteen, the police admitted me to Northern State Hospital. Drunk or drugged, I had arrived in Skagit County looking for Aunt Jo. I'd hitchhiked to Concrete from back East after my mother died. And now I've just found out that Molly had blocked my calls to Aunt Jo, confined me with red tape. What if Molly not only embezzled money but also embezzled information?"

"That's horrible! I didn't know. But, I don't follow you train of thought about the embezzlement."

"Molly was the bully staff member who flitted through the hospital reading charts and taking patients on trips to the milking barn or the cemetery. I remember thinking her odd all those years ago. I had blocked her from my memory until recently, when I found out what happened to me. At the dinner that first night I met you, her presence—even her smell—bothered me. It triggered something. I think Molly's practice has always been to compromise people to her advantage. She must have collected information that she could sell or use against her targets."

Exhausted from thinking about her past, she sat back down and stared at the manifest report, trying to concentrate on the areas that had sent deliveries.

Spencer leaned over and squeezed her shoulders. She involuntarily groaned, and the sound broke the spell of doom. They both laughed.

He smiled as if he had just discovered ice cream. "I like your groans, like an expelling of evil. And speaking of evils, I think that Molly had more knowledge and more negative connections than politicians knew. I think she bribed her way into the waste industry. Somehow she followed her obsession, my uncle and your aunt. Everything that has happened circles back to those two. Everyone else is just collateral damage."

Maria felt a tear drift down her cheek. She looked around them at the house that Jo's Spencer had built for a family. What had gone wrong so many years ago? What had kept him from coming home? "You said earlier that love is just a feeling unless trust is there. Is it possible to still trust even if the love isn't returned? I think your uncle made a commitment to the future, something beyond his individual love for my aunt. Whatever stopped him from returning to Concrete held love."

"Before I answer you, I have something to confess. You asked me earlier about the coconut painting. I brought it from Puerto Rico because I love the colors, the vibrancy, and the sway of the palm trees. I bought the painting from your sister. She is the artist."

Maria's throat closed. Her breath stopped. She felt Spencer's arms around her, holding her. Sobs came from a place so deep that she felt like she would drown.

Spencer wiped her tears and whispered into her ear, "Love endures with trust. Your sister reminds me of you, lost and vibrant, seeking, giving, and most of all filled with purpose. I don't know why you two never connected. Somehow all that is happening will make sense. Trust me."

Maria felt the gentlest of kisses on her head and then her wet cheeks. She nodded. No words came as she rested within Spencer's arms.

When the phone rang, the outside world rushed back into the room, reminding them of the mound of papers and urgency of action.

Spencer noted the caller's phone number and answered. "Russ, can you speak up? You sound upset . . . Yes, I'll head over there now. Maria is with me, and we'll swing by and get JoAnne. See you soon."

Chapter 26:
Find the Loophole

Pulling up behind Spencer in JoAnne's driveway, Maria slammed her car door shut and hurried to meet him at the entrance. Her aunt seemed relaxed as she informed them that she had made dinner. Maria quickly explained Russell's call, then headed into the kitchen to scoop up the cooler with salmon burgers and salad. By the time Maria returned, both were waiting for her in the truck.

"Thanks for making dinner, Aunt Jo. When did you have time?"

"Actually, Russell called me about an hour ago, saying he needed to round up the troops again. He refused to tell me what he had discovered. Did you two make any progress?"

Maria blushed. She still felt Spencer's soft kisses on her cheeks and knew that this shared moment had already affected their course. She felt a reluctance to re-enter the present, not knowing if they could alter the future, let alone reconcile the past. But Spencer's face had shifted fully into the present. Mouth set, he drove in silence.

JoAnne had sense enough not to pry. They traveled the next ten minutes thinking their separate thoughts. Unlike at Spencer's house with its motion detectors, the driveway to Russell's home remained dark. Maya's barking announced their arrival, and within moments, the kitchen and porch light shone down the pathway.

While Spencer helped her aunt with her wheelchair, Maria entered the kitchen. "Russell, I'm in the kitchen. Aunt Jo made us dinner."

"I'll be there in a second. You know where all the plates are to set the table."

Seconds turned to minutes, and finally Maya came into the kitchen and nudged Maria's leg. Her heart skipped a beat, worried that Russell had fallen. She turned to follow Maya and nearly collided with Russell in the hallway.

"Slow down, girl. I should have said I'll be there in a few minutes. I forget that my body moves slower than my mind."

Maria found Russell's arm and helped him into the kitchen. He sat there staring out at JoAnne and Spencer as they made their way inside. Maria pretended that all was well, that Russell had made a joke. But Maya knew better, watching the slow, careful movements of her owner. Ever loyal, she lay by Russell's feet, her paws touching his shoes.

As usual, JoAnne came to the rescue, wheeling herself around the kitchen to find a vase for flowers, a pitcher for water. She hummed a song Maria remembered from her childhood: "Whatever will be, will be. The future's not ours to see. *Que sera, sera.*" Maria had never noticed the Spanish words before. The irony of connections to Puerto Rico didn't really matter, as the words in any language made sense.

Russell barely ate, leaving his salad and picking at the salmon burger. Maria knew he couldn't wait politely until the dinner ended to talk, so she decided to break one of her aunt's cardinal rules.

"Aunt Jo, even though we haven't finished eating, let's listen to what Russell has to say. There is no reason to make small talk when we have large issues to discuss."

Her aunt nodded her agreement. Russell drank some water and began.

"Since our visit upriver earlier today, Ralph and Rocky discreetly asked questions about the McCains' activities. My ham radio buddies sounded the alarm through the airwaves, and the buzz is that lots of the folks in the valley have fallen ill with unexplainable symptoms. The worst hit have been kids and old folks like me."

Russell paused and drank more water, as if it could help wash down his words. He looked out into the sky at the stars, searching for guidance, before he continued.

"Up until now, the cases seemed isolated. But with Molly's hospitalization and the Health Department's involvement, records from the last ten years show what some of the upriver folks already knew. Deaths that may have been declared as natural causes were the result of years of toxic exposure. Word is that the Health Department will be asking all of us for blood samples." Russell's voice cracked, and drained by the inference, he sat back in his chair.

JoAnne gasped and covered her mouth.

Maria needed to hear their thoughts, so that as a group they could act on the worst-case scenario. "Russell, are you saying that maybe your Emma died unnaturally, that she would still be alive?"

Spencer reached over and placed his hands on Russell's shaking shoulders.

Russell closed his eyes for a moment and then took a deep breath. "Emma used to say, 'It isn't spilled milk that you have to worry about but the stench if you don't clean it up.' Emma's time was up, and I'm not going to second-guess the cause. I won't lie to you—I'm so angry I could spit on Molly McCain. But I guess she has done worse to herself. I'm ashamed I didn't catch on sooner."

Spencer stood and began pacing. He walked around the kitchen table so many times that Maria got dizzy. JoAnne had pushed all her food around the edges again. Maria realized the wisdom in JoAnne's insistence on keeping mealtime talk light. Her own appetite had disappeared with Russell's shaking and the statement that the most vulnerable were the elderly and the younger children.

"Russell, from what you just said, you and Aunt Jo are susceptible. I'm worried that your systems have been compromised. First thing tomorrow, you are both going down to the Health Department."

Russell put his hand up, palm facing outward. "You haven't heard all that I have to say. It gets worse. Ralph gave Spencer a packet that Ralph's father left after he died. The packet held a letter from your Spencer, JoAnne. He meant to come home to you. That was clear. But the hard part to understand was his warning about Molly McCain. Just like my Emma warned me, Spencer warned his friend Ralph Senior."

JoAnne kept her hand over her mouth. Maria scooted her chair back and kneeled by her.

"Aunt Jo, you can take your hand off your mouth now. Remember, you are supposed to feel. Say something, cry, throw a fit. The only way we can move forward is to release the anger. This is no longer just about us. We need to protect the community."

Slowly JoAnne put her hand down. Her moist gaze met Maria's, shifted over to Spencer's face, and then settled on Russell's shaking frame. "Russell, you and I can't go backward. Molly McCain has no power unless we give it to her. Lies slipped through cracks because we let them. Not anymore."

With JoAnne's declaration, the room righted itself. Spencer returned to his seat, Russell snorted like a dragon, and Maria felt air re-enter her lungs.

Maria looked over at Spencer. He had lived with someone who was a ghost to everyone in Concrete, yet even he didn't know the reasons for his uncle's desertion. Lies settled deep once they slipped through the cracks.

Russell had more to say. "My call into Mourning Dove this afternoon went unanswered. Either the radio waves were jammed, or he just didn't respond. I'll try again later, but until then, I need help gathering information. Unless we find out the how, the authorities will find a scapegoat. Even with Molly in the hospital, she's laid out a plan that blames others, mainly Mourning Dove. The agencies have so many loopholes in their regulations that they can't act. Everyone stretches the rules, everyone is guilty, and that's what Molly wants. Excuse me for saying this, but she has us by the balls until we can expose her."

Spencer shook his head. "First off, I will not refer to my great-uncle as Mourning Dove. And excuse me for getting annoyed, but we have to cut out the bullshit. Everyone must come forward with what they are hiding. As long as my great-uncle keeps quiet, or we behave too civilly, Molly wins. No one can conceive of an elderly lady causing so much havoc. All the environmental regulations were meant for law-abiding citizens, but those who choose to find loopholes can and will. I'd like to put Molly's neck in a loophole."

Russell grimaced. "Spencer Senior also made a suggestion—more of a demand. He insisted that we act as a team, sharing all the information no matter how trivial it might seem, to stop Molly and at the same time working to contain or remove the toxic waste. Just finding the disposal areas won't stop what Mourning Dove—I mean, Spencer T—calls the *false links* Molly has formed over the years. Even from her hospital bed, Molly manipulates."

With each of Russell's statements, JoAnne's eyes blinked, and the impact on her aunt's health worried Maria. Russell implied that Molly's plots continued and that JoAnne's one love knew all of what went on in Concrete. Two powerful entities were controlling their lives, and they were pawns.

"Russell," JoAnne asked, "how can Spencer T know so much about what is happening here in a town over three thousand miles away from Puerto Rico, and how can Molly dictate our lives from her sickbed? We talk about loopholes, but are there leaks of another kind?"

Maria felt a soft nudge on her leg, and she looked over at Spencer. Even within his stern eyes, she saw that he cared. He reached across the table and squeezed her hand. Maria reached over to her aunt's hand and squeezed, and she followed suit, taking Russell's hand. Somehow, linked, they had forged a family unit.

Sparks of life came back into Russell's eyes, and his gaze went outside toward the night sky. "I'd like to believe that I wasn't just a gossip, that my age and past jobs in Skagit Valley working with the foresters, the fishermen, and the farmers made me a trustworthy person. Confidences occurred without expectations. We helped each other out not because we had to, but because there was an understanding, a respect. We followed rules or skirted them slightly, trusting that our intent was for the larger good. Maria, you and your Spencer share the same respect for the valley and upriver, and you two help by giving a fresh view. I know so much because of my ham radio buddies, as well as word of mouth. News also travels three thousand miles away because of luck and my diligence."

JoAnne spoke in a whisper. "What else does our Spencer from the past say? What other information is there from upriver?"

"The story from three thousand miles away causes me pause. Apparently, Rosie, JoAnne's new medical advisor from Puerto Rico, called a Dr. Knobs at the Skagit Valley Hospital. He is an old friend of hers, and she wants to see the doctor when she comes to visit you, JoAnne. Dr. Knobs answered the call while he was in Molly McCain's room and said your name out loud."

Russell paused, fiddling with the food on his plate. "Coincidences can be useful. This is where Spencer T learned of Molly McCain's reach. Even though Molly appeared to be suffering another heart attack, while the two doctors were on the phone, Molly heard everything. Within an hour of the original phone conversation, one of Spencer T's disposal companies called about a lost shipment, an investigation, a threat from an inspector. The inspector stated the complainant's name as Molly McCain."

At this point, JoAnne pushed her wheelchair away from the dinner table. She turned her back to all of them, eyes fixed on the window and the dark sky. In a firm voice, loud enough for the three of them to hear, she delivered her thoughts. "I would dismiss this as folly, coincidences, but I did that once before. Molly McCain is like a worm that replicates itself when parts get cut off. For some reason, my name, my very being, causes a venomous reaction. I won't make the same mistake as before. Molly's power is in our disbelief, our good hearts, our failure to believe in calculation and manipulation. My best defense against Molly is Molly. Rosie's call, in Molly's mind, revealed a weakness in my physical state, maybe in my mind. If Molly believes I'm vulnerable, she thinks that she gains. For her, winning means that I have lost something she wants. That is the key. Her measure of winning involves loss. In the short time I've been working with Rosie, I've learned that vulnerability means I am human, and declaring I have a need shows I'm strong. Molly believes that to hurt me all she has to do is to accuse Spencer T, make him the culprit, the bad guy. Molly's revenge has no substance if we know it exists."

Her aunt's words sounded brave, and they made sense if the only judge was JoAnne. Agencies liked finding answers that showed them in a favorable light. Blaming someone from outside the community would serve them well. Since revenge was outside the scope of the agencies, Maria wondered how to act on the knowledge of Molly's reprisals. Within the next few days, JoAnne and the group would be sweeping the area for toxic waste disposal sites. Ironically, the entire Skagit Valley was at risk because of Molly's revenge. Who else in the community had fallen out of favor with Molly and had experienced her malicious ways? If the holes in the evidence were too wide, the fear too strong, Molly might still win.

"Russell," Maria said, "besides the attempt at blaming Spencer T, what else did you discover? Spencer and I realized that Molly must have connections, that over the years she had found ways to circumvent the system. Something else happened, or you wouldn't have called us here tonight."

Russell smiled for the first time that evening. "I think Molly is too blind to see her own weaknesses. Now that she is in the hospital and the Health Department has jurisdiction over the case, she has lost some of her control. One of my ham radio buddies works in the lab at the hospital, another for the hazardous waste task force, and I found out they also tested Frank. His blood levels showed some oddities—not as severe as Molly's but significant enough for them to question him. His answers triggered a site investigation at Molly's farm, and they searched her house with a warrant. Besides the grave sites with dead sheep, they found phone records connecting her to Puerto Rico as well as a stack of very old mail addressed to JoAnne, Maria, and myself."

Russell sat calmly after he delivered this news. Fireworks exploded in Maria's head. JoAnne wheeled her chair around with such force that she banged into a table and knocked over a lamp. As Spencer righted the lamp, Russell leaned forward.

"This is where we tighten the noose. Molly's deception goes beyond loopholes. No matter what else we can prove, mail fraud is a federal offense."

Maria closed her eyes, let the tears seep through the slits. She thought about Monica. Letters searching for her, letters of love. The hole in her heart ached with the red lies. A failure to believe, a failure to pursue had kept this wound open too long. *Oh, Monica, how could I have doubted?*

Chapter 27:
Attitude: Stable Position

JoAnne slept fitfully, the nerves in her legs on fire, her heart pumping turbulent feelings of shame, guilt, and loss. Every inch of her body ached. Overwhelmed, her mind imagined, over and over, opening a stack of very old mail. How could she have allowed Molly to steal her life?

Mail fraud might put Molly in jail, but the damages to JoAnne's relationship with Spencer T, Maria's connection to her sister, and the health of the community had already occurred. JoAnne felt violated, imagining her lover's letters in the hands of Molly. Shivering with disgust, she turned on the bedroom light and scooted off the edge of her bed and into her wheelchair.

As she wheeled herself into the kitchen, she noted her reflection in the French doors. For some reason, the disheveled hair, the skimpy nightdress, and the determined jaw gave her comfort. Molly couldn't take her essence away. JoAnne saw herself: the pilot, the lover, the aunt, the gardener, the old woman she had become. She remembered flying for the first time. Trying to understand the concept of a plane's integrity had pushed her to mature as a pilot. After landing a Beech 18 through strong crosswinds, her instructor had posted on the wall of the cockpit: *Each plane has an attitude, a position in the air. Your job is to create a positive stability, where the plane returns to neutral when you release the control stick.*

Molly's nature perpetually remained in negative stability. JoAnne felt the pulls of time, the failing of obscured view. Closing her eyes, she remembered flying when visibility ceased to be the measure of direction, when the wind, clouds, and wide expanse of wings hid the sky markers. Forced to use her internal sense of balance and to rely on the instrument panels, she had weathered many a storm to land safely. Now grounded, JoAnne looked for more than a neutral attitude. She had to regain the control stick, move beyond Molly to a positive stability. Without that, her life stalled in a tailspin of lost hope.

After making a cup of hot chocolate, she sat at the kitchen table with a clean sheet of paper and a newly sharpened pencil. She drew lines horizontally and vertically, creating a grid. She sketched the river and mountains of Skagit County, the small townships of Lyman, Hamilton, Birdsview, Concrete, and all those leading to Marblemount. JoAnne marked Hamilton Logging, the composite factory, gravel pits, refurbished state parks, Northern State Hospital, the cement silos, and any area that contained industrial business or abandoned space. Engrossed in mapping, she didn't hear the bedroom door open upstairs or the quick steps of her grandniece Maria.

"Good morning, Aunt Jo. You woke up before the sun or the birds."

JoAnne lifted her gaze slowly. Maria stood with her arms across her chest and wearing only a t-shirt that came to her mid-thigh. Her hair had the rumples of sleep, and her eyes were red and swollen.

"I guess you couldn't sleep either, but I think I fared better than you. I have some garden-fresh cucumbers in the refrigerator. Put a slice over each of your eyes."

Maria got the slices and sat next to her. "Good idea, making a grid of the area. We can get a topographic map from the Civil Air Patrol for the mountain areas and farms. Are you setting up a command center?"

JoAnne smiled at how easily they slipped into the planning and organizing, just as easily avoiding the hard conversations about Molly and the letters. "I remembered my first lesson in flying, when the instructor talked about attitude, knowing where the plane became stable, how to right the position. Flying lessons apply to real life. As much as Rosie wants me to feel, deal with my emotions, and redirect the synapses of my brain, sometimes feelings don't matter as much as action. A cool head, planning, and intuition bring a pilot down safely. If we are to survive Molly's shenanigans, Maria, we have to use our training and instinct."

Leaning back, half slumped in the kitchen chair, Maria held the cucumber slices to her eyes. "Aunt Jo, how is it that people like Molly create such ugliness, mess up the natural balance? I'm having a hard time understanding the forethought needed to craft such an imbalance. A plane is constructed to find stability, and nature's design seeks a balance where relationships for plants and animals thrive. If I put my emotions aside, as you say, and use my training, my intuition, it means that Molly at my age or younger plotted to destroy you and anything that you touched. She purposefully sought a negative balance aimed at toppling you. I am just collateral damage."

JoAnne let Maria's words float. Reaching across the table, she picked up an old plastic sharpener and twisted her pencil until the shavings left a fine point.

"There isn't a cure for Molly or people like her. Theirs isn't a sickness. If I mapped out Molly's behavior, I'd start with a need unfulfilled. Molly isn't satisfied with her first actions. Her need is bottomless, so she sharpens her skills and again intentionally acts, but now her intent also contains greed. With each victory, she feels powerful but not satiated. The fallout of damage increases, and her intent and greed now turn into a fixation. I may have once been a target for a reason, but now all that remains is her fixation."

Maria removed the cucumbers from her eyelids and placed them in the compost bin below the kitchen sink. She stretched her arms above her head, the t-shirt rising to reveal her belly. JoAnne shook her head, smiling at the simple beauty of youth. Even though JoAnne's age more than doubled Maria's, her cells remembered the freedom, the unencumbered abandonment that came before thought.

"Aunt Jo, thank you for your love. Without it, I would have drifted so far off course, and my attitude toward life would be colored dark with negatives and lies. Molly has no idea of the good acts that followed because of her misdeeds. Last night, I cried myself to sleep, feeling so cheated and wrong for not having pursued my sister. When I get the guts to call, I still have the opportunity to continue our relationship. Collateral damage or blessing, reframing my past helps me chart a new course."

She blew out a breath. "But enough talk about Molly. I'm with you on getting down to the specifics. When I talked with Spencer, I misspoke about using laser equipment to find the waste sites. I still might be able to get the equipment from my employer, but not fast enough, and the weight would be problematic. Your grid, beefed up with data, is the right approach."

JoAnne nodded. Her mind wandered backward to a time before 9/11, a time when hazardous waste, toxic chemicals, and the environment took a back seat to world problems. In the 1940s of World War II, fighting for the country was an honor and a duty. The attack on Pearl Harbor brought the war to America, and the goal to win didn't consider consequences. Her Spencer had worried about the nuclear bomb, but his dedication to his country outweighed his objections. As an engineer, his role to solve problems came first, and his belief that science had all the answers deceived him. That deception had nothing to do with Molly.

"Maria, before 9/11 the regulations for waste disposal had less oversight, almost nonexistent. The lies of science go back to the Cold War, to a time when we all believed that science plus war meant a quick end to fighting. Back then, Molly acted as an opportunist, lying and using the system for financial gain. She had no idea that this one lie would accumulate in toxicity. I don't think that today she could continue bringing nuclear waste into Skagit County, as they'd be banned or tied up in red tape with deliveries to legal disposal areas.

"You're too young to remember, but in the early 1970s, Puget Sound Power and Light proposed a nuclear power plant on Bacus Hill, near Lyman. I'm sure that Molly and Frank worked behind the scenes for rezoning to speed up the process and pushed for the nuclear power plant. Locals objected. Puget Sound Power abandoned the idea in 1979, after Skagit County voters and Skagitonians Concerned About Nuclear Power nixed it in the polls.

"Today, there won't be a vote for laws that already exist. You can't vote on a process that contains and enforces illegal dumping. Thwarting Molly McCain will take more than a village, but we'll have to rely on the locals to spot the black lies."

Staring at the grid, Maria looked at the demarcations of possible burial sites. Her fingers traced lines on the maps, air routes of the pilots coming to the Concrete Fly-In, and the Skagit River's path.

"Aunt Jo, I need to eat something, feed my brain."

Ten minutes later, Maria returned with a spread of toast, eggs, potatoes, and coffee. JoAnne cleared space for the breakfast, noting Maria's plate where the two sunny-side up eggs formed the eyes of a face; the toasted bread, the ears; and the hash browns, a beard. She smiled at the endearing habits of her grandniece.

Just as they finished their meal, the phone rang. They looked at the clock. 7:00 a.m.

Maria made for the phone. "Who would be calling us this early?" She answered, "Yes, I recognize your voice, Rosie. My aunt is at the kitchen table, I'll bring her the phone."

JoAnne almost grabbed it from Maria's hand. "Rosie, sorry I missed your call the other day." Her voice was unsteady. "What news do you have?"

Rosie, apparently with only a quick layover in Florida, was on her way. She would be seeing Dr. Knobs about the illness in the valley. Rosie had made inquiries about Molly McCain, since the name seemed familiar. At the university where she did her research, she had found documents of medicinal waste signed for by a company called MMC. One of the documents has the signature of Frank McCain. Rosie corroborated the various pharmaceutical companies, and further investigation found that the materials came to Concrete, Washington, actually diverted from another company with a similar name, NMC.

When JoAnne asked who was coming with her, Rosie sidestepped the question, asking JoAnne instead about the progression of her nerve sensations, then had to hang up to catch her flight. JoAnne sat holding the phone, shaking her head.

Maria cleared the dishes and listened to JoAnne's half of the conversation with Rosie. Letting the words drift at the back of her mind, Maria envisioned her sister as a teenager, the age when she left for Puerto Rico. She could see Monica in a skirt and blouse, books piled on the table as she rushed to make them breakfast and assured Maria that life would be better someday. Maria imagined she could hear her voice through the airwaves, superimposed on the voice of Rosie, who could see Monica anytime. Her sister's most comforting saying was, "You never know what will happen when you turn the corner." Knowing that both her sister and her Spencer had shared time with Rosie caused her heart to beat faster. Maria wanted to fast-forward so she could turn the corner, see Monica, and feel free of yearning.

By the time Maria returned to the table, JoAnne had hung up the phone. Silence stretched.

"Aunt Jo, your face is red, your eyes teary, and your jaw stiff. Are we flying in stable air, or are there more bumps?"

JoAnne sharpened the pencil again, taking her time to make the point tip equal on each side. She smiled and looked up at Maria. "Rosie will be here tomorrow, two days early. Her concerns for my welfare and yours and everyone in Skagit Valley elevated after she talked with Dr. Knobs." She explained about Rosie's discoveries of the McCain waste shipments.

Maria fidgeted, impatient for news of who would be on the plane with Rosie. "This explains part of how Molly worked, but don't keep me waiting to hear what we both want to know. Is Monica or your Spencer on the plane with Rosie?"

JoAnne broke the pencil point as she pressed down on the grid. Her hands shook until she folded them together and placed them on her lap. "Rosie's answers aren't always intelligible. I want her to be direct, but she talks as if she knows things I don't. She senses that I want something, and she isn't the one to give it to me. I can't explain exactly, but she doesn't want an emotion to guide me.

"I can't repeat her exact words, but it was something like, 'You give a gift without expecting a reward, a letter because you feel you have something to share. Feelings always exist, whether they are reciprocated or not. Whoever comes with me is the person I need to bring. It doesn't mean others are absent. If I tell you something you don't want to hear, will it change this moment? Work on this moment, not the next.'

"Maria, I think she wants us to find the attitude of our plane, the place in our own life where we are stable. Or Rosie simply wants to protect me from disappointment, wants me to not give up my internal strength. At my age, feeling is what makes life worth living."

"What did you promise this Rosie, 'the All-Seeing'?"

"Sarcasm doesn't become you, Maria."

"I'm afraid we will be blindsided again. Trusting too easily."

Maria wrapped her arms around her chest and held tightly to the flimsy t-shirt, to the bones protecting her heart.

"Oh, Maria, that is exactly what Rosie is saying. The trust she wants us to have is not in her, or hers to give. It is in our own judgment. If I had trusted my love for Spencer T and his for me, I would not have accepted the lies planted by Molly. Nothing would have stopped me from searching for him. My Spencer's demons, his reasons for staying in Puerto Rico, must be more important than feelings. His feelings for me will always exist. And your sister—you'll find what you find.

"Now to answer your original question, I promised Rosie that I would go to the Health Department to get tested and encourage every-one who resides here do the same."

Maria dropped her arms from their hold around her upper torso and gave her aunt a kiss. The day finally seemed to take form. "Okay, we should get going. Is there anything else I need to know?" The two of them were hardwired for action.

"Yes. According to Rosie, Spencer T contacted various research centers in the Pacific Northwest, the universities and other centers where they have been experimenting with the blue goo he invented for containment of toxic waste. Most of them are just around the corner from Concrete, a short flight away. When we find the various burial sites, the centers will be ready to assist us."

"Aunt Jo, aren't we jumping ahead of ourselves? There is no chain of command here. All the agencies have been alerted by the Health Department of the situation. We can't just create a command center in isolation."

At this, JoAnne nodded slowly. "Let me reframe that. We will work simultaneously with the agencies. I'll contact Dr. Knobs directly, since he found the worst contaminant, Molly, and has contained her. He can tell the other agencies of our plan. We need to work fast, and unencumbered by red tape. In a case like this, civilians with a background in air patrol and systems can be more effective. Rosie arrives tomorrow, flying directly into the Concrete Airport. I'll meet her there, and we can establish a real command center accessible to the pilots and the agencies. I'm sure Russell and Spencer will participate."

Maria sprinted toward the stairs to get dressed, but JoAnne called her back.

"One thing Rosie mentioned that has me puzzled: A foundation from Seattle sent her a check in the mail for research and development. The anonymous donor specified the monies be used for two purposes. One is Rosie's research with the *linea* vine, its function in the regeneration of nerves, and the second is to promote research to contain toxic waste. This money only adds to my pondering of the other trust money. The sudden windfall of money to Rosie has me stymied. Rosie welcomed the donation."

Maria rubbed her arms, tried to push the hairs down as goose bumps moved across her body. "Aunt Jo, you said it before. There is someone looking out for us, trying to counter Molly. I'll take it as a silver lining. Let's get moving. First your tests, then to the command center."

Chapter 28:
Concrete Command Center

The town of Concrete might have slept through the night, but Russell couldn't be sure, as his ham radio buddies filled the airwaves with chatter. Most of the talks centered on the Health Department's decree, demanding all residents take a blood test in order to find those affected by toxic contaminants. No one demands anything of those living upriver. They lived away from the towns for privacy, to get away from the eyes of the government. Russell painstakingly countered their logic with that of the power of Molly McCain, the threat of her actions, and the resulting damage to their own land and health. At one point, he felt like a politician, declaring their best interests were at stake, that their refusal to act would allow a vagrant bully to skirt laws, laws meant to protect them. The clash of private and public needs buzzed like the chainsaws of their pioneer forefathers.

After going up and down the stairway from the kitchen to the basement more than a dozen times, Russell and Maya made their beds by the radio. Russell dozed fitfully with Maya at his feet, wet nose and warm body watching over him. His visit to the Health Department had left him with too much to ponder. His blood showed signs of low white blood cells and a slight case of anemia. This was the good news, indicating only a slight exposure to internal radiation, fixable with antibiotics and iodine. The presence of dioxins revealed a mixture of toxic elements present in the water. The most alarming result from the blood tests revealed a lack of oxygen throughout his system, clearly not a contaminant issue but an indication of a failing heart.

Emma came to him in his dreams, his whole being absorbed in the smell of her skin, the floating fragrances of their intimacy. She lingered in his system. She breathed for him and kept his heart going. Waking to a skipped heartbeat, labored breathing, and the licks of loyal Maya, Russell moved mentally quicker than his legs or arms allowed. Gathering the scattered bedding, he mounted the stairs to the kitchen, creaking with each step, an echo of bones and loose nails.

"Good girl, Maya. I'll let you out in a minute to romp with the birds. With all the chatter in the airwaves, you'd think birds wouldn't be able to fly. Used to be they'd get caught in the telephone wires, but now we can communicate without lines, something you and my Emma have always done. Go on, now, go outside while I ready us for the patrol."

Russell made himself a bowl of cornmeal mush with leftover bacon drippings, filled up his thermos with coffee, and loaded the truck with his ham radio equipment. By the time he had finished, Maya sat by the passenger door, ready to jump inside. He rolled down the windows, letting the cool morning breeze pass through and giving Maya her watch post. The drive to the airport took less than ten minutes—no traffic, no distractions, only the quiet before the storm.

He headed toward the lights, the museum hangar, per JoAnne's instructions, their meeting time still an hour away. The lights meant JoAnne and Maria were too anxious to rest. He pulled up next to Spencer's truck, realizing much of Concrete had left sleep behind.

Maya led the way, rushing into the opened hangar doors, sniffing and greeting everyone with a wag of her tail. She settled down by JoAnne's wheelchair. Russell lumbered in behind Maya, carrying his radio and maps. He noted the freestanding chalkboard, three laptop computers, a printer, and an empty table.

JoAnne patted Maya and greeted Russell with her first command. "Russell, plop your radio down on that empty table. I've got the chalkboard and a bulletin board ready for the maps. What did you bring?"

"All business, are we? I brought news from upriver. They are ready to work with us, be part of the land patrol. They'd rather be out looking for problems than go to the Health Department for a blood test, and I can't say that I blame them. Doctors always find problems. I convinced the old-timers that the common enemy is Molly McCain. Her actions flow through the valley up and down the river, spewing who knows what. With so many abandoned roads from the Department of Natural Resources, only those living in the area, those who hunt, fish, and perhaps skirt the law, know where to look for the buried waste. Maybe this one time, the call of the common good will suppress the fear of government interference into their lives."

By the time Russell finished his speech, Spencer had the ham radio set up and the rest of Russell's gear inside. Spencer thumbed through a stack of maps and papers from old industrial and logging sites, part of Russell's business past. JoAnne and Maria waited, watching the scene.

Russell winked when he caught JoAnne's eye. "Who would have put us all together, generations apart, on a mission? JoAnne, I never flew a plane or ventured outside of Skagit County, but I've traveled up and down the river, up and down this valley. I may be old, but old is what we need. The new generation has their cell phones. I have my ham radio and so many stories."

JoAnne wheeled her chair over to Russell's radio center. She examined the maps and opened yellowed charts of logging camps, farming areas, and fishing sites. Russell's past life was held in the creases, the years of knowing a land and its community.

"Thanks, I knew I could depend on you. Spencer brought with him the most recent hiking maps for this area, as well as the USGS quad maps. They break the areas up into roads, rivers, hills, and include back roads. Between the two sets of maps and online images, we can find what we need. My plan is to use the grids for the flight patterns of our veteran pilots."

Maria stood beside JoAnne and let her aunt take the lead. JoAnne had explained that searches hadn't changed much over the years; the basic principles remained the same. This hangar would act as the center hub, receiving information and directing the volunteers. Rules of coordination made sense out of what seemed a vast task.

Maria looked worried. "What about the lack of tower control at the Concrete Airport? How do we maintain contact with the ground force? I know that on the day of the fly-in, all the pilots depend on the command frequency of 122.9. Chaos would reign otherwise. How do we keep the ground forces informed without ham radios and keep sensitive information away from the likes of Frank?"

Russell chuckled, Spencer hid his grin behind his hand, and JoAnne pointed her pencil at her cell phone.

"Don't ever forget the obvious. We might be restricted from having the latest technology of detection, or for that matter radios, but we have what civilians call the digital cell phone. Everyone will have my cell phone number. They'll call in the sightings."

Maria laughed and finished her aunt's sentence: "And snap a digital photograph of what they see. Our computers and printers will let us see through their eyes."

Russell sensed the nervousness behind the laughter. Making a joke had always been his way to diffuse tension or let situations settle, but he felt anything but settled. For so many years he'd played the role of detective and informant with his radio buddies, but now their role held the spotlight.

He cleared his throat. "My gear's been in my basement for so long I can see the oily imprints from my fingers. I started working with the ham radio after World War II. The handler, Mourning Dove, became my first and most loyal voice from outside the mainland. Spencer, thanks for reminding me the other day that his call name obscured facts, made him less a person and the facts more surreal. All of us who served our country have names and families. Our real mission is to live life peacefully, and being here with all of you reminds me of loyalties that go beyond family. Sorry if I'm being maudlin. Worry does that. I haven't been able to connect with your uncle for a few days now. It's as if he has disappeared. Our invisible lines of communication have always been a comfort of sorts, especially since my Emma died."

Spencer fidgeted with the last of the wiring for the printer. "Russell, you just gave two speeches in the last few minutes, more words than I've known you to spout since I've been hanging out with you. No need to worry. My uncle texted me that he would have Rosie make contacts for the magnetic mop and gels to help soak up and counter the effects of the toxins. When he gets involved in a project, he has no outside schedule—days and nights become one."

Russell drank from his thermos and made a motion to toast the group. Maya moved from JoAnne's wheelchair to lay her head protectively on Russell's feet.

On JoAnne's airport radio, the red light flashed. Through the static, a pilot was checking for other planes in the vicinity, and they heard multiple answers. Without a tower, these calls gave pilots the power to know their surroundings, warn other pilots in the area, and call for help if needed. With no flight plans filed, they could only guess at the identity of the arrivals.

Maria ran outside with Spencer, acting as both the welcoming committee and the flaggers. The sun burned through the clouds, making a path straight to the runway. The first plane, an Aeronca L-16, swooped down on all three, a landing considered a ten for those measuring the proficiency of the taildragger. Maria signaled a thumbs-up to the pilot. Right behind the Aeronca, a Boeing Stearman PT-17 missed the three-point landing and bounced slightly but still held true to the runway.

Planes circled around the runway in a choreographed dance, until the next five planes lined up in a sequenced formation to land. Through the airwaves, the pilots communicated in a language of rules, etiquette, safety, and good airmanship. The sleepy town of Concrete woke to an airport transformed into a strategic hub of expert pilots.

Russell watched the landings and noted the planes and pilots as they made their way off the runway. The official date for the annual fly-in was the third Saturday in July, but pilots often came a day or two before to camp and tell flight stories. JoAnne's and Maria's calls to veteran pilots drew in the crème de la crème. New faces, new energy, just as Russell found his own energy waning.

He stood up and walked over to JoAnne's desk. "What can I do to make your job easier?"

"I've got charts of the general area set up on the bulletin board," JoAnne replied. "Once we see the type of planes available, the experience level, and the number of pilots, we can assign areas. Make a sign-in sheet. If anyone is here unofficially from the Civil Air Patrol or the Cascade War Birds, send them right over to me. Civil Air Patrol pilots work as an auxiliary to the US Air Force. Today, they would be footing their own gas bill to help us out. If our hunches pan out, they'll call the big guys in and make the search for toxic waste official."

Russell feigned enthusiasm. He had his doubts, not about finding toxic waste but about the timeliness of saving those affected. "Don't worry about that. Molly and Frank aren't smarter than us, just more devious. They have had years of honing their lying skills, but us old farts know how to sniff out a skunk. We'll have the advantage looking from the air. We'll find evidence of burial sites."

"To help us with the aerial photos, Russell, I'll need you to find someone with expertise in the use of online aerial maps. Spencer says there are digital photos of the area from years back, ones that zoom in and out. We'll be looking for differences in the terrain—brown spots, seepages, disturbed earth."

Russell obeyed, quickly setting up clipboards for the volunteers. Work helped keep his mind off his body. He wanted to ask JoAnne about her visit to the Health Department. She never complained, seemed to have the energy and strength of a mother bear. But now wasn't the time to ask her about the blood test results, especially since he didn't want to offer his own yet.

Instead, he filtered through the list of pilots filing into the hangar. The early birds tended to be from the Civil Air Patrol. The more recent arrivals worked as crop dusters, flying their planes low and targeted. They swarmed around JoAnne to study the grid and divvy up the work.

Outside the hangar, Maria and Spencer were staring up at the sky. Russell, waiting for the arrival of more pilots, watched the two as they laughed and pointed upward. Their ease with one another filled Russell's heart with a sense of longevity, a sense of caring and love that would continue even if his bloodline didn't. Childless, he wondered if this, too, was the fault of Molly's messing with nature.

Suddenly Maria and Spencer ran down the runway. Russell watched as a Grumman Goose attempted a landing. The pilot either misjudged the runway, or his cargo load, or had minimal experience with conventional landing gear. The plane drifted and crabbed, zigzagging along the runway. The smaller tail wheel had come down seconds after the two front wheels, causing a small bounce and a twirl. Struggling to avoid a ground loop, the pilot finally straightened out the Grumman.

What happened next had Russell rushing out of the museum hangar. Instead of greeting Maria and Spencer, the pilot ran over to the McCain hangar. He banged on the door, waited less than ten seconds, and headed back to his plane. Out of breath, Russell stood by the Grumman wing waiting.

"Saw you had problems landing. We've got some veteran pilots here who could help you."

The pilot walked around Russell, shooing him away like a fly. "No need, just move out of my way. I've got deliveries to make. I must have got the time or place wrong. I'm on a schedule. Thanks."

Russell stood taller, letting his body block the entrance. "Where did say you came from?"

"I didn't. Now move, or I'll move you."

Russell took his time, letting Spencer reach the plane. Spencer circled the plane, studying the tires, touching the wings, acting as if the plane held a special interest.

"Sorry you are in such a hurry. Our annual fly-in starts tomorrow. Your Grumman Goose would fit right in with all the refurbished planes. Looks like you might be more adept at landing on the water or a beach than on a runway."

At this, the pilot mounted the plane, shut the door, and started his engine. Russell and Spencer backed away. Russell took out paper and pen from his pocket and noted the registration numbers. He would let his radio buddies track the plane down and then have Customs, or Homeland Security, or any agency that would listen, find out about the cargo.

Russell's hands shook, and he bent over trying to catch his breath. Maya came running from the hangar as Spencer supported Russell from behind.

"Russell, slow down," Spencer said. "Lean on me. I think the adrenaline kicked in too fast. I'll help you get back to the hangar."

In between his wheezing and slow walk, Russell blurted out his suspicions. "That's got to be another delivery of canisters. Frank is holed up at the hospital. He didn't show. Maybe I can find out something."

Spencer nodded and then pointed to Maria, who was flagging another plane down. The Twin Beech taxied down the runway, past the museum hangar, and over to the helicopter pad, where a Secret Service helicopter had just landed. One passenger, a male, deplaned and immediately entered the helicopter. The copter lifted off the pad and headed west. A second passenger, a small woman, deplaned and slowly walked toward the museum hangar. They all arrived almost at the same time.

"Hi, I'm Rosie, and you must be Spencer and Russell. I assume the flagger is Maria, and that JoAnne is holding down the command center."

Chapter 29:
Bird's Eye Perspective

Loyal to her assignment as a flagger, Maria resisted the pull of her legs to run and investigate the Twin Beech that had just taxied to the helicopter pad. Instead, she pulled out her binoculars and scanned the skies. Emotionally split, her two selves vied for attention. The first self saw with the eyes of a pilot wanting to fly, strapped to the runway with clipped wings as a flagger and concerned with traffic safety. The second self, acting as an adult and missing a sister, believed with the innocence and passion of a child that the new arrival came on the wings of her sister's spirit. Every fiber of her being sensed that the woman walking toward the museum hangar would be Rosie, Maria's connection to Monica.

Maria's binoculars drew in the skyscape. She noted the crisp clouds high in the sky, Sauk Mountain to the east still waking to the day. No planes in sight, nor the distant rumble of motors signaling an incoming flight. She waited, hoping that JoAnne would send out someone to relieve her from flagging duties. Two young cadets, dressed in khaki uniforms, answered Maria's wish as they huffed their way toward her.

"Hello, I'm Cadet Carl Songbird, and this is Cadet Joan Songbird from Civil Air Patrol Squad 46. On orders from our incident command officer, we've come to relieve you of your flagging duties."

As they saluted, her split selves melded together. She studied the two young volunteers, not more than thirteen or fourteen. "I'm Maria. Is this your first time out in the field?"

Simultaneously they answered, "Yes, sir—I mean, ma'am."

Volunteerism began at an early age in the Civil Air Patrol. She thanked the kids and offered them her orange batons. Politely refusing, each one pulled a pair of batons from their backpack. They were clearly prepared with radios, water, snacks, and an eager attitude. Maria saluted them again and ran to the museum hangar, her heart racing in pace with her legs. Overcome with anticipation, she felt as young as the cadets and as old as Russell.

The museum hangar had morphed into an actual command center. JoAnne still sat at her post near the bulletin board, but an older gentleman with a cap bearing the initials *IC* stood by her side, clearly the incident commander. Maria sighed with relief, noting that this would be a *B* mission, kept local and paid for by the volunteers. Everything would be unofficial but done with the utmost professionalism. Reading the IC's uniform, she noted his name, Bill Lindbergh.

"Aunt Jo and Incident Command Officer Lindbergh, thanks for sending relief. I'm reporting back for duty. What can I do?"

Maria prayed silently that she could attend to her heart's needs, selfish as that felt. She would still do everything required for the search, even if it kept her from learning more about her sister. Refusing to look at her aunt, Maria kept her eyes fixed on the IC. The room felt too tight, too quiet. Russell had disappeared, as had her Spencer. Maria expected to see Rosie conferring with her aunt, and Rosie had vanished, too.

"Maria." JoAnne's voice was shaking. Her hands were held tightly on her lap, her eyes moist, her lips trembling. "Maria, Rosie is in the back room with Russell. Russell says we are fussing too much, says he just got winded from running. Rosie and I will have time to talk after she goes to the hospital to meet with Dr. Knobs. Could you take care of Russell and Rosie? I don't think I can handle more right now."

Maria noted the familiar return to official roles, the cover to hide their emotions. Their awkwardness hid the fear, the threat of honesty. Hurrying to the other side of the table, she embraced her aunt. "I know you're worried, Aunt Jo. Relax. With the Civil Air Patrol, we have a chance. They'll find the evidence to stop the McCains. I'll take care of Russell and Rosie."

A tight squeeze from her aunt sent her off, and Maria headed toward the back room through a dark hallway. She pictured Spencer's home, the motion lights that shone in the dark. Maria needed lights to show her the way, not through the hall but toward her heart. Why did she believe that Rosie would be that light?

Maria expected the worst, thinking that Russell would be struggling to breathe, that she'd have to rush to the hospital on a lifesaving mission. Instead, there was Russell charming Rosie. The two sat facing one another, sharing coffee from Russell's thermos. Rosie turned to Maria and raised her left eyebrow in an informal salute, still keeping her eyes on Russell, who was saying, "Rosie, if I were a tad bit younger, I would ask you out. But I'm glad to hear that you have a beau, someone who knows how to work the land and be loyal to someone as sweet as you."

Maria cleared her throat so Russell could hear her come up from behind him. She placed her hands on his shoulders, feeling his bones through his shirt and the shallow breath that followed his words. "Russell, Aunt JoAnne told me that you were ailing, but it looks to me like you were flirting with our guest."

Russell's faced turned red, and his eyes broadcast his sweet-devilish look.

Rosie took his defense. "Maria, we haven't been introduced yet, but you look so much like Monica. Russell talked to me about missing his Emma, and then he asked me if I was married. I take his flirting as a compliment. His real question goes deeper. I told him that I was no longer married but had a beau. Russell lucked out, finding his lover and mate on the first try."

Hearing Monica's name and that she looked like her sister jump-started Maria's heart. She felt her knees begin to buckle and pulled up a seat by Rosie. How had this small woman with wild spiraling black hair become intimate so quickly? Maria sensed calm, an openness that slipped through her barriers. "Aunt JoAnne said you need a ride to the hospital to see Dr. Knobs. I can drive you there."

Russell stood slowly, bowed ceremoniously toward Rosie, and started down the hallway.

"Russell, are you sure you feel well enough to work?" Maria asked.

He turned back to face them. "Rosie has the power to mend a leaking heart. I've got work to do with ground patrol, and the ground operation branch director needs my ham radio assistance. I'll catch you both later."

Rosie waved goodbye, acting as if she belonged among them. Literally having dropped from the sky, she faced Maria as though they were already long-time friends and confidants. She apparently knew no other way.

"Rosie, do you have any luggage or things to bring to the hospital? I can help you to my car."

She smiled, her olive skin crinkling around the eyes. "Just this bag with the notes for my lecture at WWU and some information Dr. Knobs needed. I'm ready when you are."

As they left, Maria waved to JoAnne and Russell. No one had said anything about Spencer. He'd been gone since Rosie arrived. Maria worried, but kept her thoughts to herself. Or so she thought.

They traveled in a comfortable silence without the pressure of words.

Maria rolled down the car windows and listened to plane engines circling the airport, preparing for landing. She envisioned the new cadets, anxious and serious, waving them along with their unseasoned orange batons. She kept her lips sealed, not wanting to break the silence, not wanting to ask questions. Her mind was still stuck on Spencer's disappearance.

Rosie sat low in the car, barely seeing over the dashboard. She hummed the tune Maria recognized from childhood, "*Que sera, sera, what will be, will be.*" Her heart fluttered, flapping wings of memories. Although she kept her lips sealed, tears leaked from her eyes. Rosie repeated the chorus three more times before Maria finally let her thoughts spill out.

"Did you know that Monica and I sang that song when we were little kids? It was one of the songs that kept hope in our hearts."

Rosie turned to face Maria. Hers large, dark eyes penetrated Maria's protective shell. She nodded more in understanding than with an answer. "That song is one my grandmother sang to me. I have not been blessed with children, but I can see why your mother taught you and your sister the words. When I first met Monica, she stared at me the same way, in disbelief and with a little fear. Do you still have hope in your heart?"

Maria's knee jerked at an imaginary obstacle in the road, and the car swerved ever so slightly. She herself had been accused of being blunt, but Rosie really dove in. She let the question sit between them, let her feelings catch up to the meaning. She remembered the pains of the earlier years after her mother's death, the journey from there to here, what it was like to grow up in Concrete, and the struggles of being Maria.

"Yes, I do have hope. I was lucky enough to have Aunt JoAnne as my mentor. She saved me from going astray. I was a mess with my mother's alcoholic abuse and then death. I drifted so close to being what I hated in my mother. I couldn't hold on to the good, especially when I lost contact with Monica. I lost a piece of my heart."

"Monica never left you. Not a day goes by that she doesn't honor you. Her story is as convoluted as yours, but it belongs to her. She runs a café, and each of her dishes carries a memory. My favorite dish is called 'The Falling Star.' Monica makes a pocket out of a banana leaf, and inside she roasts pieces of coconut in the shape of a star. She sprinkles it with honey. I see her eat this dish often, especially on days when a rainbow appears after a sprinkling of rain."

Maria felt like she needed windshield wipers to clear the tears away. Thankfully she turned into the hospital parking lot without incident. Rosie handed her a handkerchief.

Before she let Rosie disappear into the hospital to talk with Dr. Knobs, Maria needed to warn her about Molly. As kind and as powerful as Rosie's disposition felt, Maria feared that Molly's tentacles reached beyond the lies that still held the town, JoAnne, and herself. She wasn't sure that Rosie could withstand the cold calculations of a person who got pleasure from creating loss.

"Rosie, you have no idea how much it means to me, your sharing the description of Monica's favorite dish. I still have an envelope where I saved our falling stars, saving them for a rainy day. I only just found out that Monica years ago sent letters searching for me. Molly McCain stole them. Beware of her."

Rosie seemed unfazed at her declaration. She patted her bag of information as if this were armor enough, but Maria doubted that Molly would be powerless against Rosie's truths.

"Maria, I can still see fear inside you, and Molly's power lies within that fear. I have no real power against her, but Molly will lose this battle she fights. She fights herself, lies to herself first, so that it gives her the conviction of moral honesty. Exposure gives us the opportunity to cut her tentacles that have a hold on others. She will never see her own wrongs. Our first line of defense is showing truths that counter her lies."

"I agree, but I still think Molly unleashed more than toxic waste. Is it horrible for me to want her gone, to die an evil death? Her actions polluted so many worlds. I hate her. Just the thought of her makes me feel dirty, contaminated with her evil."

Rosie's eyebrow lifted, and her lips pursed. "You ask a thoughtful question. I think they call it 'getting what is coming to you' or your 'just desserts.' Life is full of surprises, none of which we can control, or should. Molly's fate belongs to Molly. You aren't a horrible person because you have a horrible thought. Even if Molly were to disappear today, she has left an imprint. But so has your aunt and your sister. Which impression do you want to honor, give your energy to? Don't focus on Molly. Work on the positive changes you will make."

And there it was, so simply stated. Maria's deeds counted. The antidote to Molly's deceitful and evil behavior began with Maria herself. She saw the catch-22, the irony, the risk.

"Rosie, certainly you are armed with more than my future good deeds. I understand that I can influence those around me, take the lead in finding the toxic waste, but Molly's actions impacted more than just my aunt, me, and Spencer T."

Maria realized that Rosie wasn't talking about just Molly's actions.

Rosie nudged her arm. "Stop going on and on. Park the car and come with me to meet Dr. Knobs. You aren't the only one who can make an impression. Right now, Molly and Frank McCain, the patients, are issues for Dr. Knobs. We can deal with your psychological wounds later.

The real issue is discovering what has vanished. Finding nothing seems impossible, but a wise old woman left me some clues."

Thoroughly confused, Maria parked her car and walked with Rosie into the hospital. Finding nothing seemed like a Zen puzzle. And then it struck her: Rosie was in search of disappearances. Tracking what was buried ended a cycle of toxicity, but what happened if the waste was taken elsewhere? What other community could be affected? Maria's stomach did a double flip, thinking of Spencer T's disappearance years ago and now not knowing the whereabouts of her Spencer.

Rosie took her hand and looked into her eyes. "Don't think so much. I can feel your thoughts running through your blood, and your blood pressure just elevated to that of Russell's. Stick with the facts you know."

Despite being taller than Rosie by a few inches, Maria found herself jogging to keep up with her. Dr. Knobs met them on the third floor, where patients were isolated because they were contagious, in serious condition, or had enough money to pay for a single-occupancy room. After a quick hug between Dr. Knobs and Rosie, he pulled them aside.

"Rosie, your intuition—even from Puerto Rico, close to three thousand miles away—holds merit. Molly McCain did exactly as you stated. What I mean is that her physical state shows an abuse over years of various toxic materials, but more importantly her personality splits between caustic and saccharine, revealing what I consider an abnormal projection of ill will. She fakes heart attacks while she attacks the staff with verbal abuse and accusations of patient mistreatment. The triggers for her behavior involve JoAnne's name, mention of her estate and property, and just in the last day, her brother."

Rosie nodded as if this was part of why she was here. As far as Maria was concerned, Rosie came to help her aunt with the fiery nerves in her paralyzed legs, and Rosie's inclusion in the issues of Concrete annoyed her. She felt the slow burn of anger rise to the surface as Rosie continued probing into issues that were none of her business.

"Maria, please tell Roger what you know so far concerning Molly's actions."

Maria stared at Rosie in disbelief. She had come to the hospital only as the driver, and she didn't want to talk about her past, JoAnne, or anything else. Maria repeated over and over to herself, *Stick to the facts,* but words started tumbling out of her mouth. She started with the farms, dying animals, and poor crops, and then she rolled time backward to her aunt's fall, Molly's presence, and abandonment at the quarry. She talked of her returning to the quarry this past week with Spencer and how Frank shot their tires. She mumbled about her stay at Northern State Hospital, where Molly had intervened and failed to inform JoAnne of her presence. She jumped into the manifests of shipments to the McCains' hangar, poor soil, contaminants, and finally their suspicions.

Dr. Knobs took her hand in his at some point. Rosie stood next to her, easing in close to her side. Their presence helped Maria calm down. Rosie gave her a smile as her eyebrow rose in a question mark.

"I hope you don't hate me, Maria, for making you spit out all the Molly garbage. The only way to pass through her lies and convoluted thinking is to purge. I brought you here because your aunt is too fragile at this point to even be near Molly's energy. Her physical nerve endings are aflame, and her healing process will take many forms. You, with your youth and passion, need to let the explosions occur safely. Now let's get down to business."

Dr. Knobs let go of her hand and motioned for them to follow him down the hallway. He stopped in front of Frank McCain's room. Maria looked over at Rosie and back to Dr. Knobs. The last time she had seen Frank, he had lifted her aunt off the hangar floor and declared her crazy for trying to walk. Maria started to question why they were here when Dr. Knobs and Rosie both put their fingers to their lips.

The door swung open to Frank, robed and settled in a chair by his hospital bed. He jumped up at the sight of Dr. Knobs and climbed on top of the bed.

"I didn't mean to break any of the hospital rules. When I'd go visit my mother in the nursing home, the nurses got really mad if my mom tried to get out of bed. I don't like lying in a bed when I'm not tired."

Frank looked like a kid who wanted to obey but couldn't. Maria didn't see the mean streak from the man who shot out her tires, the man who buried noxious substances around Skagit County. Clean-shaven and sober, Frank sought approval.

Dr. Knobs waved him off.

"Frank, don't worry about lying in your bed or sitting in your chair. You can sit anywhere you want in the room to read or watch TV, as long as you rest. I think you already know Maria. This is Rosie, a biologist who knows about plants and cures for diseases. I think your mother knew about Rosie's work with the *linea* vine."

Maria sat down on the chair that Frank had vacated. Rosie, still holding her precious bag of information, moved in closer to Frank. Dr. Knobs waited for his words to sink in. Frank stared at Maria and ignored Rosie and the doctor.

"How is your aunt? She needs to be careful. Her legs aren't good, never have been since the fall. My mother felt bad about that. I do, too."

Frank fixed his eyes on Maria's face. He needed something from her, more than just an answer to her aunt's condition. She searched inside for her voice, her tender side, something resembling a heart. Her rage gone, now she faced another reality, separate from Molly, from the past and her own turmoil.

"My aunt is okay, Frank. She is more worried about the dying animals and plants than she is about her legs, although they hurt. She feels things."

It was the best Maria could do. She had no more compassion than the truth.

Frank nodded, accepting her words.

"My mother worried about the land, too. She made me promise on her deathbed to fix things. I don't know how. I loved my mother. She trusted me."

At this Rosie put her hand on Frank's face. Maria thought that this must have been the first time anyone had touched him with a caress. Tears fell from the corners of his eyes. Rosie wiped them softly with a tissue.

"Frank, I never met your mother, but she was a very wise woman and kinder than most. I live in Puerto Rico. She found out about the work I do with plants that heal nerves. She must have been thinking of JoAnne's legs and that I might be able to help."

Frank jumped off the bed and hugged Rosie.

"I remember sending off a large envelope to Puerto Rico. My mother said that this was a trust, to fix what she couldn't. She sent off three more of those envelopes. Each time, she cautioned me not to say anything to Molly. I didn't ask any questions, knowing that if I knew more, Molly would push me to spill the beans. I might not be able to say no to my sister, but I know how to keep a secret. Molly can squeeze orange juice out of a rind. If I knew any important information from my job at the Public Works Department, she would force it out of me and then turn around and make trouble. I started playing dumb so she would stop prying. Acting dumb for so long, everyone forgets. Even I forgot that I had a brain with the capacity to think for myself."

Rosie nodded at Frank's logic. She gently stepped back from Frank's embrace and looked directly into his eyes. "Frank, when you buried those canisters, did you know what was inside?"

They all waited for Frank's answer. Maria wasn't sure that it mattered, but Rosie persisted, holding Frank captive with her fixed glance.

"The deliveries got mixed up. Some were from old nuclear plants. I got rid of some of those recently. Others came from pharmaceutical companies. Molly hijacked whatever she could, if it involved Spencer. Not the Spencer you like, Maria, but the older one that my sister claimed she loved. Love to Molly was the same as hate, possessive and mean. I know, because I was her scapegoat—her own brother. She is trying to blame all of this on me."

Maria thought Rosie would continue to probe with her gentle manner, but she bent her head as if exhausted.

Dr. Knobs said, "You said you moved some of the old deliveries recently. What do you mean?"

"I thought I should try and fix things, get rid of the waste. Make it better, for my mother's sake. I dug up some of the canisters buried at Northern State Hospital and put the stuff in the waste site at the composite factory."

"You can rest for now, Frank. A nurse will be in soon to give you iodine."

They walked out into the hallway. Maria felt sick and ran to find a bathroom. When she came back, Dr. Knobs and Rosie had their heads together.

Rosie whispered the dreaded words. "This is no longer confined to Concrete. Who knows where all the waste is now? This is a case of national security. I brought with me someone who has already sounded the alarm."

"Who did you bring with you?" Maria asked. "I didn't see anyone."

"Your Spencer saw my passenger get picked up by the CIA helicopter. His great-uncle went to meet with the former secretary of defense."

Maria left Rosie and ran to the car. No wonder she hadn't seen her Spencer. She drove back to the hangar not wanting to think or feel, only do.

Chapter 30:
SAR-X: Search and Rescue Exercise

With Incident Commander Lindbergh running the search and rescue exercise, JoAnne felt some of the stress lift away. Old ties run deep with pilots. These volunteers came based on a long-ago friendship. When she closed her eyes, she could imagine a different time and place, where the mission searched for downed planes and pilots. Spencer T could have been one of those lost. She never knew the real story of his disappearance and had often explained his absence as a mission gone awry. That first month after her fall, she waited for a call, a finding, a resolution.

Mind games didn't get a job done, didn't take a rescue operation closer to the truth. JoAnne's hands trembled with assumptions. She had to let all of them go.

Today's unofficial mission had less-immediate pressures. A life didn't depend on their expertise. Although JoAnne still sat at the command table, she wheeled her chair outside of the fray, preferring to take the position of consultant. She had warned Lindbergh about her fear of discovery, worried that Molly and Frank would somehow sabotage the search. JoAnne didn't trust that the hospital could contain Molly's reach.

Lindbergh's response had been matter of fact: "This is no different than any of our rescue missions. Keeping the media away is just as important as hiding facts from the enemy. The McCains can have their spies out. The Concrete Fly-In is a great cover for our low flights, and we will have our code phrases."

Lindbergh and JoAnne came up with two phrases. When one of the ground or air patrols spotted a potential burial site, they were to say, "Eagles have left the nest," or, "Beaver dammed the area."

So far, the air operations had flown over quadrants Alpha and Bravo. The safety commander ordered those quadrants searched first, since the high spots of the Sauk and Cultis Mountains became more dangerous as the day progressed, with the sun heating up the air and creating a thermal rise.

JoAnne rolled back on her wheels, tilting her chair slightly upward to see the map. She counted ten areas marked as potential sites. The flags indicated a change in color of vegetation, usually a browning or different shade of green. As one of the mission pilots had "hacked" over an area near an abandoned gravel pit, his mission scanner noted disturbed ground, large pocks, where there shouldn't have been anything but solid earth. The mission observer called in the sighting, "Beaver dams in Eagles nests." The change in wording alerted the incident commander that something was up. Lindbergh ordered the mission pilot to return to the base to explain.

Sighting after sighting, pilots came and went. The ground operations director sat by Russell. As JoAnne's energy waned, Russell's energy increased. Since his respite with Rosie, Russell stood straighter, became more engaged. His ham radio linked his buddies upriver to the air operation sightings. The map markings flagged the disposal sites along old logging roads, gravel pits, and—potentially more threatening in terms of exposure—sites along both the Skagit and Sauk Rivers. The convergence of the two rivers created a funnel for the dumping, which would spread across the county.

JoAnne had a metallic taste in her mouth. She drank water, hoping to wash the sensation away, quench a thirst perpetuated by thoughts she didn't want to pursue. She fiddled with a crumpled sheet of paper, her test results from the Health Department. Ignoring the hub of activity by Russell, she quietly wheeled herself to his side.

"Russell, do you mind my interruption? I have a question."

Russell jolted his head up, startled out of concentration. He noted the pale color of JoAnne's cheeks, the blank stare in her eyes. He stroked his chin as if he had a decision to make.

"That piece of paper you're fiddling with looks like the one I have in my pocket. Either yours is worse than mine, or I am older and can deal with bad news better."

Here it was, the truth lying dormant in the soft words of a friend. JoAnne took a deep breath and exhaled a laugh that verged on a whimper. She reached over and squeezed Russell's hand. "Nothing gets by you."

"As far as I can tell, we will live as long as we will. My tests tell me I'm older and leakier than I should be. In fact, I shouldn't be alive. I reckon yours says you'll live awhile more, but you'll get sicker without some intervention. Your friend Rosie looked into my eyes and told me to live like always. I suggest you do the same."

Living like always meant pouring her heart into what she loved. Nothing new, but JoAnne felt insatiable. Since the nerves in her legs had woken up to a slow burn of discomfort, her personal yearnings had followed suit. The test results seemed to declare there was another danger lurking in her system, that she needed to attend to her insides or meet a hairpin turn in a long, winding road. JoAnne wanted another chance, wanted to reconfigure her passive acceptance of greedy lies and the false sense of pride that had kept her safe in a fabricated reality.

"I'm anxious to meet with Rosie. Maybe she'll be able to soothe my nerves."

"My Emma always soothed mine. I don't mean what the young ones call massage, although Emma did that for me, too. She seemed to be able to see between the lines of right and wrong, between the emotions that didn't hold up to reality. With one look, Rosie was able to give me that same comfort. Here we are, trying to find where Molly McCain buried waste from all kinds of poisons, but that pathetic woman never has and never will know what comfort means. We are the lucky ones. We've known true love."

JoAnne gave him a sharp look. "Speak for yourself. Emma and you, now that was true love. I don't know if it wasn't all an illusion. I mean, with Spencer."

"It wasn't, and you know that. But to put all this nonsense to rest, I have proof—just the facts, ma'am. I managed to get hold of one of those stolen letters Molly had stashed. Don't ask me how, and I won't have to lie." Russell pulled out a yellowed envelope and pushed it into her hands.

JoAnne gasped, turning the envelope over and over, searching for the lost years, studying the scrawl of her Spencer. She pulled out the letter and read.

My dearest JoAnne,

This is my goodbye. I long for you still, but must accept that you have moved on. After all these years of silence, I will wonder no more. I wish you well, I wish you love, I wish I never left you.

Spencer T

Tears fell along JoAnne's cheeks. She abruptly wheeled herself away to the hangar door, where she could breathe in the open sky. Planes circled, touched down, lifted off. She felt as if she could lift off once more, take to the air, and fly with them. But as her heart raced ahead, she knew she needed to stay on the ground with this work, here and now.

Tucking the letter into her pocket, she returned to Russell, ignoring his questioning look. She pointed to the bulletin board, at two colors of flags crisscrossing the county, red and black. "What do the colors mean?" she asked.

"Back to business? The colors show a distinction between kinds of waste products. The more unstable areas have the black flag. I've got a feeling that soon the Civil Air Patrol won't be the only ones involved. My buddies claim a helicopter has been flying over the area with sophisticated camera equipment—the same helicopter that stopped here earlier this morning and picked up a passenger."

JoAnne didn't have a record of a helicopter checking in to the fly-in or with her at the command center.

"Am I missing something? Russell, what else do you know?"

The red face, the averting eyes, and the sheepish smile told JoAnne what she suspected. She just needed to hear her suspicions validated.

"All I know is that after Spencer and I chased down the pilot who attempted a delivery at the McCain hangar, Rosie arrived on another plane. She walked in here alone, but a CIA helicopter met her passenger. Since I haven't seen young Spencer since, I figure his uncle was the passenger."

"Didn't you ask Rosie?"

Russell put his hands up in defeat. "No, I figured we weren't supposed to know. All these years of his absence, the latest failed tries to contact him as Mourning Dove on the ham radio, the escalation of our findings, all lead me to believe he couldn't stay away any longer. The CIA helicopter made it clear that it wasn't Rosie's decision to tell me."

JoAnne pushed through the layers of crumbled dreams. The Health Department test results were as Russell stated, a warning. The letter and the news of Spencer T.'s arrival pumped new blood through her system. Heart energy, the purest and most potent, filled her with determination. JoAnne spun her chair around and wheeled herself to the command center. From this vantage point, she could watch the bulletin board, hear the incident commander, and watch for the landing of a helicopter.

She scanned the skies. The high clouds acted as a filter, keeping the air cooler and visibility clear for the low-lying search and plane landings. Cloud watching was almost like daydreaming. She remembered the quiet times on furlough when she would wait for her Spencer. Holding hands, staring at the sky, they'd make up stories, seeing a vast world of endless possibilities. Spencer always pointed at a thundercloud, dark and flat topped, declaring it an anvil ready to combine heat and metal, hammering to create a rumble. And when the rain and wind arrived, the clouds dissolved, drenching them in their future. Today, the clouds remained high—no stories, just a muted blue sky.

Watching the entrance to the museum hangar, JoAnne heard not the motor of a helicopter but the screeching tires of Maria's car braking to a halt almost inside the hangar door. Within seconds, Maria was by her aunt's side.

"Aunt Jo, Aunt Jo, do you know?"

JoAnne's lips smiled a tentative *yes, no, maybe*, half forming each word.

"Maria, all I know is that I'm watching for a helicopter carrying Spencer T. I don't know if he'll stop here or what escalated all this to warrant national and international involvement." JoAnne's hands shook as she stared out into the skies. "My hands are shaking, but really it is my heart. I don't know what to expect of my Spencer or myself. I'm afraid that his return is only because of a cocktail of waste found in the rivers, the mountains, and the roadways. I sound selfish."

Maria bent down to eye level, wrapping her arms around JoAnne.

She felt her grandniece's heartbeat against her own. Finally, JoAnne gently pushed Maria away. "Remember, I have to be able to breathe! Now tell me what I'm missing."

"Not much. I missed seeing your Spencer get off the plane and the helicopter picking him up. Rosie offered that information at the hospital after a long talk with Frank."

"And the talk with Frank and Rosie occurred because . . ."

"I know, I'm skipping around too much. Dr. Knobs and Rosie have a deeper sense of Molly's and Frank's psychological makeup than you or I have ever been able to discern. Dr. Knobs knows her triggers—you being one, and Spencer T the other."

JoAnne tapped her fingers along the arm of her wheelchair. She rolled back and forth. "Enough. I don't want to hear Dr. Knobs's feats at describing Molly's state of mind or Rosie's insightful analysis of the situation. What happened?"

Maria told her what Frank had revealed. How his mother had created trusts for JoAnne, the WASPs, Northern State Hospital, and Rosie's work on nerve regeneration. That Frank's only desire now was to fix all that Molly had destroyed so he could fulfill his mother's dying wish. "Aunt JoAnne, Molly's pull can't get past Frank's love for his mother and his devotion to you."

JoAnne's heart was pounding again. Her legs twitched, and her eyes burned. She couldn't imagine the torture Frank and his mother must have endured. "I think about heroes, those who can make a difference. Molly's mother, if I'm remembering correctly, was named Maggie. She must have suffered in silence all those years, living with a daughter who had spitefulness, anger, and meanness inside and actively spread it to others. But Maggie could somehow see beyond to the future of

249

all of us. As a mother, she found a way to counter the lies, the devious evil. She couldn't control Molly, but Maggie is why we are all here working together."

JoAnne clutched her chest, holding her heart tightly. With so many emotions tearing free, she didn't know if it could stand the strain. "Poor Maggie, she defied fate. She discovered what we couldn't face, the power of lies. She fought the battle with a steadfastness of accountability. She never wavered, not even in her death."

Maria placed her hands on the handles of JoAnne's wheelchair. "Let's go back inside. Fate alone didn't bring your Spencer in that helicopter, and your staring at the sky won't bring him here to see you any sooner. Our job now is to continue what Maggie started. Let's finish detecting and inspecting the sites. Maggie might be a saint watching from above, but we have an entire valley of concerned citizens working to find the waste sites. Stopping Molly is not our only mission. Your Spencer is here to fix what went wrong forty-five years ago. If our national security is involved, history is our story as well."

JoAnne faced the bulletin board once more. Flags, black and red, crisscrossed. She noted large X's marked over the old cement silos. Concrete's past changed in front of her eyes. "Russell, is this as bad as it looks?"

He rubbed his eyes. "Yes and no. Between the air and ground patrol, more dumping areas flagged means these are new discoveries. Some of the waste is innocuous, stable but a bother because it shouldn't be there. Metal detectors uncovered canisters in all of the old cement silos. In terms of harm, the hazardous issues occur where the red and black flags converge.

"If we ever wondered how Molly made her fortune, we know now that it was worse than the accusations of embezzlement. She took our environment and sold us down the river. Literally. She contaminated so much of our land and waters that we now have an emergency. That's the bad news.

"The best outcome is that with all of us working together, we've broken the silence of years. Our project isn't secret anymore. I think Molly is not only dying from her own poisonous concoctions but also because she can't lie anymore."

JoAnne found her fingers tapping on the armrest of her wheelchair. Nervous and unsatisfied, she barked, "I'm not looking at this philosophically. Will we be able to detoxify our land and water, now and for the future?"

Russell sat up straight and leaned his head forward. "I don't know, JoAnne. Why don't you ask the powers that be? They are standing behind you."

Chapter 31:
Connections Concomitants

Maria startled at Russell's words, and the din of the ham radio and the voices of the commanders and directors receded. Slowly, as if the frames were jammed in an old movie, her aunt turned the wheelchair around to face her old love. Her back was straight as an ironing board, her lips pressed together. She ignored all of them and fixed her intense gaze on Spencer T.

Stooped slightly in the shoulders yet taller than his grandnephew, Spencer T walked into the hangar as if he belonged. Gray-white hair and a beard framed his wide face, and he had wrinkles surrounding his blue eyes and Roman nose. Weather creased his forehead, and years of working outdoors had left his skin ruddy with sun and wind. He walked swinging his long, muscled arms in a denim jacket a size too small, and Maria saw her own Spencer in the older man's wide shoulders, the flat belly, and the slight swagger.

Maria held her breath, waiting for the unlocking of eyes between her aunt and Spencer Senior. Seconds stretched, peeling away the years, probing for old anchors. Maria forced her feet to move, needing to break the scene and release them all into the present moment.

She held out her hand. "Hi, I'm Maria, JoAnne's grandniece. You must be Spencer's great-uncle. You look so much alike. Can I call you Spencer T, or would Senior be okay?"

Maria's Spencer stepped alongside, placing his arms around her waist. His uncle moved closer, extending his hand to meet hers. Warm and worn, the fingers enfolded her hand with both strength and gentleness.

"I prefer Spencer T. Call my grandnephew Junior or whatever you two find easier. The Senior part makes me feel too old."

Her aunt recovered her voice, and with a penetrating stare, she asked, "And what shall I call you?"

Spencer T's answer came after a brief hesitation. "Anything you want. Just call me."

His simple words left the question in the air. What do you call someone you haven't seen in half a century? Where do you begin the next chapter of a story that never ended?

JoAnne kept still, the tears of years flowing, and then between crying and laughing, she made the first move. Maria had never seen her aunt dance, but her wheelchair nearly floated toward Spencer T. With an elegance bordering on old-fashioned, Spencer T bowed and swirled JoAnne around with one hand on each handle of her chair.

When the twirling stopped, he bowed again. "JoAnne, I missed your laughter. It lightens my heart to hear and see you."

Russell saved them all from an awkward transition. Although he had tears in his eyes, he knew how to balance emotions with the logistics of action.

"Glad you could join us, Spencer T. I thought I'd have to search for you in Puerto Rico, since Mourning Dove stopped answering my ham radio calls. Maybe now you can retire that call sign, since what you mourned for is right next to you. You and JoAnne can take over for me here. I need a rest—that is, unless you have a better plan."

Maria wondered if her aunt would be able to hold back her emotions. Would this be an act of bravery or a familiar role each of the old lovers could follow? Russell had bowed out of the discussion. Maria knew that they were on autopilot until the immediate concerns of the community could be resolved. Duty won.

Just like that, they fell into their roles. Without denying the long absence, the pining away of hearts they felt as committed doves, her aunt and Spencer T joined their energy. JoAnne didn't wait for an apology or explanation, and Spencer T risked rejection, while acting as only he knew how. The two studied the map and conferred with the incident commander. As the planes came in, more colored markings appeared on the map. After a while, the two came up for air.

Spencer T mopped his brow. "I can't say that I have a plan, but I have knowledge. Knowledge that has kept me away from Concrete and now brought me back."

JoAnne raised her hand to her lips, her version of holding her tongue, and then dropped it. "And someone in the helicopter that came to meet you knew of your existence, sought you out, or the reverse?"

Spencer T faced JoAnne, holding his hand to his chin and gently stroking his beard. His words came slowly, not rehearsed but from a place that mulled options and decisions with care. "Do you remember when you flew as a WASP and would return after a mission of delivering a plane that you knew inside and out? Do you remember the feeling of handing the plane over to a male pilot so he could fly it for real? Which one of you was the real pilot? Did your job end after the handoff, or did you track your plane, report on its strengths and weaknesses? Was your loyalty a fleeting moment or based on a larger purpose? I don't expect an answer. I ask only so I can explain that the question you asked me has more answers than you gave me questions. One answer alone would be a lie. Communicating truth is harder."

He took a breath. "I'm not sure which came first. Simply stated, I have been talking with the former secretary of defense because he retired to Concrete, which I still consider my home. He lives and breathes the air where you live, he cares about Highway 20, and he carries with him institutional memory. Although he is retired, he holds secrets, decisions, and knowledge of events and issues none of us need to know or will know. The helicopter came because I called, but since my ill-fated flight during World War II, I have always been on the Department of Defense's radar."

Her aunt, with all her poise and intelligence, listened with the attention of a woman who served her country. She also listened with her opening heart.

Maria was younger and impatient. "Spencer T, are you trying to tell us that you never retired from the government and have been working secretly with them since the 1940s? Your grandnephew disappeared when you arrived here today. He lived with you and ran your vineyard. My aunt might not ask you these questions, but I want to protect her heart, and I need to re-establish a sense of trust."

Russell coughed and pointed his finger at her. "Mourning Dove—I mean, Spencer T—I told you this one would push us all to uncover more truths. Maria isn't satisfied with half answers."

"And she shouldn't be. Maria, I can only answer the first part of your question. The second belongs to my grandnephew. If I'm guilty of anything, it is loyalty. Loyalty led me to protect the people I love and care about. My work during World War II had its secrets, but I was an engineer with the responsibility of taking care of a plane sent to Ramey carrying an experimental bomb. The crash left the cargo vulnerable, unstable. Months later, we all witnessed the devastation of the nuclear bomb in Japan. My goal since that moment was to protect, find solutions to the remnants of hazardous waste. My research all these years has been funded by various agencies, and retiring was never an option.

"Denying loyalty and love isn't an option, either. I would have returned sooner to Concrete and JoAnne if I had known more. The problem with engineers is that they deal best with facts. Data, letters, and responses factored into each of my decisions, and I have to take responsibility for that. What-ifs don't count in retrospect. Molly McCain filled in the gaps. She was never on anyone's radar, not mine nor the government's. No one ever factors in the frailties of human nature."

Before Maria caught herself, she blurted out one of her unfiltered reactions. "Good speech if you were running for office."

At this, she felt the stern eyes of her aunt on her. "Maria, hold your tongue. Sharpness doesn't become you. If we are looking for blame, we can place it on Molly, on the government, on ourselves for not staying the hard course. Or we can find new truths, something more than lies."

Maria closed her eyes, humiliated in her smallness. Tears fell along her cheeks. Her Spencer's hand gently brushed them away, and then he kissed her cheek.

Spencer T faltered, turning to JoAnne. "I failed to believe you cared. The unanswered letters hardened my resolve, and I gave up my heart. I chose to work harder and care less about you, JoAnne. I knew you would survive."

Spencer jumped to his uncle's defense. "Your life isn't why we are here searching for illegal waste. We all need to concentrate on fixing this mess. JoAnne makes a point, which is that Molly McCain is now irrelevant. Uncle T, why did the former secretary of defense arrive in that helicopter?"

As soon as the words *secretary of defense* were uttered, the room shifted. Lindbergh, along with Safety Command Officer Wiggins, who loomed large like a wolf protecting its pack, walked over from the command board.

"If there is something you need to tell me," Officer Wiggins said, "this would be the time. I have at least ten pilots out hovering in the air and about forty responders on the ground. If there is an issue that would put them in harm's way, the search will be called off."

Lindbergh nodded, acknowledging the gravity of Officer Wiggins's role. "JoAnne, we are here on your behalf, unofficially, but we still abide by the rules of the Civil Air Patrol. What has changed?"

JoAnne deferred to Spencer T, nodding in his direction, letting go of the controls, and passing a baton of trust. No longer on the defense about his past, Spencer T moved into the role of directing and conferring. Maria noticed the decisiveness in his jaw, a tilt to his chin that brought his eyes into plain view.

"The former secretary of defense is here unofficially. He has sensitive information about other local sites that have been sanctioned to dispose of hazardous waste. One of our factories here locally builds components for our national defense, and his concern is twofold: breach of security and unintended contamination. Historically the Pacific Northwest has fostered many programs that aid the United States through research. We may live in a small town, but our role has always been large. Molly McCain's small lies, her personal vendetta, and her bullying to find out information have violated the security of the nation. His job is to put her to rest. Ours is to pull together and become our own heroes. Searching for all the possible sites of illegal burying is the safer of the operations. The danger comes with the removal. Hopefully my last forty years of researching materials that can absorb the toxins will allow for safe disposal."

Lindbergh and the Officer Wiggins returned to their posts. Russell walked over to Spencer T and gave him a hug. Maya followed by his side, sniffing the ground, watching to keep her master safe. Russell put a hand down, patting Maya's head.

Maria cleared her throat. "Aunt Jo, thanks for keeping me in line."

"You're like Maya, trying to protect me. You have been my anchor throughout these years."

Maria looked over at the two Spencers, the older and younger version, studying maps, talking with Russell and the other directors. Her gaze across the room embraced all the volunteers from the Civil Air Patrol, an infrastructure held together not with the genetics of family but the blood, sweat, and tears of commitment.

"Are you still going to Puerto Rico?" Maria asked.

Her aunt bent her head, held her hands together as if in prayer. She seemed far away. Maria wondered if she was lost to her, claimed by another, and she felt the shaking of her foundation.

"Plans change. I have to deal with some health issues before I can work with Rosie. The toxic levels in my blood are higher than is healthy for a woman of my mature age. I'll need some treatments."

Once again, a truth had spilled out that superseded assumptions. Maria's selfish needs had created a hole where none existed, and now she had worry where a moment before she had disappointment. Before she had a chance to ask her aunt about it, Rosie and Dr. Knobs walked in with a stately gentleman.

The way he dressed said casual, but the stance, the assured walk, and the entourage of men dressed in suits, wearing earpieces, and standing outside the museum hangar told her that this man was their former secretary of defense.

This time, Maria wasn't the bold one breaking the ice. Her aunt wheeled herself past Maria and sat in full view of the new arrivals.

The secretary took the lead. "You must be JoAnne Kraft, the famous former WASP who has spearheaded this search. I'm here unofficially to thank you for honoring your country, then and now."

Maria wasn't fooled, and she doubted her aunt was. She knew that thanks from the government, no matter how heartfelt, came with conditions. JoAnne's services as a WASP had never met such attention, but now she shook the secretary's hand, all the while keeping her gaze strong.

"I accept your thanks, but typically the next line is, 'Thank you for your service, but we won't be needing you in the future.' Quite frankly, Sir, I won't be dismissed. That happened once, it won't happen again. My loyalty to our country goes beyond my service as a WASP and now as a citizen. Service, knowledge, giving, caring, all of these can't be dismissed."

Maria almost applauded her aunt. The Spencers and Rosie all had grins of pride on their faces. Something other than a dismissal came with the secretary's thank you.

"Well, JoAnne, I am happy to hear that. I have an offer for you. After talking with Dr. Knobs, Dr. Nazario—or as you know her, Rosie —your old friend Spencer, and the distinguished gentleman with the ham radio, I was convinced that I need you to help quietly and quickly clean up this mess. Not the physical work, but connecting the dots, going back to your service as a WASP, all the way up until the present. Molly McCain represents a threat to all of us. Presently we have rendered her physically inoperative, but not her psyche. What I mean is, we need to figure out how one bully can create so much havoc, gaining power without being detected or stopped."

Her aunt sat with her hands quietly folded in her lap, but Maria witnessed the twitching of her legs, the emotion of years rushing through her. She looked at all of them as only she could—dignified and humbled.

Finally, JoAnne spoke. "I have my conditions. First, you must follow through and reward our past WASPs, and second, you must be lenient with Frank McCain, as his life has been twisted beyond anything you can imagine. His heart is purer than his actions. You say you have rendered Molly McCain inoperative, and that needs an explanation. And before I wither away, I demand that you personally make sure those regulations are enforced, that the citizens of Skagit Valley have transparency and access to those who will listen and have the power to act."

The former secretary of defense listened with more attention than Maria had seen from any of her superiors at work. He jotted down all of her aunt's demands. He looked at his watch as if he had to leave, but instead pulled up a chair.

"JoAnne, thanks for your honesty and leadership. Retiring and living here along Highway 20, I never suspected the power of a community. I chose my home based on beauty, and now I know there is a dedication and sense of fairness. This is a rare commodity. In answer to your requests, acknowledgement of the WASPs has been a long time in coming. They will be recognized, receive commendations for their past service, and will be eligible for health benefits.

"As to Frank, Dr. Knobs and Dr. Nazario have also made this same request. Frank's mental state is fragile, though his health will improve. He has already given us information that will help us find the illegal burial sites, and I promise the charges will be minimal. Finally, the issue of Molly. That is harder, because prison wouldn't be bad enough for her. She will stand trial, and I will recommend that she be stripped of all her worldly goods as a settlement toward all the damage she has created. Molly is very ill. She should be isolated in a place where no one will ever see her again."

As patriotic as the best of them, Maria couldn't help but feel that everything was being tied up in a too-neat package. Skeptical, she found herself retreating. She felt a gnawing of injustices and wanted to scream out, *What about my aunt's legs, the nerves, the absence of love? How about Emma dying too early? How about me?*

Maria made eye contact with Spencer. He seemed far away, caught up with the power of resolution, his world intact. She searched for a sign that she had a place in his heart, and all it took was his hand touching his lips, a kiss sent through the air. Maria had to believe that their connection counted. Rosie slowly moved away from the doctor and the former secretary of defense and came by Maria's side, holding her gaze with her luminous eyes.

Maria whispered to Rosie, "My aunt won't be going back with you to Puerto Rico. She isn't healthy enough."

Rosie took Maria's hand and encased her fingers and palm in both of hers.

"Maria, would you like to travel back with me? I know Monica would love to see you."

She thought about truths and lies and keeping centered. About her sister, and how she must need her as much as Maria needed her. She glanced over at her aunt with Spencer T, and Russell with Maya, his protector. She watched the Civil Air Patrol continue working. Maria thought about the things she admired in all of her friends and family—kindness, generosity, understanding, honesty—and how easily all this could be destroyed by greed, meanness, and lies. Maria knew her answer.

Before she spoke, the former secretary of defense turned to face them.

"Rosie, I hope Maria answers yes. I have arranged a flight that leaves after your conference. It can accommodate three passengers."

Maria looked over at Rosie and then at her Spencer.

Chapter 32:
Beginnings Never End

Maria pressed her nose against the window to stare down at the clouds. For most of the flight, she had slept as darkness blanketed the skies, and she had taken refuge in dreaming. Flying as a passenger left her the luxury of free and unfocused thought. Her hand still held Spencer's hand, and his snores, not recognizing the rising sun or her accelerated pulse in anticipation of touchdown, complemented the quiet hum of the US military-designated plane.

Although Rosie sat across the way, Maria felt her presence as a magnet. They had only exchanged a few words since leaving Concrete, but each conversation drew Rosie closer into Maria's heart. Nothing passed through the eyes of Rosie without making an imprint. As she had so aptly demonstrated, knowing a person had nothing to do with time frames.

Maria closed her eyes, recalling their send-off to Puerto Rico. JoAnne had sat at the head of the dining room table, dressed in her seasoned white linen dress. Spencer T presided from the opposite end, with Russell to his left and Rosie on Russell's right. Maria and her Spencer sat next to one another. Russell, bless his heart, had made the toast.

"To new beginnings. May we always listen to our hearts."

To this, Spencer T had nodded and raised his glass, but instead of toasting JoAnne, he turned and faced Maria.

"To the daughter I never had, but who gave my love JoAnne so much happiness."

JoAnne drank and ate with an appetite that showed a hunger couched in comfort. Her garden-fresh green beans, corn on the cob, and grilled Chinook salmon disappeared with everyone's slow, appreciative bites. Maria felt the ease of family and a flow of energy that had been so glaringly absent at the dinner just two weeks before. Between tears and laughter, she caught her own reflection in the window. She seemed taller by at least an inch—longer in stature, wider in her heart.

The meal had ended with Rosie holding Russell's hands. She had stared at the veins, as if she could see the blood flowing. Kissing the tips of his fingers, she whispered in his ear. Maria heard only Russell's response: "My Emma would have liked you."

To JoAnne, Rosie gave one of her cryptic comments. "You'll never lose your nerves. Work first on generating warmth from within. All synapses meet in the heart."

JoAnne had simply replied with a smile that emanated through her eyes and the flush of her cheeks. Spencer T counter-toasted Russell and Rosie's words with what must have held him together for almost a half of a century: "There is no end to our beginning, only detours that take us back to our true colors."

Now, as Maria stared out the plane window, she thought about the colors of lies, the colors in her life, the lies that had darkened the horizon, the accumulation of misunderstandings, the refusal to see truths. She wondered what color she was and the color of the man who held her hand. Was there a color for devotion and consistency, or for that matter, was absence a non-color, a void so deep that neither white light nor black light entered? For the briefest of moments, her thoughts felt tainted as she remembered Molly's intentional lies. Molly's was a life devoid of light.

Rosie must have sensed her train of thought, for she leaned closer to speak softly across the sleeping Spencer. "If you stare at the clouds long enough, the light shines through. The sun is behind the clouds, not always visible. An old friend of mine, Don Tuto, used to say that the only way to see is to use all your senses as if you were blind. He worked in caves. Your sister can tell you about him. During her darkest times, she learned to follow her inner light, which I think encompassed all she loved."

Spencer's snores ceased as the engine shifted speed, the drone softening to a slow deep hum, adjusting the plane for their descent. Any second, the pilot would open the flaps for the landing gear. They dropped below the clouds, and the sky opened up. Maria could feel as well as see the green of lush vegetation, the olive palm fronds waving in the wind, the brown coconuts, the white sand, the blue of the ocean. She felt what could only be expressed as a rainbow of colors flooding her system.

A gentle bump, as the tires hit the tarmac of the old Ramey Air Force Base, woke Spencer to attention. His grin expressed a joy of another life, one that Maria hoped encompassed her. As they deplaned, he held back, taking her hand, looking into her eyes. His gaze revealed the sparks of life in his blue eyes that she had first noticed only two weeks prior.

His wink felt like a kiss and a promise of a future. "Here is to a beginning that will endure."

Maria walked off the plane, not as an eight-year-old lost without a mother or sister but as a woman of twenty-six years with newfound love. She looked all around, unsure of who or what to expect. Then she saw her, Monica, her sister, racing out onto the tarmac, her dark hair flying behind her, her orange-flowered sundress announcing she loved life with all of its sensuality. True colors. Even with her eyes shut, Maria could smell and feel Monica's sweet essence of honey.

Monica's embrace was more than a hug. Held within her arms, Maria felt the purity of her love.

"My star, here you are."

About the Author

Abbe Rolnick grew up in the suburbs of Baltimore, Maryland. Her first major cultural jolt occurred at age 15 when her family moved to Miami Beach, Florida. To find perspective, she climbed the only non-palm tree at her condo complex and wrote what she observed. History came alive with her exposure to Cuban culture.

After attending Boston University, she lived in Puerto Rico, where she owned a bookstore. *River of Angels* flows from her experiences there and is the first novel in her Generations Series. She continues with *Color of Lies*, the second novel in the series, bringing the reader to the Pacific Northwest where she presently resides. Here she blends stories from island life with characters in Skagit Valley. The third in the series, *Founding Stones*, will be published in 2019, and continues with characters from her two previous novels.

Her recent experiences with her husband's cancer inspired *Cocoon of Cancer: An Invitation to Love Deeply.* (2016) It's a love story that shares intimate tips for caregivers and family.

Tattle Tales: Essays and Stories Along the Way (2016) is a compilation of twenty years of writing.

An avid world traveler, Abbe can be found with her husband Jim in Africa, Southeast Asia, South America, Sri Lanka, the Middle East, and other exotic countries when they aren't at their home amid twenty acres in Skagit Valley, Washington, or visiting with her grown children and grandkids.

To learn more about her writings, Abbe's Notes and Abbe's Ruminations, visit her website, www.abberolnick.com.

Abbe welcomes questions and requests for speaking engagements. She'd love it if you posted your reviews of her writings on Amazon.com and Goodreads.com. Spread the word virally and by word of mouth to all book lovers.

COLOR OF LIES
Reading Group Question and Topics for Discussion

1. What are your "tells," small indicators that let the observant know what you feel? Can you describe the various "tells" of each character mentioned in the first chapter?

2. Why would someone destroy a flower? What is the difference between a mean person and a bully?

3. When is it okay to tell a white lie? Does JoAnne lie to others? What are lies of omission—whom do they protect?

4. Russell knows the history of the community and more. Matters of the heart act as his guide or barometer in all his decisions. Give some examples of his version of truth and how his philosophy keeps peace within the community.

5. Are there Molly McCains in your life? How do you protect yourself from intentional manipulation? How does conflict avoidance perpetuate bullying?

6. Love and family circumstances, powerful motivators, dictate in part the path of an individual. How have Maria and Molly used their circumstances?

7. Toxic land and toxic behavior accumulate. What lessons did the community learn in hindsight?

8. What truth does JoAnne refuse to see, and what lies does she tell herself to survive?

9. Prejudices, based on judgments, tend to skew facts to create a sense of truth. How do judgments of those who live upriver skew facts? Discuss the concept of labeling: "outsiders," "insiders," "Tar Heels."

10. Could Spencer T have acted differently? Can understanding bypass a lie or truth? When does forgiveness begin?

Preview from *Founding Stones,*

GENERATIONS OF SECRETS, BOOK THREE

What Defines Us May Kill Us

Records Group F-444 documents of the Jewish emigration from the area of Pale.

Kiev 1905, a time young Abraham would never forget but refuse to remember. He ran from gaslight pole to gaslight pole, milepost to milepost. Now, after months of rigorous nightly forays, he could travel twenty miles an evening. His city, awash with chaotic and fabricated anti-Jewish riots, forced family after family to leave southern Russia. He left as the day ended, traveled in the dark to the city of Hamburg, Germany. It was too dangerous and expensive to use the train system, so he slept at safe houses till he reached port, where the Bulgaria set sail in three weeks. He left behind the pogroms and with it his seven dead siblings, his feeble and tormented parents. If all went as planned, he'd emerge in the Americas as someone new.

Besides food and another pair of shoes, Abraham's haversack held falsified papers. Clean-shaven, he looked less like an Abraham, more like an Edward or Eduardo. His practiced English and Spanish sounded passable to the uneducated ear. For the last time, he reviewed the sacred Torah's words. From now on, he'd be a Christian. May god forgive him and save his life for a good purpose.

Abraham ran through the night, hid among the trees, under rocks, and in barns. He gathered fragments of stones, pieces of the world he knew. Nothing he took could identify him. He memorized smells, the movement of the wind. He foraged mushrooms, ate roots. After three weeks of running, he boarded the ship. He used the last of his savings to travel steerage, rested for a week, and emerged from the transcontinental ship ride as Eduardo, not the Edward he had hoped for. Stormy weather had blown the ship off course. Instead of New York, he entered the coast of Costa Rica—a nobody to become somebody.

MORE BOOKS BY ABBE ROLNICK

Cocoon of Cancer: An Invitation to Love Deeply

A book of inspiration, *Cocoon of Cancer: An Invitation to Love Deeply* is for those diagnosed with cancer, their caregivers, families, and staff. This collection offers an insider's look at the way life changes forever when the word *cancer* is uttered. The essays and poems reflect an attitude of wonder, defiance, acceptance, and beauty through the painful journey.

Sometimes raw, letters to and from friends voice the unspeakable. The scientific voice of Jim, the patient, comes through when he has the energy to speak. His wife and caregiver Abbe witnesses and documents the signs of distress, gains, losses, and the new equilibrium that forges deep love. More than anything, this is an invitation to feel and find comfort.

Abbe also offers invaluable insights with her *Caregiver Tips, Questions I Still Ponder*, and *Questions for the Reader to Ponder.*

. . . . .

. . . Rolnick (River of Angels, 2010, etc.) deploys her writer's craft to evocative effect in this collection. She conjures up several striking images, not only her cocoon analogy, but also her comparison of Jim's "secret strength" to "upside-down dogwood flowers." Yet Rolnick isn't simply lyrical; she also provides unsparing glimpses into the challenges and struggles faced by this couple, which she makes clear were made bearable by their loving connection and the ideology that "Finding joy is a choice." . . . this collection delivers instructive, uplifting testimony. A positive, perceptive primer for cancer patients and caregivers.

—Kirkus Review

Enlightening . . . . I highly recommend this book for patients and families undergoing the sometimes confusing, often fearful, and yes, at times even joyful, process of cancer care.

—Dr. Bruce Mathey, Skagit Regional Cancer Clinic

Cocoon of Cancer *is a poetic, poignant, and scientifically accurate memoir. Abbe's Care Giver's Tips add insights to those who will identify with similar thoughts and feelings.*

—Dr. Fred Appelbaum, Executive Vice President,
Fred Hutchinson Cancer Research Center &
Executive Director & President, Seattle Cancer Care Alliance

Tattle Tales: Essays & Stories Along the Way

Abbe Rolnick—teller of tales, celebrant of life, world traveler—offers visions from the heart in this collection of short stories and essays. Explorations of whimsy and wisdom take the reader from the basement of a young girl learning about the Holocaust via a repairman, to a literal and psychological deep dive in the Caribbean, to the humble truths of a dung beetle in Africa, and all points in between. The author's keen perception and compassion light the way.

• Short Story Finalist, 2011 80th Annual *Writer's Digest* for, **Swinging Doors.**

• Short Story Finalist about Family, 2009, *Cup of Comfort,* **You've Got a Match.**

. . . . .

In Tattle Tales, *Abbe Rolnick's joie de vivre is evident. These stories and essays take you to an inner realm where Abbe, the observer, contemplates an ever-changing landscape called life. Her enthusiasm and passion thread through each thoughtful piece. Enjoy* Tattle Tales.

—Mary Elizabeth Gillilan, Editor, *Clover, A Literary Rag*

. . . The most memorable entries are those that skew toward fiction; "Lace" is a particularly lovely example of Rolnick's mastery at conjuring images of such things as handmade lace and deep-sea diving, which highlight the allure of travel. The essays, while engaging, tend to tread more familiar ground, such as post-divorce dating, and it's occasionally challenging to keep track of the author's autobiographical details . . . . Rolnick offers many observational gems to enjoy. Resonant reflections from a skilled literary artist.

—*Kirkus Review*